THE CSIs GATHERED AROUND THE BODY, LIKE MOURNERS AT A WAKE.

Novak's bloodshot eyes stared blankly at the ceiling; a thin film had already formed over the lifeless orbs. Catherine looked at David, curious to hear his conclusions. "David?"

"COD appears to be a single GSW to the chest." He pointed at the hole in the wall she had noticed earlier. It was right by the door, about six inches to the left of where they had entered the office. "Possibly a through-and-through. Rigor and body temperature puts the time of death at approximately eleven p.m."

Brass nodded. "Which agrees with the initial reports from the witnesses."

That makes life easier, Catherine thought. Maybe this would prove to be a straightforward case of death by misadventure. She put herself in the place of the alleged shooter, suddenly finding herself face-to-face with a masked, chainsaw-wielding assailant. Catherine could see why she might have shot the actor in self-defense. *Under the circumstances, I might have fired, too.*

"Do we have a weapon?"

Brass produced a Smith & Wesson revolver, already sealed inside a plastic evidence bag. Catherine raised an eyebrow. "You doing our job for us now, Jim?"

He shrugged apologetically. "One of the witnesses, a tech guy on the film crew, had already taken possession of the gun before we arrived. He turned it over to the first officer on the scene."

Catherine frowned. She would have preferred to have collected the weapon herself from its original location, but she couldn't blame the bystanders for not wanting to leave a loaded weapon lying around. Especially after what they had just witnessed. *Maybe it won't matter,* she thought. From the sound of it, there was little question as to who pulled the trigger.

"Anybody else touch the victim?" she asked. "Aside from David, that is?"

"'Fraid so," Bra⸻⸻⸻⸻⸻⸻⸻⸻mbers tried to help Nova⸻⸻⸻⸻⸻⸻ff his mask and everyth⸻⸻⸻⸻⸻⸻erine wanted to hear. "S⸻

It was starting t⸻⸻⸻⸻⸻⸻⸻d the evidence before the⸻

Original novels in the CSI series:

CSI: Crime Scene Investigation
Double Dealer
Sin City
Cold Burn
Body of Evidence
Grave Matters
Binding Ties
Killing Game
Snake Eyes
In Extremis
Nevada Rose
Headhunter
Brass in Pocket
The Killing Jar
Blood Quantum
Dark Sundays
Skin Deep
Shock Treatment
Serial (graphic novel)

CSI: Miami
Florida Getaway
Heat Wave
Cult Following
Riptide
Harm for the Holidays: Misgivings
Harm for the Holidays: Heart Attack
Cut & Run
Right to Die

CSI: NY
Dead of Winter
Blood on the Sun
Deluge
Four Walls

CSI:
CRIME SCENE INVESTIGATION™

SHOCK TREATMENT
a novel

Greg Cox

Based on the hit CBS series CSI: Crime Scene
Investigation produced by CBS PRODUCTIONS,
a business unit of CBS Broadcasting Inc.

Executive Producers: Jerry Bruckheimer,
Carol Mendelsohn, Anthony E. Zuiker,
Ann Donahue, Naren Shankar, Cynthia Chvatal,
William Petersen, Jonathan Littman

Series created by: Anthony E. Zuiker

POCKET STAR BOOKS
New York   London   Toronto   Sydney

Pocket Star Books
A Division of Simon & Schuster, Inc.
1230 Avenue of the Americas
New York, NY 10020

First Pocket Star Books paperback edition December 2010

POCKET STAR BOOKS and colophon are registered trademarks of Simon & Schuster, Inc.

For information about special discounts for bulk purchases, please contact Simon & Schuster Special Sales at 1-866-506-1949 or business@simonandschuster.com.

The Simon & Schuster Speakers Bureau can bring authors to your live event. For more information or to book an event contact the Simon & Schuster Speakers Bureau at 1-866-248-3049 or visit our website at www.simonspeakers.com.

Cover art and design by David Stevenson

Manufactured in the United States of America

10 9 8 7 6 5 4 3 2 1

ISBN 978-1-4391-6080-0
ISBN 978-1-4391-6928-5 (ebook)

1

JILL WOOTEN FELT like she was being watched.

A double-decker bus pulled away from the curb, leaving her on a dirty sidewalk a few blocks north of Fremont, on the outer fringe of the downtown tourist traps. Neon signs, nowhere near as impressive as the ones over on Glitter Gulch, drowned out whatever stars might have been shining in the clear night sky. Instead of big casinos, only souvenir shops, fast-food places, tattoo parlors, and liquor stores lined the street. Light traffic cruised past without stopping, en route to less seedy destinations. A cold winter wind blew litter across the pavement.

She glanced around nervously. She didn't exactly have the sidewalk to herself, but there weren't a whole lot of people out and about. Most of the tourists were patronizing the big-name attractions farther west, like Neonopolis and the Fremont Street Experience. After a typically balmy afternoon, the temperature had been dropping precipitously ever since sundown, driving everyone indoors. Jill wished there were more pedestrians around. She shivered, and not just because of the cold.

Maybe this was a bad idea. . . .

A horn honked at the intersection, startling her. She nearly jumped out of her skin. Her heart pounded and she needed a second to recover. Was this what a panic attack felt like?

Knock it off, she scolded herself, dismayed at how jumpy she was. This was no time to let her fears get the better of her; she had to bring her "A" game to this job interview. Her bank account was getting seriously depleted. She really needed this gig.

Worried about her appearance, Jill checked out her reflection in the glass window of a discount electronics store. An attractive redhead in her early twenties gazed back at her; a curvy figure good enough to land the occasional modeling job, but not frequently enough for her pocketbook. Lustrous auburn curls tumbled past her shoulders. She was dressed warmly but stylishly in a tight pink sweater, a leather miniskirt, leggings, and boots. A push-up bra enhanced her natural attributes, but not too much. She wanted to look sexy, not trashy. Like a high-class hostess instead of a hooker. Her purse, a designer knockoff she had picked up at the mall, was slung over her shoulder.

She peeked at her watch. It was nearly ten-forty-five p.m. Kind of late for a job interview, but people in Vegas kept all kinds of hours. Supposedly, this was the only time the club owner, a Milton Boggs, had been available. Jill hoped everything was on the level. According to her friend Debra, this place was legit, but Jill couldn't help worrying. A pretty girl had to be careful in Sin City; there were all sorts of creeps and predators out there, as Jill knew from experience.

Debra had better know what she was talking about. . . .

Quickening her pace, Jill headed east across Las Vegas Boulevard. Her heels clicked against the pavement. The pedestrian crowd thinned out even more as she headed away from downtown. Despite herself, she kept glancing back over her shoulder. The crisp December night seemed to be getting colder by the minute; Vegas's desert climate made for warm days and freezing nights. She found herself wishing she had brought a jacket, even though that would have slightly spoiled the effect. An ominous warning echoed at the back of her mind:

"You better watch your back, 'cause I'm coming for you. Don't even think you can get away from me. You're going to die screaming. . . ."

Footsteps came up behind her. Alarmed, she looked back to see only a tired-looking Hispanic woman carrying a load of groceries. Jill gasped in relief as the other woman passed by. For a second there, she had been worried. No, not just worried, she admitted to herself.

Terrified.

Geezus, she thought. *I'm a nervous wreck.* Not that anyone could blame her, under the circumstances. She considered turning around and going home. If she managed to catch the next bus, she could be back in her apartment, behind closed doors, in less than an hour. It was awfully tempting. Did she really need the job that much?

Yes, actually.

Mustering her courage, she continued on her way. A couple of drunken college boys staggered out of a strip club on her left, then hailed a cab. Raucous laughter and music escaped the club before its door swung shut again. Jill paused briefly in front of the club. She couldn't help wondering if they were hiring. She hadn't stooped that low yet, but if she didn't land some paying work soon, she might have to review her options. The unfortunate possessor of two left feet, she had been too unco-ordinated to make it as a showgirl on the Strip, but she guessed that places like this were a lot less picky. They weren't exactly about the choreography, after all.

A vivid flash-forward, of her "dancing" in front of a mob of leering leches and pervs, was enough to send her scurrying past the club. *I can't believe I was actually considering that,* she thought, appalled at how desperate she'd become. *All the more reason to make sure I ace this interview.*

She pulled an index card from her purse and double-checked the address. "439 Zeller Avenue" was scribbled on the note in her own handwriting. "Corner of 7th and Zeller."

A street sign confirmed that she was nearing her destination, which proved to be in the least prosperous neighborhood she had seen yet. Empty storefronts were boarded up. Rolled-down metal doors protected the few remaining businesses, most of which had closed for the night. Graffiti defaced the walls and windows. Cigarette butts, fast-food wrappers, and the occasional used condom littered the pavement. Jill watched her step as she counted down the numbers over the doors until, finally, she reached 439.

It was hard to miss.

WaxWorkZ was a new nightclub with a spooky wax museum theme. The two-story brick building had been freshly painted black. Life-sized wax figures posed like mannequins in the storefront windows, against a red velvet background. One display depicted Jack the Ripper creeping up on an unsuspecting victim. The other featured a pale, raven-haired woman bathing in what appeared to be a tub of human blood. Plastic molding in the shape of dripping wax hung from the marquee above the entrance. The name of the club was spelled out in glowing red neon letters upon the marquee. OPENING SOON! proclaimed the banners stretched across the windows. No lights escaped the hidden interior of the club.

Looks like the right place, Jill thought.

Supposedly, the club was looking for hostesses and professional eye candy to adorn their grand opening next weekend. Jill had landed similar gigs in the past; event planners often arranged to have plenty of youthful sex appeal at openings just to create an enticing atmosphere. In theory, she could pick up a nice paycheck for doing nothing more than mingling and looking hot.

I can do that.

She took a second to pull herself together. Peering into the window, she checked her hair and makeup one last time before approaching the entrance. Despite the lighted marquee, the club was still a few nights away from opening. According to Debra, WaxWorkZ was the first part of a revitalization plan intended to turn this whole neighborhood around and draw some tourist dollars away from Fremont Street. Jill guessed that the owners had gotten the property for a song.

She glanced at her watch. 10:50. Her appointment wasn't due until eleven, so she was still a few minutes early, but she was anxious to get off the chilly, semi-deserted street. She looked up and down the sidewalk one more time, just to make sure she wasn't being followed, then rang the buzzer. An electronic gong sounded somewhere inside the club.

Long moments passed, but nobody came to the door. Jill paced restlessly, worried about missing her interview. She stared at the number above the door. This was the right address, wasn't it? *Don't be silly,* she told herself. How many wax museum-slash-nightclubs could there be, even in Vegas? This had to be the place, so how come nobody was letting her in? *Do I have the right day? The right time? What if I was supposed to be here at eleven* a.m.*?*

Had she already blown the interview?

She rang the buzzer again, more insistently, but still found herself stranded on the sidewalk. A tinted glass door offered her no view of what was going on inside. She placed her ear to the door, hoping to hear footsteps drawing near, but heard only the fading echoes of the gong.

10:58.

Oh, no, I'm going to be late, she fretted. Trying the door, she was surprised to find it unlocked. She pushed it open and stuck her head inside. "Hello?"

Not wanting to spend another moment on the lonely sidewalk, and afraid of missing her appointment, she stepped into the foyer. The air-conditioned interior was only slightly warmer than the frigid weather outside. Dim blue lighting cast shifting shadows on the glossy black walls. A long red carpet was flanked by rows of waxwork villains behind red velvet ropes. Footlights in the floor lit up the figures, who were posed atop squat black pedestals.

In keeping with the morbid atmosphere, the wax statues were a rogues' gallery of famous murderers of fact and fiction. Charles Manson, an "X" carved upon his forehead. Hannibal Lecter, complete with muzzle and straitjacket. John Wayne Gacy in full clown makeup. "The Son of Sam," talking to an evil demonic dog. Freddy Krueger, brandishing his razor claws. Natalie Davis, "the Miniature Killer," decorating a blood-spattered dollhouse. Vlad the Impaler. Lizzie Borden. Bonnie and Clyde. Janos Skorzeny. Rasputin. The Las Vegas Headhunter, holding up a shrunken head. . . .

Ugh, Jill thought. She shrunk away from the gruesome figures. One particular waxwork, a looming behemoth sporting a hockey mask and a silent chainsaw, reminded her of the gory slasher films her psycho ex-boyfriend used to force her to watch. Craig would have eaten this place up; he had loved horror movies, the bloodier the better. She shook her head in disgust. *Give me a good romantic comedy any day.*

The door swung shut behind her. She gulped at the sound.

The scary statues were not doing her jangly nerves any favors.

"Mr. Boggs?" She crept forward tentatively. "It's me, Jill Wooten. I'm here for the interview?"

Heavy black curtains hung before her, at the far end of the foyer. A glimpse of light shone through a crack in the drapes, luring her forward.

"Hello . . . ? Is anyone here?"

The spooky silence was not a good sign. She was tempted to give up and go home, but that meant venturing out into the streets again—and maybe applying for work at the strip club.

Not a chance, she thought.

She headed deeper into the club, through a gauntlet of eerie wax effigies, whose unblinking glass eyes seemed to track her as she made her way apprehensively down the carpet. The shifting blue lights made the sculpted murderers appear to move, at least out of the corner of her eye. A cold draft rustled the fabric of their costumes. Once again, as on the street, she felt predatory eyes upon her. The hair rose up on the back of her neck. Goosebumps sprouted beneath her sweater. The heels of her boots sank into the red carpet, muffling her tread. Her heart was going a mile a minute. She could hear her own breathing.

Or was that someone else?

Why the hell would anyone want to party in a spooky joint like this? Jill had no intention of ever setting foot in WaxWorkZ again, unless she was paid. She nervously fingered her purse. A heavy weight within the purse reassured her . . . somewhat. *You can do this,* she told herself. *They're just made of wax.*

She pushed through the curtain to find a lounge, bar, and dance floor waiting for her on the other side of the drapes. More wax figures, equally menacing, lurked in shadowy nooks and alcoves. A fountain of bubbling wax percolated in the center of the dance floor. Frozen sheets of wax flowed down the walls. Looking around for the source of the light, she spotted a door, slightly ajar, behind the bar area. Polished wax letters read EMPLOYEES ONLY.

Was that where she was supposed to go?

"Hello? Mr. Boggs?"

The unbroken silence unnerved her. Why had nobody come to greet her? Worst-case scenarios flashed across her brain. What if the club had been robbed or broken into? Maybe Mr. Boggs was lying dead or injured in the back room? Suppose his attackers were still there?

Screw it, she thought. *No job is worth this.*

She started to turn back, only to be halted by a muffled groan from the room ahead.

"Shit," Jill said. Now what was she supposed to do? The poor guy sounded like he needed help. *Maybe he's having a stroke or a heart attack,* she thought. He might need medical attention. . . .

Jill figured she had no choice but to investigate. Her mouth as dry as the desert, she went behind the bar and slipped through the door.

"Mr. Boggs? It's me, Jill Wooten?"

She discovered what appeared to be an empty office. A laptop computer sat atop a gray metal desk. An enormous flatscreen TV hung upon the wall to her left. A calendar by the desk counted down the days to the club's gala opening later this week. A replica iron maiden was propped up in one corner. A phone rested in its cradle. Invoices and resumes were piled in an in-box. A half-empty bottle of water suggested the club's owner hadn't gone far.

Aside from the looming medieval torture device, the office was reassuringly normal compared to the macabre decor of the public areas. To her relief, the room did not appear to have been ransacked, nor were there any signs of a struggle. Jill relaxed a little. Surely any thieves would have absconded with the laptop and flatscreen TV. She didn't see any open safes either.

So where was Mr. Boggs?

Maybe he'd just needed to hit the men's room?

Another strangled groan dispelled any such hopes. Her heart sank as she realized the whimpers were coming from the iron maiden. The rusty metal sarcophagus was large enough to hold an adult man or woman. The cabinet was cast in the likeness of an unsmiling female figure. A vertical seam down her front divided a pair of closed metal doors. A narrow air hole parted her iron lips. An agonized moan issued from the gap.

Someone was definitely trapped inside.

It took all her courage not to run screaming from the club. Trembling, she walked over to the iron maiden. She heard the groan again; there was definitely someone trapped inside. She nervously took hold of the metal doors, which felt cold and metallic. Against her better judgment, she pulled them open. Rusty hinges squeaked like they were in pain.

"Oh my God!"

An older guy, who she assumed was Milton Boggs, was trussed up inside the iron maiden. Bound and gagged, he struggled futilely to free himself. A steel collar was locked around his neck, holding him fast to the spiked inner walls of the torture device. Chains pinned his arms to his sides. His craggy face was contorted in fear. An ashen complexion was almost the same color as his disheveled gray hair. Bright red blood smeared the front of a rumpled white business shirt. Frantic eyes were wide with panic. He looked scared to death.

So was Jill.

A towel or cloth was jammed into his mouth. Jill couldn't make out what he was saying, but she guessed he was freaking out. She recoiled in horror, uncertain what to do. "Holy crap! Who did this to you?"

She stared at the heavy-duty locks and chains. She wanted to help the poor guy, but didn't know where to begin. The crimson stains on his shirt looked way too fresh for comfort. Her gorge rose. She glanced around fearfully, just in case Boggs's attacker was hiding somewhere, but didn't see anybody else. It seemed like they were alone, thank God.

"Hang on," she told the guy, resisting an urge to run for the nearest exit. "I'm calling 9-1-1." She fumbled with her purse, trying to find her cell phone. *Please*, she prayed, *let me have remembered to charge it!*

The phone call alone was not enough to calm Boggs. He went crazy inside the iron maiden, rattling his chains in a violent attempt to break free.

The iron collar dug into his neck as he strained at his bonds. He shouted at her through the gag, like he was trying to warn her. The last of his blood drained from his face. Bulging eyes stared in fright, not at Jill, she realized too late, but at *something* behind her. The office door slammed shut.

The roar of a chainsaw drowned out her scream.

Jill spun around to see the hulking chainsaw maniac from the lobby. Crazed bloodshot eyes glared at her from behind the expressionless hockey mask. The madman wore a grimy flannel shirt under bloodstained blue overalls. Heavy boots stomped across the floor. He brandished his whirring weapon, its jagged teeth spinning too fast to see. The chainsaw's engine growled ferociously. Noxious exhaust fumes invaded Jill's lungs. Her phone slipped from her fingers.

No! she thought. *This can't be happening!*

The waxwork figure, impossibly come to life, lumbered toward her, holding his chainsaw aloft. Jill stumbled backward, shrieking. Inside the iron maiden, Boggs flailed about uselessly. Jill stared into the rabid eyes of a lunatic. A crazy thought popped into her brain.

Craig?

Panicked, convinced she was only seconds away from being chopped to pieces, she thrust her hand into her purse. She took out a .38 revolver and swung the business end toward her attacker. There was no time to think or even aim carefully. She pulled the trigger.

The muzzle flared. A deafening report shook the office. The recoil knocked her into the desk, bruising her hip. The startled slasher staggered backward, then toppled onto the floor. The growling chainsaw fell from his grip, landing on the carpet a few inches away. It sputtered and fell silent. Bright arterial blood spurted from his chest. Hot droplets spattered Jill's face.

Her limbs turned to rubber. She could barely hang on to her gun, which suddenly felt like it weighed a hundred pounds. Leaning against the desk for support, she watched the wounded maniac twitch upon the floor. He tried to lift one hand. Gloved fingers clawed at the empty air. Jill didn't dare look away. In the movies, the killer never stayed dead, no matter how many times you shot him. . . .

"Oh, God! What did you do?"

A closet door swung open at the rear of the office. A strange man, wearing a baseball cap, a khaki jacket, and some sort of headset, burst into the room. A bearded jaw dropped at the sight of the dying madman. "Matt!" he cried out. "Oh shit! Matt!"

Confused, Jill lifted her gun. She swung it toward the newcomer, her finger poised on the trigger. The man's face went pale. He scrambled away from her, almost tripping over his own feet. He threw up his hands. "Wait! Don't shoot! It's just a TV show!"

What?

Jill didn't understand what was happening. Looking back toward the closet, she glimpsed a hidden room on the other side of the wall. More people were crowded in the doorway. They seemed torn between rushing to the madman's side and hiding from Jill's gun. Scared eyes watched her nervously. To her surprise, Jill spotted a familiar face.

"Debra?"

Like the others, her friend looked shocked and horrified. A sob tore itself from her throat. "Oh God, Jill. I'm so sorry!"

Debra was the one who had set up this interview for her. But what was she doing here now? And who were all these people?

"Please, lady," the man in the baseball cap said. A logo on the cap read *Shock Treatment*. He approached her cautiously. "Just put down the gun, okay?"

She had almost forgotten about the gun. She stared at the name on his cap.

A TV show? This was all just pretend?

Jill dropped the gun onto the desk. She grabbed onto the desk to keep from falling. The truth was starting to sink in. She found it hard to breathe.

Jesus, what have I done?

More people poured into the room. Ignoring Jill, they rushed to the bleeding man on the floor. "Matt?" A lean, tanned man with a ponytail tried to push his way through the crowd to get to the gunshot victim, but a woman with a first aid kit got to him first. "Everyone get back!" the medic ordered. "Give him some air!"

Ponytail gave the patient room. He chewed anxiously on his knuckles. "Matt?" he called out again. "Stay with us, Matt!"

The hockey mask came off, revealing the face of a perfect stranger. A lantern jaw, heavy brows, and a crooked nose gave him the look of a thug or bouncer. Mussed brown hair needed combing. His skin looked pale and clammy. Unable to speak, he coughed up blood.

Not Craig, Jill realized numbly. *It wasn't Craig at all.*

Debra pushed her way through the chaos to get to Jill. She threw her arms around her friend, apologizing over and over. Her tears soaked Jill's shoulder. "I'm sorry! I'm so sorry!"

"Has anyone called 9-1-1?" Ponytail shouted. "We need an ambulance!"

It was already too late. A final spasm shook Matt's body. His arms and legs went limp. His eyes glazed over. The blood stopped pumping from his chest.

The "chainsaw maniac" died before Jill's eyes.

"Are we still filming?!" Ponytail angrily kicked the silent chainsaw across the room. *"Somebody tell me we're not filming!"*

2

It WAS WELL past midnight when the CSIs arrived at WaxWorkZ.

Catherine Willows surveyed the scene from the passenger seat of a black Denali as Nick Stokes pulled up to the curb. Police cars were already parked in front of the nightclub, along with Jim Brass's unmarked Taurus and the coroner's wagon. As usual, the forensic team was the last to arrive. Yellow crime scene tape sealed off the front entrance, while uniformed police officers kept curious onlookers out of the way. A small crowd, comprised of both locals and obvious tourist types, mobbed the sidewalks on both sides of the street. Curious eyes scoped out the excitement. News of the shooting had clearly traveled fast.

"What's supposed to be the story here?" Nick asked. The broad-shouldered Texan hit the brake. A blue baseball cap covered his short brown hair. Catherine had briefed him on the basics on the way there. "We talking a homicide or a prank gone wrong?

"That's what we need to find out," she replied, reluctant to jump to any conclusions until they had thoroughly reviewed the evidence. Her predecessor, Gil Grissom, had taught her that. Keep an open mind until all the facts were in. Now that she was in charge of the night shift, Catherine subscribed to the same philosophy. Strawberry-blonde hair framed her face. Shrewd blue eyes had been trained to take in every detail. She glanced back over her shoulder at Greg Sanders, who was occupying the backseat of the SUV. "So, you were saying you've actually heard of this show?"

"You bet." He leaned forward, poking his head between Catherine and Nick. Tousled brown hair was stylishly mussed above his animated features. The former lab rat prided himself on his extensive knowledge of modern pop culture. "*Shock Treatment* is basically a horror-movie version of *Candid Camera.* They scare the crap out of unsuspecting victims, while filming the whole thing with hidden cameras."

"Never heard of it," Catherine admitted. Then again, what with working nights and raising a teenage daughter, she hadn't had much time for watching TV even before she was promoted to supervisor. These days she was lucky if she could squeeze in a movie rental on her days off. "Is it new?"

"Nope," Greg informed her. "It's been running on cable for at least five seasons now." His enthusiasm for the program was obvious. "You should have seen the flesh-eating virus episode. The victim practically had a meltdown before they let him in on the gag."

Nick scowled. "Making people think they're in actual danger? Sounds kind of sadistic to me." He gave Greg a dubious look. "You actually watch this stuff?"

"Sometimes," Greg confessed a trifle sheepishly. Suddenly, he didn't seem quite as proud of his expert status. He withdrew back into his own seat. "Call it a guilty pleasure."

"Or maybe just guilty," Catherine said.

Nick killed the engine. Catherine stepped out of the heated Denali into the frigid night air. A blue jacket and gloves fit the weather. FORENSICS was printed in block letters on back of the jacket. WILLOWS was written in smaller type above her chest, across from an LVPD star patch. She fished her metallic silver field kit out of the back of the Denali and headed for the entrance. Nick and Greg followed after her, lugging their own kits. She hoped that three CSIs would be enough for this call.

Unfortunately, the media had already arrived in force. A news copter hovered overhead, making Catherine glad that the crime scene was safely indoors. She'd had too many outdoor sites disturbed by the backwash from an overeager copter. Camera flashes and spotlights nearly blinded her. Reporters shouted questions at her, which she studiously ignored. A Channel 8 news van circled the block, looking for someplace to park. It was obvious that the press had already gotten wind of the show-biz angle.

Terrific, she thought sarcastically. In her experience, excess media attention just brought down more pressure on the crime lab and made her job that much more difficult. The fact that a TV show was involved, even an obscure cable program, meant publicity, gossip, and all sorts of public-relations baggage to deal with. *Ecklie is going to be all over this.*

She flashed her ID at the uni in charge, who lifted the yellow tape to let the CSIs through. Later on, they would have to bag the yellow tape and take it back to the lab for processing, just in case any trace evidence from the scene had transferred to it. At least once, they had actually cracked a case by isolating some cobwebs that had been accidentally carried out by a careless first responder. A mosquito caught in the webbing had contained DNA from the perp, blowing his alibi. Catherine had made sure to look over any crime scene tape ever since.

Escaping the reporters and their cameras, they entered WaxWorkZ. The club's dimly lit foyer was a literal chamber of horrors, and not in the bloody sense they were used to. They paused on the red carpet to take in the display. Catherine hadn't seen this many hardcore killers since her last trip to the penitentiary.

"Wow." Greg gawked at the macabre figures. "Not exactly Madame Tussauds quality, but pretty good."

Catherine was less amused. She got enough of murder and mayhem every night at work. She grimaced at the sight of the Miniature Killer immortalized in wax. "Okay, that is way too soon."

Natalie Davis had committed suicide in her prison cell only three years ago, after nearly killing Sara Sidle. Resurrected in effigy, she tended to her gruesome dollhouse with meticulous care, an inscrutable smile upon her bland, unassuming features. Catherine was glad that she hadn't assigned Sara to this call.

"Tell me about it," Nick agreed. He shook his head disapprovingly. "Is it just me, or does this place remind you of Millander?"

Paul Millander, another notorious serial killer in their past, had manufactured grisly Halloween novelties for a living, churning out severed rubber heads, arms, hands, and feet, some of which he'd used to plant bogus prints and impressions at crime scenes. He'd also managed to produce several genuine corpses before the CSIs had finally brought him to justice. Like Natalie Davis, he had ultimately cheated the executioner by taking his own life.

"No," Catherine said. "You're not the only one."

Now was no time for a trip down memory lane, however. She mentally shoved the disturbing recollections into the past. Millander and the Miniature Killer were dead. She had a new case to focus on. Scanning the lobby, Catherine noted a conspicuous gap in one line of figures. An empty pedestal was positioned between John Wayne Gacy and Lizzie Borden.

Wonder who used to be there?

Another cop met them at the end of the carpet and escorted them to the actual site of the shooting, which turned out to be a back office behind the bar. The body of the victim lay on his back on the floor.

The front of his blue coveralls was soaked in blood. The clotted stains were still shiny and damp, indicating that the blood had been spilled in the last few hours. A gunshot wound in his chest left little doubt as to the cause of death. A hockey mask lay near his head. Blood spatter stained the walls and furniture. An untouched void on the desktop indicated the possible location of the shooter. Catherine winced at the sight of smeared red footprints all around the body; too many people seemed to have stomped all over the evidence. A single bullet hole could be seen in the wall by the door.

A chainsaw rested on the carpet about a yard from the body. Catherine did a double take at the incongruous power tool.

And was that an iron maiden in the corner?

What the hell?

Captain Jim Brass was already on the job, along with David Phillips, the assistant medical examiner. Dave appeared to have completed his preliminary examination of the victim, and was now waiting for Catherine and her team to release the body. Both he and Brass were keeping their distance from the corpse to avoid disturbing the blood and footprints more than they already were. Catherine appreciated their caution, but was not surprised. The two men had been working hand-in-hand with the crime lab for over a decade now; Brass had even supervised the forensics unit for a time before returning to his true calling as a detective. They knew the drill.

"Welcome to the house of wax," Brass greeted them, looking and sounding nothing like Vincent Price. A Jersey accent testified to his roots in Hoboken. A dour, hangdog face conveyed the impression that few things surprised him anymore. A star-shaped badge was pinned to the lapel of a tan sport coat.

"What did we miss?" Catherine asked.

Brass pulled out his notebook. "The victim is Matt Novak, an actor on the show. According to multiple witnesses, who were filming the whole thing from the next room, Novak surprised the shooter, one Jill Wooten, as part of a hidden-camera stunt. She surprised *him* by pulling out a gun and putting a bullet into his chest before anybody could say 'cut.'" He put the notebook away. "Guess his performance was a little too convincing."

"Talk about dying for your art," Catherine said. She peeled off her winter gloves and replaced them with thin white latex. "And the chainsaw?"

"A noisy prop," Brass reported. "All bark, no bite."

Catherine took a closer look at the chainsaw, wanting to quickly eliminate it as the murder weapon. A gloved finger gingerly touched one of the jagged teeth, which bent backward when she pressed on it. The teeth weren't metal at all, she realized, just rubber painted metallic silver. *Guess that explains why the carpet isn't all chewed up.* The harmless prop would have generated lots of noise and smoke, but no real danger. Not that any frightened "victim" was likely to notice.

The CSIs gathered around the body, like mourners at a wake. Novak's bloodshot eyes stared blankly at the ceiling; a thin film had already formed over the lifeless orbs. Catherine looked at David, curious to hear his conclusions. "David?"

"COD appears to be a single GSW to the chest."
He pointed at the hole in the wall she had noticed
earlier. It was right by the door, about six inches to
the left of where they had entered the office. "Possibly a through-and-through. Rigor and body temperature puts the time of death at approximately
eleven p.m."

Brass nodded. "Which agrees with the initial reports from the witnesses."

That makes life easier, Catherine thought. Maybe
this would prove to be a straightforward case of
death by misadventure. She put herself in the place
of the alleged shooter, suddenly finding herself face-
to-face with a masked, chainsaw-wielding assailant.
Catherine could see why she might have shot the
actor in self-defense. *Under the circumstances, I might
have fired, too.*

"Do we have a weapon?"

Brass produced a Smith & Wesson revolver, already sealed inside a plastic evidence bag. Catherine
raised an eyebrow. "You doing our job for us now,
Jim?"

He shrugged apologetically. "One of the witnesses,
a tech guy on the film crew, had already secured the
gun before we arrived. He turned it over to the first
officer on the scene."

Catherine frowned. She would have preferred to
have collected the weapon herself from its original
location, but she couldn't blame the bystanders for
not wanting to leave a loaded weapon lying around.
Especially after what they had just witnessed. *Maybe
it won't matter,* she thought. From the sound of it,
there was little question as to who pulled the trigger.

"Anybody else touch the victim?" she asked. "Aside from David, that is?"

"'Fraid so," Brass answered. "A couple of crew members tried to help Novak before he kicked the bucket. Took off his mask and everything." He knew this wasn't what Catherine wanted to hear. "Sorry."

It was starting to look like half of Las Vegas had handled the evidence before they'd got here. The chaotic scene, with the panicked film crew desperately trying to save the dying actor, explained the flurry of bloody footprints. She sighed in resignation, accepting the situation for what it was. This wouldn't be the first time would-be Good Samaritans had messed up her crime scene.

"But here's the good part," Brass added. "We've got the entire thing on film." He gestured around the room, pointing out the location of the various hidden cameras, including the TV screen, a small mirror, and a smoke detector on the ceiling. "From multiple angles, they tell me."

"Okay, that's convenient." She welcomed the windfall. Archie in the A/V lab had some work ahead of him. "I'm going to want every frame of that footage."

"Way ahead of you," Brass said. "I've already told these folks not to erase a thing. We've got all the cameras locked down."

Catherine expected nothing less. "Great."

Taking possession of the gun, she turned her attention to the body. Flashbulbs strobed the office as Nick and Greg took numerous photos of the late Matt Novak. Shutters clicked rapidly until they were satisfied that they had every shot they needed. Catherine hung back, supervising, while the guys lifted the confusing mélange of footprints onto clear plastic gel filters. The body's supine position suggested that much of the blood had collected in his chest, cutting down on the size of the blood pool around him. Nonetheless, they would have to collect the carpet as well, once it no longer had a corpse lying on it. She walked around the body one last time before deciding that there was nothing more to be learned from its placement here. "Okay," she said. "Let's get Mr. Novak on his way."

While Greg labeled the footprints, Nick helped David flip over the body. Sure enough, an exit wound in his back confirmed that the bullet had passed all the way through him. They zipped the cadaver into a pristine white body bag made of polyvinyl chloride. The white fabric ensured that loose bits of trace evidence could be easily spotted should they fall off the body in transit. They loaded the body onto a gurney and David wheeled him out the door. Matt Novak's next starring role would be at the morgue. The violent circumstances of his death mandated an autopsy, although Catherine would be surprised if Doc Robbins turned up anything unexpected. How Novak had died appeared obvious. Why was another matter.

The big question: was this just a tragic accident— or something more premeditated?

"How about the witnesses?" she asked Brass.

"We've got them herded upstairs," he informed her. "In the VIP lounges. Officers are keeping them apart until we can take their statements."

Catherine nodded. Separating any suspects and

witnesses was standard protocol. You didn't want them comparing notes with each other. Even if there was no deliberate attempt to fabricate a phony story, too much chatter could mess up people's memories, make them start to second-guess their own initial impressions. You wanted each person's account, exactly as they remembered it, not some sort of consensus version.

"And the shooter?" she asked.

"Pretty messed up," Brass said. "No surprise. Paramedics are checking her out now." He cocked his head toward the north wall. "There's a bunch of studio trailers parked out back. I figure we can question people there. Give your guys plenty of room to work in here." Nick and Greg were busy rolling up the carpet. "I'm going to talk to the shooter first. You want to sit in?"

Probably not a bad idea. She needed to check the woman's hands for GSR anyway, to confirm that she had indeed fired the fatal shot. "All right." She packed up her field kit and addressed Nick and Greg. "You guys finish working the scene. Brass and I are going to ask some questions."

"Whatever you say, boss." Nick took a breather before lugging the carpet out to the SUV. He unzipped his jacket to cool off. "We can handle things here."

"Don't I know it," she said. After taking charge of the night shift, she had drafted Nick as her second-in-command. So far, that was turning out to be one of her better executive decisions. "Keep me posted."

She vacated the office with Brass, leaving Nick and Greg to collect the remainder of the physical evidence, including the bullet in the wall. She knew she could count on them to make sure everything made it safely back to the lab.

"Okay," she told Brass. "Let's find out just what sort of colossal screw-up we're dealing with here."

The trailers in the parking lot were of the sort used by film crews when shooting on location. Catherine had been in several such trailers before; she'd lost track of how many movies and TV shows had been filmed in Vegas. It was a popular location. Crossing the lot, she noticed that one of the trailers was larger and more impressive than the others. It was at least two stories tall, seventy-five-feet long, and looked big enough to house a decent-sized crime lab.

Wonder who rates that one?

The other four trailers were of less titanic proportions. Brass led her to a silver Airstream trailer a short hike away from the back door of the nightclub. A bored-looking uni was standing guard outside the trailer. An ambulance was parked nearby.

Brass rapped on the trailer door. A young paramedic answered. A stethoscope hung around her neck. The name on her jacket was EXTON.

"How's she doing?" Brass asked.

"Still pretty shook up," Exton said, "but not in shock. I gave her a mild sedative." She shrugged. "Not much else I can do here."

"Had she been drinking?" Catherine asked. Alcohol was frequently a factor in accidental shootings.

Exton shook her head. "She's clean. Didn't seem to be high either, although we didn't test her for drugs. She said she hadn't taken anything. I didn't see any reason to doubt her."

Catherine trusted the paramedic's assessment. You didn't need to be drunk or high to be scared by a man with a chainsaw.

"Thanks," Brass said. "We'll take it from here."

Exton cleared out, and the investigators climbed into the trailer. They closed the door behind them to keep in the heat. Vinyl flooring led them past a built-in dinette and wardrobe. Sandwiches, popcorn, a vegetable platter, and a pot of coffee had been laid atop the dining table. Catherine was tempted by the coffee. It was looking like they had a long night ahead of them.

They found Jill Wooten in a dressing room near the rear of the trailer, seated on a stool in front of a makeup table. An ambulance blanket was draped over her shoulders. Shaky hands clutched a cup of coffee. Model-pretty good looks showed through her obvious distress. Large green eyes were red from crying. Tearstains streaked her cheeks. Her makeup was a mess. A tight pink sweater was splattered with blood. Catherine put her in her early twenties, only a few years older than her daughter, Lindsey. A maternal instinct threatened to compromise Catherine's objectivity, but she knew better than to see Lindsey in every troubled young woman she encountered on the job. That wasn't good for anyone.

"Ms. Wooten?" Brass introduced himself and Catherine. "We have some questions we need to ask you."

Jill gave them a confused look. "But I already told a policeman what happened."

"We need to hear it again," Brass explained. "A

man is dead. We need to make sure we understand the circumstances."

She nodded. "I understand." She sat up straight, bracing herself for the cop's questions. Her voice was hoarse. "What do you want to know?"

"Why don't you start at the beginning?" he suggested.

"Okay." She put down the coffee cup and took a deep breath before diving in. "I had a job interview tonight. My friend Debra told me they were hiring girls for the opening." A worried look came over her face as she realized how that sounded. "Not for anything sexual. Nothing like that. Just to glam things up, you know?"

Catherine understood the concept. "Got it. You were just supposed to be window dressing."

"That's right." Jill sounded relieved at having that cleared up. "Anyway, when I got here, the front door was unlocked, but nobody seemed to be around. There was a light coming from the office, though, so I checked it out. That's when I found that guy chained up in the torture thingie."

"Wait a second," Catherine interrupted. "There was a man in the iron maiden?"

"Uh-huh. An old guy with a gag over his mouth. I tried to call for help, but then that freak with the chainsaw came at me—" Her voice faltered and her eyes welled with tears. "I swear to God, I thought it was for real! It was like something out of a horror movie. I'd never been so scared in my entire life. I thought he was going to chop me to pieces!"

Brass took a Kleenex from his pocket. Crying victims and suspects were par for the course. "Okay, take your time," he said a little more gently than usual. Catherine wondered if he was identifying with the poor girl. She recalled that he had once shot and killed a fellow officer by accident. That was something you never forgot. He handed her the tissue. "Whenever you're ready."

Jill needed a moment to recover. She dabbed at her eyes with the tissue. She wiped her nose on her sleeve. "You know what happened next," she said between sniffles. "I pulled out my gun and shot him."

That was the part Catherine didn't get. "You always bring a gun to a job interview?"

"Not usually," Jill admitted. "But . . . I've been getting these horrible phone calls lately, threatening me." She shuddered beneath her blanket. "In fact, I got a call just a couple of hours before I left my apartment tonight. No way was I going out after dark without my gun."

Catherine exchanged a look with Brass. Maybe this case wasn't as straightforward as it first appeared.

"These calls," Brass asked. "Any idea who's making them?"

"Oh yeah," Jill said. "I can't prove it, but I'm pretty sure it's my psycho ex-boyfriend, Craig. He's a real creep, started stalking me after we broke up. For a second tonight, I honestly thought that chainsaw guy was Craig." Anger flushed her ashen cheeks. "He always loved that slasher movie crap. Should've tipped me off that he was no good. I even had to get a restraining order against him. You can look it up. His name's Gonch. Craig Gonch."

"We'll do that," Brass promised. "Can you recognize his voice on the phone?"

Jill hesitated. "I'm not sure. It sounded like him, sort of, but it was all whispery, you know, like he was trying to disguise it or something." Her face curdled in contempt. "Sneaky S.O.B."

"What about caller ID?" Catherine asked.

"No luck," Jill said glumly. "He blocked it somehow."

That information would still be on file with the phone company, Catherine knew. With any luck, Archie could track down the source of the calls. Unless the caller used some sort of disposable cell phone.

"Did you save any of the calls?" Brass asked.

"You bet I did!" she declared. "In case I needed to get another restraining order."

"Good," Catherine said. "We can get copies off your voice mail." She made a mental note to look into subpoenaing the ex's phone records as well, if it turned out that there might be more to this shooting than met the eye. The anonymous calls might have been just a coincidence, but, if nothing else, it sounded like they were a contributing factor to what happened tonight. If that was *really* why Jill had brought a gun to the club.

They couldn't rule out the possibility that Jill had shot Matt Novak on purpose.

"Let's get back to the actual shooting," Brass suggested. "You had no idea who was attacking you when you fired at Mr. Novak?"

"Novak? Was that his name?" Jill started to fall apart again. Tears gushed from her eyes. "Oh my

God, that poor guy! I can't believe I really killed somebody!"

Brass offered her another tissue. "What about when his mask came off? Did you see his face?"

"Yes, unfortunately." She squeezed her eyes shut to block out the image. "I'm never going to forget it!"

"Did you recognize him?" Brass asked.

"No." She hesitated. "I don't think so."

Catherine picked up on her uncertain tone. "What do you mean?"

"Now that I think of it, maybe he looked a little familiar." She paused to search her memory before opening her eyes again. "Like maybe I've seen him on TV?"

Possible, Catherine thought. Novak was an actor, even if she had never heard of him. Maybe he had done some other TV spots or commercials. *We should look into his credits.*

"You never thought it might just be somebody playing a trick on you?" Brass asked. "In a spooky place like that?"

"No!" she blurted. "Not after I found Mr. Boggs in that metal coffin thing, all bloody and everything." She pulled the blanket tighter around her. "You have no idea how scared I was!"

She struck Catherine as sincere. "This *Shock Treatment* TV show? Were you familiar with it?"

"A little," she confessed a bit defensively. "Craig liked to watch it, back when we were together. But that didn't even occur to me tonight. I thought it was all real!" The sniffles started up again. "Who was this Novak guy? Do you know? Did he have a family?" Her questions dissolved into sobs, and she buried her face in her hands. "Omigod, I killed him. I really killed somebody!"

Sedative or not, Jill looked like she was at the end of her rope. Catherine judged that they wouldn't be getting much more out of her tonight. At least nothing useful.

Brass seemed to agree. "All right, Ms. Wooten. We're almost done now. But I'm going to have to ask you not to leave town until this is all cleared up." He took her address, then handed her his card. "Give me a call if you remember anything else."

Jill got up to go.

"Not quite yet," Catherine told her. "I need to get your fingerprints and check your hands for gunshot residue." She opened up her field kit and took out some moist swabs. Her gaze fell upon Jill's blood-splattered sweater. The pretty pink top was evidence now. "And I'm going to need your clothes, too."

"Oh," Jill said.

3

"HELLO? IS ANYBODY there?"

Rita Segura rapped against the locked glass doors. Frosted white letters, etched into the glass, identified the business as THE NILE, A SALON & SPA FOR DISCRIMINATING MEN AND WOMEN. A sign posting the hours reminded her that the spa didn't open until eight, but Rita couldn't wait that long. She could feel a migraine coming on. She needed one of The Nile's special massages now. *If we move fast,* she thought, *maybe we can nip this headache in the bud before it gets too bad.*

She tapped her toes impatiently on the sidewalk. Exclusive boutiques, cafes, and clinics faced the palm-lined walk of an upscale "lifestyle centre" in southwest Vegas. Rita usually enjoyed window shopping here, but this morning she was in a hurry. A petite Latina still a few years short of thirty, she had driven straight to the spa from her home nearby. Designer clothing flattered her trim, attractive figure, which she took great pains to maintain. A fur wrap protected her from the early morning chill. Gucci sunglasses shielded her sensitive eyes from the sunrise. A cool breeze rustled her dark brown hair, styled in a short wavy bob. Manicured nails massaged her left temple, which was already starting to throb. A telltale aura flickered ominously at the periphery of her vision.

She stopped kneading her head. It wasn't helping. *Come on*, she thought. *Somebody help me.*

She peered through the glass doors, hoping to catch a glimpse of movement. The lights were on inside, giving her hope that some of the staff had already arrived. The lobby was decorated in an ancient Egyptian motif. Bamboo plants and leafy papyri rose from glazed earthenware vases. Hieroglyphs were painted on the walls. Sandstone tiles, looking like they'd been chipped off the pyramids, fronted the reception desk, which was, maddeningly, as yet unoccupied. Flowing water trickled over a shallow artificial stream. Rita prayed that the staff was just in the back somewhere. Her knuckles rapped against the door.

"Hello?"

She was half-convinced that no one could hear her when an exotic presence emerged from the rear of the salon. Rita gasped in relief as she recognized Alexandra Nile, the owner of The Nile. A decade or two older than Rita, Madame Alexandra was clad in a flowing silk kaftan embroidered with stylized lotus fronds. Jet-black bangs (dyed, no doubt) hung beneath the saffron turban wrapped atop her head. Crystal earrings dangled from her lobes, and a silver ankh hung upon her chest. Turquoise bracelets adorned her wrists. Open-toed sandals peeked out from beneath the hem of her robe. Impeccable posture added inches to her height.

Thank God, Rita thought. *I knew I would find somebody here.*

Madame Alexandra approached the entrance from the other side. Kohl-lined violet eyes regarded Rita through the glass. Her gaunt, immaculate face held a quizzical, slightly annoyed expression. She glanced pointedly at her watch.

"Ms. Segura?" she asked. Rita was a regular at The Nile. "I'm afraid we don't open for another hour."

"I know, I know." Rita raised her voice to be heard through the glass. "I hate to impose on you like this, but I feel one of my bad headaches coming on, and you know your massages are the only things that stop them." Rita had tried acupuncture, biofeedback, meditation, Botox, and every medication under the sun, but nothing had worked for long. She winced in pain, the pressure building in her temple. Even with the shades on, the light was hurting her eyes. "Please. I have an important luncheon this afternoon, and I don't want to have to cancel."

Madame Alexandra frowned, clearly reluctant to open early. "I don't know. . . ."

"Please!" Rita implored. She knew she was one of Madame Alexandra's top customers, and had talked The Nile up to all of her high-society acquaintances. Surely that counted for something. "I would be so grateful if you could just squeeze me in early. As a personal favor?"

The salon owner vacillated, perhaps weighing the negative consequences of disappointing so influential a client. Rita regretted throwing her wealth and status around, but didn't see any viable alternative. The prospect of facing today's busy social calendar while fighting a raging migraine was just too ghastly to be contemplated.

"Just this once," she pleaded. "You're the only place in town that has the treatment I need."

"This is true," Madame Alexandra conceded. Sighing, she bowed to the inevitable and unlocked the door. "I suppose we can make an exception in an emergency."

"Thank you so much!" Rita rushed into the lobby before the other woman could change her mind. Things were starting to look up; there was still time to halt the migraine in its tracks. "I won't make a habit of this, I promise."

Madame Alexandra waved away her gratitude. "Do not trouble yourself." Now that the decision had been made, the glamorous spa owner was all hospitality. Her rotund tones held an upper-class, vaguely British accent of questionable authenticity. "We wouldn't want to see one of our favorite clients suffer."

"That's very generous of you." Rita basked in the soothing atmosphere of the lobby. Middle Eastern music played softly in the background. Incense perfumed the air. Shelves of lotions and other personal care products were on display next to the reception desk. An indoor stream flowed through a gap in the tile floor. Bamboo and palm fronds added a touch of nature to the waiting area, where a couch and chairs surrounded a low ebony coffee table. New Age magazines fanned across the tabletop. Flyers and pamphlets promoted various spiritual retreats and workshops. Gods, goddesses, and pharaohs reigned in two dimensions upon the painted walls. A bas-relief sphinx presided serenely upon the sandstone front of the reception desk. The miniature Nile babbled softly over polished stones.

Yes, Rita thought. *Today is looking better already.*

Mercifully, Madame Alexandra did not keep her waiting. She clapped her hands. "Heather!"

A fit young blonde answered her summons. In keeping with the spa's theme, she wore a pleated white linen dress with sandals. Freckles dotted her rosy cheeks, which held traces of baby fat. A sandy yellow pixie cut gave her a gamine look. "Yes, Madame Alexandra?"

"Ms. Segura requires a serpentine massage immediately," the spa owner informed the masseuse grandly. She had the air of an empress issuing a decree. "Is the Cleopatra Room prepared?"

"Yes, Madame," Heather answered. "All set."

"Excellent." Madame Alexandra guided Rita back toward the dressing rooms. "Heather will be with you as soon as you're ready."

Rita sighed in anticipation. She could feel her whole body relaxing already. Even the pressure in her skull seemed easier to bear. "You're a lifesaver, Madame Alexandra. I won't forget this."

The older woman airily dismissed her praise. "Please. It's the least we can do for you." They stepped into a corridor and she veered away to the left. "I'll be in my office if you need anything."

"I think I'm fine," Rita said. "Thanks again."

She knew the layout of the spa by heart. Finding her way to the dressing rooms, she enjoyed having the whole place to herself. She made a mental note to send Madame Alexandra a thank-you note later, and perhaps a deluxe fruit basket or bouquet of flowers. Eager to avail herself of The Nile's unique services, Rita wasted no time undressing. Hanging her wrap and designer clothes in a convenient locker, she changed into a white terrycloth bathrobe and slippers before scampering down to the Cleopatra Room at the end of the hall. A profile of the legendary queen was painted on the door. Rita didn't give it a second look before slipping inside.

"The usual treatment?" Heather asked her as she entered. A clean white towel was draped over the girl's arm. A second towel was already spread out atop the massage table. A clear glass cupboard held various massage oils and lotions. An electronic towel warmer, which resembled a large metal toaster, sat on a countertop next to the sink. A classical painting of Cleopatra lounging on a barge was framed on one wall. Wall sconces flickered softly. The dim, subdued lighting was easy on her eyes. The tile floor felt warm beneath her slippers.

Accustomed to the graceful decor, her gaze was immediately drawn to the chamber's most singular accouterment, which sat atop a carved ebony cabinet against the back wall. A rectangular glass vivarium held at least a dozen snakes of various sizes and colors. Their sinuous bodies slithered over, under, and across each other, beneath the warming glow of a heat lamp. As always, Rita was fascinated by the nesting reptiles. Largish king and corn snakes, at least three feet in length, mingled with smaller garter snakes. Smooth, shiny scales varied in hue from one end of the spectrum to the other. Yellow racing stripes ran along the length of thin black snakes. Brightly colored bands circled their bodies, dividing them into segments. Iridescent checkers and blotches added to their visual allure. Unblinking reptilian eyes gazed back at her. A forked tongue flicked at the glass between them.

"Yes, please."

She swiftly disrobed and lay facedown on the cushioned massage table. The room was warm enough that her bare skin didn't feel at all chilled. Heather laid her towel across Rita's rear end in a token concession to modesty. "Looks like you've been working on your tan," the masseuse observed, admiring the client's evenly toned skin. "I'm jealous."

Rita appreciated the compliment, but was in no mood for small talk. A pang in her temple started to spread to her forehead. She sensed they were running out of time. "Hurry, please."

"Of course," Heather assured her. "Coming right up."

Rita turned her head sideways to watch the masseuse in action. She braced herself for company as Heather slid open the lid of the vivarium and took out two large handfuls of hissing snakes. The serpents squirmed restlessly, trying to escape, but Heather managed to hold on to all of the tangled reptiles. Scaly coils wrapped around her wrists and forearms.

"Here we go," she said.

Without further ado, Heather gently deposited

the snakes onto Rita's back. Their cool, dry bodies undulated across her naked flesh. Agitated by their sudden change in location, they attempted to flee in every direction, but Heather deftly herded them back toward Rita's spine, braiding them together to slow their escape. The larger, heavier snakes kneaded her deep tissues, while the smaller serpents fluttered across her skin like caressing fingers. Despite the heat lamp, their cold-blooded bodies were chilly at first, but she knew from experience that her own innate warmth would soon heat them up. A scaly belly slithered down her spine.

"Ah," Rita sighed rapturously. "Just what I needed."

Serpentine massages were the latest therapeutic craze. According to Madame Alexandra, the practice had originated in Israel a few years back, but was slowly making inroads into America's trendier enclaves. The sinuous motions were said to relieve tension, soothe sore muscles, and even cure migraines. As far as Rita knew, The Nile was the only salon in Vegas currently offering the treatment, but she'd heard rumors that some of its competitors, and even a couple of the big resort hotels on the Strip, were thinking of adding live snakes to their spas and health clubs. *Seems like a natural for the Luxor*, she thought, *or maybe the Bellagio*.

She settled in to enjoy the experience, luxuriating in the unique sensation of the snakes writhing all over her nude body. There was something undeniably sensual, and maybe even a little erotic, about it. *No wonder Eve had succumbed to the Serpent*, she mused; Rita felt like she had snuck back into the

Garden of Eden. A forked tongue tickled the back of her neck. She felt the pressure on her temple ease. Her eyes stopped hurting. Just as she'd hoped, the headache was already fading away.

Maybe she could make that luncheon after all.

Just as she was drifting off on a tide of bliss, however, she was jolted by a sudden sharp pain at the base of her neck. What felt like tiny needles pierced her flesh.

"Christ!" she yelled out. "I've been bitten!"

Her dreamy swoon evaporated. Her neck stung like blazes. Alarmed, she sat up abruptly, spilling the snakes onto the floor. The towel slid off her behind, landing unnoticed at Heather's feet. Glancing down, Rita was horrified to see a banded red, black, and yellow snake still hanging on to her throat, its fangs sunk into her jugular. The snake bounced against her bare shoulder, swinging back and forth like a scaly pendulum. An angry popping noise emanated from somewhere inside the creature.

"Crap!" she shrieked. "It won't let go!"

Heather's face was pale. She backed away fearfully, like she was on the verge of bolting from the room, while the spilled serpents scattered across the floor in all directions. She jumped in fright as a thick orange corn snake slithered across her foot.

"Omigod!" the girl blurted. "That's not supposed to happen!"

"I know that, you idiot!" Rita crouched atop the massage table, which was now an island of refuge surrounded by a sea of hissing menaces. Meanwhile, the banded snake's jaws were still clamped onto her neck. "Don't just stand there! Do something!"

Heather glanced longingly at the door. She inched toward the exit. "Maybe I should get Madame Alexandra?"

"Don't you dare leave me!" Rita snapped, close to hysterics. She started to reach for the snake herself, then yanked her hand back, afraid to touch it. The pain was getting worse by the second. She wasn't sure how much longer she could stand it. "Get it off me!"

"O-okay," Heather stammered. Mustering her courage, she darted forward and grabbed onto the vicious creature's tail. Rita screamed as the snake's fangs were painfully ripped from her body. Heather yelped as well as she flung the snake against the nearest wall. It smacked against the plaster, then slid down onto the floor with the rest of the snakes. Heather scooted into a corner to get away from the swarming serpents. Hisses and pops assailed the women's ears.

Rita's hand went instinctively to her throat. The torn skin was wet and sticky. Blood trickled from a ring of ragged teeth marks at the base of her neck. Her fingers came away from the wound. They were red at the tips.

I don't understand, she thought. *That's never happened before.*

A tingling sensation seemed to spread from the bites. Her pulse pounded in her ears. Was it just her nerves, or was she starting to feel faint? She found it hard to swallow.

"Oh crap," she whispered hoarsely. "Get a doctor. Call 9-1-1!"

Heather tried to calm her. "Don't worry. It will be all right. None of our snakes are poisonous."

Rita wasn't so sure of that. Her vision blurred, double vision splitting Heather into shimmering blond twins. A cold sweat broke out over her exposed body. Her eyelids drooped. A trickle of drool leaked from the corner of her mouth. She suddenly felt weak and lethargic. The damn migraine came back full force, squeezing her skull like a red-hot vise. She panted raggedly, finding it difficult to breathe. Her arms and legs went limp and rubbery. Nausea turned her stomach. She could barely keep her eyes open.

What's happening to me?

The door slammed open. Two Madame Alexandras burst into the room. "What's going on?" she demanded. "Why all the shouting?" Her exotic features reacted in shock to the serpentine chaos in the Cleopatra Room. Loose snakes darted toward the open door, while Heather cowered in the corner. Rita swayed unsteadily atop the massage table. Blood dripped from her wounded throat. The room started to spin around her. Blackness encroached on her vision.

"It bit me," she whimpered. "It freakin' bit me. . . ."

Rita tumbled off the table onto the floor. She collapsed atop the warm ceramic tiles.

Hissing furiously, the snakes slithered away from her body.

4

JIM BRASS WAITED outside the makeup trailer while Jill Wooten changed into a jumpsuit under Catherine's supervision. He suspected that Jill was probably happy to get out of her blood-splattered attire. Chances were, she never wanted to see those clothes again. Brass knew the feeling. He still remembered the day he had accidentally shot Officer Martin Bell during that firefight six years ago. He had never been able to put on the jacket he'd worn that day again. Too many painful memories. Eventually, he'd tossed it in the trash.

Good riddance.

He loitered at the foot of the steps, wishing he had put on a heavier coat. Dawn was hours away and they still had several more principals to interview, not to mention the rest of the TV crew. He figured he was going to be here past sunrise at least. In the meantime, the temperature had to be in the thirties. His breath frosted before his lips. He began to regret vacating the trailer while Jill changed. Chivalry was a bitch.

Footsteps echoed behind him. He turned to see a uniform, Officer Pennington, escorting another witness toward the trailer. Debra Lusky was the next item on Brass's to-do list. According to Jill, her friend had steered her toward tonight's "job interview" at WaxWorkZ. Which meant that Debra had set her friend up for a little *Shock Treatment*.

Wonder how she feels about that now?

He looked Debra over as she approached the trailer. Compared to her redheaded, modelesque friend, she struck him as a bit on the plain side. Of medium height and weight, she trudged glumly toward the detective, wearing slacks and a stylish wool blazer that he guessed she had bought especially for her big debut on TV. Straight brown hair was cut in a short, professional bob. Her defeated expression and body language hinted at a guilty conscience. She dragged her feet across the pavement.

"Here she is, Captain," Pennington told Brass. Pennington was a burly Filipino who looked like he put in plenty of time at the gym. "I told her you wanted to talk to her."

Brass gruffly acknowledged his service. "Thanks."

Debra and her escort had reached the foot of the steps when the door to the trailer swung open. Catherine's voice could be heard inside. "You're free to go, Ms. Wooten. Thank you for your cooperation."

Jill emerged from the trailer, clad in an unflattering orange jumpsuit. Another uni stood by a few yards away, waiting to drive her back to her apartment out past Tropicana. Jill froze atop the steps as she spotted the other woman below her. Her knuckles tightened on the rail. "Debra?"

"Jill?" Debra hurried forward, leaving Pennington behind. She held out her arms in sympathy, like she couldn't wait to give her friend a hug. "Oh my God, Jill. How are you doing? I am so sorr—"

She didn't get to finish her apology. "You lying bitch!" Jill snarled, her face twisted in rage. "How could you set me up like this? Do you realize what you've done? This is all your fault!"

She lunged at Debra. *Oh hell*, Brass thought. Reacting quickly, he grabbed onto Jill's waist before she could add assault and battery to her rap sheet. He struggled to hold on to her. She was stronger than she looked. "Whoa there! We don't need any more bloodshed tonight."

Pennington stepped in front of Debra, just in case Jill got loose. Visibly shocked by her friend's reaction, Debra shouted past her guardian, trying to justify her actions. "But . . . it wasn't supposed to be like this! It should have been fun!"

"Fun?" Jill stopped squirming, but her fury hadn't cooled a bit. She glared angrily at Debra. "You call this fun? I killed a man because of you! Do you get that? He's dead!"

Debra flinched as though she had been slapped. "Please, Jill. You have to understand. I didn't mean any of this. If I'd had any idea things would turn out this way . . ."

"Shut your lying mouth!" Jill put her hands over her ears. "I don't want to hear any more bullshit from you." She smacked herself in the head. "I

should have known better than to friend you again.
This was all about getting back at me, wasn't it? You
jealous little slug!"

Okay, Brass thought. *This is getting interesting.* He
observed the confrontation through narrowed eyes.
He had not arranged this run-in on purpose, but
it was turning out to be more informative than he
could have anticipated. Now he just needed to keep
Jill from adding to tonight's body count. *Good thing
she doesn't have another gun on her.*

Drawn by the commotion, Catherine poked her
head out of the trailer door. "Everything under control out there?"

"I think so," Brass muttered. He loosened his grip
on Jill, but didn't let go.

Debra kept trying to defend herself. "No! It
wasn't about that, I swear. You're my friend, Jill!"

"Not anymore." Jill twisted in Brass's arms, turning away from Debra. "Please," she begged him, "get
me away from her. I can't stay here any longer."

"All right." Brass decided it was time to break this
up. He turned Jill over to Pennington, who kept a
tight hold on her arm as he escorted her to a waiting patrol car. The wary uniform clearly wasn't
going to give Jill a chance to make another lunge at
Debra. The last thing they needed was a brawl on
their hands.

Unfortunately, Debra didn't know when to shut
up. She shouted at her friend. "Jill! Listen to me,
please! I didn't mean any harm. We can work this
out!"

"Save your breath." Jill didn't even look back. Instead she quickened her pace.

Pushing her luck, Debra started to hurry after her. "Jill, wait! We need to talk about this!"

"Excuse me, Ms. Lusky." Brass intercepted her before she got too far. He laid a restraining hand on her shoulder. "You're going to have to talk to Jill later, if she's so inclined. Right now I'm afraid you and I need to have a little chat."

"What?" she said, still distracted by Jill's icy exit. Her shoulders sagged in defeat as she watched the patrol car carry Jill away. Damp eyes remained fixed on retreating taillights until they finally disappeared into the late-night traffic. She whispered softly to herself. "I'm sorry, Jill. Please forgive me."

Brass tried again to get her attention. "Ms. Lusky?"

"Yes?" She finally remembered Brass was there. "Oh, right." She turned to face him. Her bland, nondescript face looked a few years older than Jill's. Sparkly white teeth, her most attractive feature, were ready for their close-up. "My apologies, Captain. This has been very traumatic for all of us. I'm sorry you had to see that."

I'm not, Brass thought. He felt like he'd learned a lot, even if he didn't entirely know about what. He indicated the trailer. "Please step inside. We have some questions for you."

"Of course," she said, more cooperative now that Jill was gone. "I understand."

He followed her into the trailer, where he introduced her to Catherine, who was placing the blood-stained sweater and skirt into a labeled brown paper bag. They escorted her back to the makeup station, where she plopped down on the same stool Jill had used before. Judging from that shouting match outside, the seat might be the last thing they would share for awhile.

"Jill's right hand tested positive for GSR," Catherine updated him. "No surprise there."

"Good," Brass said. Surprises were overrated, especially in murder investigations. So far everyone agreed that Jill Wooten was the shooter.

I can live with that.

Debra was still apologizing for the ugly incident in the parking lot. "Just so you know, we're not usually like that. Jill is just overwrought. Small wonder, after what she just went through." She shivered from head to toe. "What we all went through."

"Uh-huh." Brass maintained a neutral tone. "And how exactly do you and Jill know each other?"

"We used to be roommates," Debra answered. "Until about a year ago. We've been friends, on and off, ever since."

Brass wondered about that "on and off." He'd gotten the impression that there had been some bad blood between them at some point. Jill had been kicking herself for making friends with Debra again. *What's that all about?*

"Do you think she'll ever forgive me?" Debra fretted. Their falling-out appeared to be preying on her mind. She chewed on her nails. "Is that even possible?"

"I couldn't say." He got down to the business at hand. "How do you figure into what happened here, Ms. Lusky?"

Debra slumped upon the stool, unable to meet his eyes. "It's true. I set her up for the show. Told her I had a line on a job opportunity for her. I'm a copywriter at the local ad firm. I claimed our company was handling the promotion for the club's opening." She looked up, seeking understanding. "But it was just supposed to be a harmless TV stunt. I mean, you've seen the show, right?"

"I can't say I've had the pleasure," he said dryly.

"Well, that's how it works," she explained. "Friends or family members set up their loved ones to get 'Shock Treatment' every week. And everybody has a big laugh afterward. No one's ever gotten hurt before. Honestly, I thought Jill would find the whole thing fun and exciting, and that the TV exposure might even help her modeling career." A bitter smile lifted her lips. "I thought I was doing her a favor."

Ironic, Brass thought. *If she's telling the truth.* "Guess it didn't work out that way."

"No," Debra admitted. "But how was I supposed to know that she'd be carrying a gun?"

Catherine raised an eyebrow. "You didn't know about the threatening calls she'd been receiving?"

"Calls?" Debra looked confused. "What calls? From whom?"

Brass noted her blank expression. If she really didn't know about the calls, then maybe the two women weren't really as close as Debra seemed to believe. You'd think Jill would confide in her friends about something like that.

"That remains to be determined." He consulted his notebook. "Are you familiar with her ex-boyfriend? Craig Gonch?"

"That jerk? Sure. We were still roommates when

they broke up. He didn't take it very well, to say the least." She gave Brass a puzzled look. "But what's that got to do with anything? As far as I know, he's been out of the picture for awhile."

Brown eyes widened as she put the pieces together.

"Oh my God. You think she had the gun because Craig's been stalking her again?" She sighed and shook her head. "Oh, poor Jill. I had no idea." She stared bleakly at the floor. "I still can't believe she really shot someone!"

Brass shrugged. "Guess you didn't know her as well as you thought."

5

THE SPA WAS located on North Durango Drive, near
Summerlin. A pricy neighborhood, Dr. Ray Langston noted. It made a pleasant change from the skid
row motels and filthy alleys his career change as a
CSI often brought him to. The Nile appeared to
be the last place one would expect to find a crime
scene, although Ray had come to learn that murder could be found almost anywhere. Even better
than the sanitary surroundings, however, was the
conspicuous absence of the coroner's wagon. David
Phillips was nowhere to be seen. Instead Ray spotted a van belonging to the Las Vegas Department of
Animal Control.

"No body?" Sara Sidle asked. Obviously, she had
noticed David's absence as well.

"The victim was still breathing, barely, when the
EMTs arrived," Detective Vartann informed them.
The veteran cop met them in the salon's elegant
lobby, wearing a dark suit, hawkish features, and a

characteristically grim expression; Langston wasn't sure he had ever seen Vartann smile. "She was rushed to Desert Palm Hospital."

A former physician, Ray was relieved to hear that the patient was still alive. A distinguished-looking African-American male in his late forties, he wore a neatly pressed sports jacket with no tie. A professorial air betrayed his past as both an MD and college instructor. Short black hair was showing traces of gray. He took off his sunglasses. "What's her prognosis?"

"Not sure," Vartann said. He was only a few years younger than Ray. "We're still waiting to hear back from the hospital."

"Beats waiting to hear from the morgue," Sara commented. The thirty-something brunette had left the crime lab a few years before Ray had joined the team, but had recently returned to help out on a temporary basis. Ray appreciated the chance to learn from her experience. Only a level-2 CSI at the moment, he was eager to advance to the next level. Sara was already a level-3, like Catherine, Nick, and Greg. After two years on the job, Ray didn't feel like the new guy anymore, but he knew he still had a lot to learn. Sara looked over the lobby. "So where's our crime scene?"

"This way," Vartann said. "If there actually was a crime. We're still trying to work that out." He led them down a hallway profligately decorated in pseudo-Egyptian kitsch. Shouts and heavy footsteps escaped a closed wooden door. A painted profile of a regal Egyptian beauty, sporting an asp-crowned beaded headdress, and embossed gold type identified the chamber beyond as the Cleopatra Room.

Sara raised an eyebrow. "Cleopatra? Wasn't she killed by a snake?"

"An asp," Ray confirmed. "In retrospect, perhaps not the most auspicious of names."

"Or too auspicious," Sara said.

Vartann ignored their banter. "Careful," he warned. "It's a zoo in there . . . literally." He rapped on the door. "All clear?"

"Okay," a female voice called out from inside. "But make it snappy!"

The detective cautiously opened the door, just enough to slide through sideways, then beckoned for the CSIs to follow him. "Step lively. Some of our 'suspects' are still trying to stage a getaway."

They entered to find a scene of slithery pandemonium. A pair of sweaty Animal Control officers, in blue uniforms, were busy rounding up what appeared to be several runaway snakes, who were scrambling all over the floor. A glass vivarium atop a low wooden cabinet appeared to be the original source of the infestation. The officers chased the snakes around an empty massage table.

Ray quickly pulled the door shut behind him. He backed up against the door to keep out of the way of the outnumbered snake wranglers. He glanced at Sara. "Hope you don't have a problem with snakes."

She scoffed at the notion. "I'm married to Gil Grissom. I'm used to all sorts of creepy-crawlies."

Good point, Ray thought. He recalled her husband's extensive collection of ants, spiders, cockroaches, and other insects, which Ray had taken the opportunity to inspect prior to Grissom's departure.

They watched as a snake catcher extracted a writhing eight-inch corn snake from behind a radiator. Long metal tongs extended the woman's reach, allowing her to safely grasp the snake a few inches behind its neck. She pulled it from its hiding place, then grabbed onto its tail with her free hand before depositing it back into the vivarium, which had a sliding glass lid. A yard away, on the other side of the massage table, her partner used his own tongs to prod a recalcitrant black kingsnake into an overturned plastic bin. Once he had the snake fully inside, he swiftly snapped on a ventilated lid. Trapped, the snake hissed unhappily inside its prison. Several more snakes, hoping to escape their comrades' fate, slithered for cover.

Ray winced inwardly at all the activity messing up their crime scene, but acknowledged that it was unavoidable in this instance. They could hardly work the site with a lively passel of snakes swarming underfoot. He surveyed the room from against the wall. His gaze zoomed in on the massage table and vivarium. Discarded towels littered the floor. Specks of blood could be spotted upon the rumpled white fabric.

Sara was already thinking ahead, too. "We're going to need those snakes," she informed the Animal Control team.

"All of them?" a stocky Asian woman asked. A shield-shaped badge identified her as Brookston.

"I'm afraid so," Sara said. When collecting evidence, it was always better to have too much than too little; you never knew what inconspicuous detail could break a case wide open. She peered at the tangle of reptiles in the vivarium. "Do we know which snake is our perp?"

Brookston shook her head. "Sorry. We've been too busy rounding them up to try to sort them out." She helped her partner, whose name was SWEED, dump the contents of his bin into the tank, before looking around for her next scaly target. "And the masseuse who witnessed the attack is long gone."

"How is that?" Ray asked, surprised to hear it. "Don't we need to question him or her?"

"Her." Vartann scowled at his notepad. "One Heather Gilroy. She ran off before we got here. Hasn't been seen or heard from since."

"Well, that's suspicious," Sara observed. "She got something to hide?"

Ray was wondering the same thing. "What exactly happened here?"

Vartann crisply brought them up to speed. "Our vic, Rita Segura, a local who lives in Summerlin, showed up this morning for a 'routine' snake massage, only to receive a nasty bite on her neck. She had a severe reaction, the owner called 911, and here we are."

"Snake massages." Sara rolled her eyes. "Now I've heard everything."

"I thought you didn't mind snakes," Ray reminded her.

"I don't," she insisted. "But that doesn't mean I want them crawling over me." Her face wrinkled in disgust. "I think I'll stick with shiatsu."

Ray couldn't argue with that. Watching his step, he wandered over to inspect the snakes in the vivarium. He was no herpetologist, but his medical training and practice had familiarized him with most of the venomous snakes native to North America. Looking over the undulating contents of the tank, he didn't spot anything that resembled a rattler. *Makes sense,* he thought. He couldn't imagine anyone volunteering to have a rattlesnake applied to their bare skin. "I'm guessing our culprit is some variety of coral snake," he theorized. "Which can be easily mistaken for more harmless species."

A quick scan of the tank's contents revealed a couple of banded red snakes that bore a resemblance to more venomous species. A coral snake would have blended right in, unless you knew what you were looking for.

He addressed the snake wranglers. "You folks seen a coral snake yet?"

"Don't know," Brookston said. "Like I said before, we've mostly just been chasing them. We haven't really had the chance to give any of them a once-over." She cursed under her breath as a small, striped garter snake eluded her. "Plus, to be honest, we don't deal a lot with reptiles. Stray cats and bad-tempered dogs make up most of our calls. Not sure I'd recognize a coral snake if I saw one."

"Understood." Ray appreciated her honesty. As he recalled, the coral snake was notoriously reclusive, accounting for less than one percent of reported snakebites in any given year. He couldn't recall ever actually treating a case before. He figured they would have to examine the snakes more thoroughly back at the lab. "We should notify the hospital that we believe their patient was bitten by a coral snake."

In a case of snakebite, knowing which antivenin to administer could often be the difference between life and death. He just hoped that Desert Palm had an adequate supply of the correct serum, or Rita Segura could be in serious trouble. And, of course, there was always the danger of an allergic reaction to the antivenin itself. . . .

"I can do that," Vartann volunteered. He took out his cell phone and immediately dialed the hospital.

"So how dangerous are coral snakes?" Sara asked.

Ray searched his memory. "Bites are uncommon, but potentially life-threatening. Their fangs deliver a potent neurotoxin which, left untreated, can paralyze the breathing muscles and also lead to cardiac arrest. The venom often takes several hours to take effect, but our vic appears to have been unusually susceptible to the venom. The fact that she was bitten on the neck, as the initial reports suggest, probably contributed to the rapidity of her reaction. Bites to the face and trunk are the most dangerous. In this case, the venom might have gone straight into her jugular."

"Lucky her," Sara said.

Vartann put away his phone. "Okay, I informed the docs at the hospital of your suspicions." He watched the Animal Control team continue their wild snake hunt; it looked like they weren't going to be finished anytime soon. Vartann glanced at his watch, then nodded at the CSIs. "While these guys finish up, I'm going to interview the owner of this illustrious establishment. Either of you interested in taking part?"

"Sure," Ray said. Meeting an interesting assortment of people was one of the perks of the job, and a frequent source of valuable information. Besides, he was just getting in the way here. He glanced at his cohort. "Sara?"

"You go." She pulled on a pair of latex gloves and gestured at the vivarium, whose cold-blooded population was steadily growing, thanks to the persistent efforts of Brookston and her partner. "I want to check that tank for fingerprints. See if anyone has been tampering with the snakes who shouldn't have been."

"Good idea," Ray said. Chances were, a coral snake had ended up in the spa's supply by mistake, but they couldn't rule out the possibility that someone might have added a venomous snake to the mix on purpose. *In which case,* he thought, *we could be talking attempted homicide—or worse if the victim doesn't survive.*

Sara waved him away. "Have fun talking to the snake lady."

"I'll try not to make an asp of myself," he replied with a grin. He and Vartann exited the room, being careful not to let any stray serpents out. An amused chuckle escaped his lips. This was probably the first time his prime suspects had ever tried to flee the scene without benefit of legs, let alone been literally cold-blooded. Although, come to think of it, he had investigated at least one case of death by falling turtle. . . .

They found the spa's owner in her office at the other end of the hall. A police officer stood by to make sure she didn't get a chance to coach her employees on what to say. Ray assumed that the rest of the staff were being kept isolated as well. Aside from the runaway masseuse, of course. Tracking Heather Gilroy down and getting a statement from her was obviously going to be a priority.

Alexandra turned out to be a middle-aged woman of somewhat exotic appearance. Jet-black hair matched the kohl highlighting her eyes. Crystal and turquoise adorned her ears, neck, and wrists. She sat behind an antique bamboo desk. Shaking hands held on to a steaming cup of herbal tea.

Her office was equally colorful. A potted papyrus plant sprouted in the corner behind her. An eclectic collection of crystals, idols, and amulets crowded her shelves. The sacred Eye of Horus was painted over the door, watching protectively over the office. A polished quartz scarab served as a paperweight. A small ceramic statue of Hathor, the Egyptian goddess of beauty, blessed the proceedings from her perch on to the windowsill. A filing cabinet, personal planner, and in-box served more prosaic functions. A scented candle perfumed the air.

Vartann took care of the introductions. "This is Dr. Langston from the crime lab. He'll be assisting in our investigation."

"*Crime* lab?" Kohl-lined eyes widened in dismay. A quasi-British accent sounded more affected than genuine. "But there's been no crime here. This is all some sort of terrible mistake!"

Ray didn't blame her for being upset. According to Nevada law, the owners of dangerous animals could be held legally liable for any serious injuries resulting from bites or other mischief. One way or another, she could be facing criminal and civil penalties. Not to mention a lawsuit of catastrophic proportions.

Vartann sat down opposite the distressed spa owner. Ray did the same. The detective took out his notebook. "Why don't you tell us all about it?"

"I wish I could help you, gentlemen!" She took a deep breath in an attempt to compose herself. "But I don't understand any of this. Our snakes are perfectly harmless!"

"Apparently not all of them." Vartann got right down to business. "So you say Ms. Segura arrived early this morning for her massage?"

"Yes, an hour before opening." She displayed a trace of irritation. "It was quite irregular, to be sure, but she was very insistent."

"Really?" Vartann asked dubiously. "She was that keen on having live snakes dumped on top of her?"

"Don't sound so skeptical, Detective," she chided him. "Serpents have been associated with healing since time immemorial. The ancient Mesopotamians believed snakes to be immortal, achieving rebirth every time they shed their skins." Her spiel had a well-rehearsed tone to it. No doubt she was accustomed to people resisting the idea of snake massages. "Indeed, to this day, the medical profession is symbolized by a serpent entwined around a staff."

Ray nodded. "The Rod of Asclepius, not to be confused with the Caduceus, which features *two* snakes." Although deriving from different mythological roots, the two symbols were often mistaken for each other and used interchangeably. "Moses also healed his people with a staff topped by a serpent."

"Precisely!" She beamed at Ray as though she had just found a kindred spirit. "Our serpentine brothers and sisters are meant to soothe those in need, not inflict pain on the innocent.

"Uh-huh." Vartann sounded unconvinced. "Too bad it didn't work out that way."

"I assure you, I feel absolutely terrible about this," she said. "Ms. Segura is a very dear friend of this salon. It grieves me deeply that she's come to harm."

Ray wondered again if anyone could have deliberately added a coral snake to the vivarium in the Cleopatra Room. "Did she have an appointment? Did anyone know she was going to be receiving a snake massage this morning?"

"Not at all. It was completely spontaneous. We were not expecting her at all." Alexandra Nile frowned at the memory. "Truth be told, it was actually something of an imposition. I routinely avail myself of the serpents' soothing caresses every Monday morning, before we open our doors, to ensure that my body and spirit are in tune and fully prepared for the inevitable stresses of the coming week. But this morning, I sacrificed my own treatment to accommodate Ms. Segura." A sudden gasp escaped her lips. A hand went protectively to her throat. "Good heavens! I just realized . . . that could have been me!"

Interesting, Ray thought. Perhaps Rita Segura had not been the intended victim at all. "Do you know of any reason why someone might want to harm you?"

Madame Alexandra's hand came away from her

throat. "Don't be absurd. I'm in the business of helping people. Why would anyone want to hurt me?" Her eyes narrowed as the full implications of Ray's question sank in. "But . . . you don't actually think that someone arranged this on purpose, do you? That's ridiculous."

"We're not ruling out any possibilities," Vartann said. He took control of the interview again. "These snakes of yours, any more on the premises?"

"No." She clung to her teacup with both hands, visibly unnerved by the disturbing turn the conversation had taken. Worry lines cracked her immaculate makeup. "The Cleopatra Room is currently the only therapeutic space set up for the serpentine massages. The rest are reserved for more conventional treatments." She sighed ruefully. "I had been contemplating adding vivariums to some of the other chambers, to keep up with the demand, but I suppose I shall have to reconsider those plans in light of these unfortunate circumstances."

"You might want to hold off on that," Ray agreed. The attack on Rita Segura was unlikely to increase the popularity of the snake massages. The Nile would be lucky if the bizarre incident stayed out of the papers. "And are the snakes kept in the Cleopatra Room at all times?"

"Naturally," she stated. "In deference to our more sensitive clients."

"Yeah," Vartann said. "I can see where some people might not like seeing them carried from room to room." He grimaced in sympathy. "Can't say I blame them."

"Snakes are not repulsive, Detective." Madame

Alexandra segued back into lecture mode. "They have been part of nature for over one hundred and thirty million years. Did you know there are over two thousand different species? And that many life-saving medicines have been derived from snake venom?"

This was true, Ray conceded. Not just antivenims, but also blood thinners and other pharmaceuticals had been developed from the unique properties of snake venom. Including promising new treatments for lupus and other disorders.

"Right." Vartann cut off her sales pitch. "So where exactly do you get your scaly miracle workers?"

"Our serpents are supplied by a supposedly reputable dealer, a man named Chip LaReue." She spelled out the name for their benefit, then moved quickly to deflect any blame from herself. "If you wish to know how a venomous adder invaded this sacred temple of healing, I suggest you talk to him."

"We'll do that." Vartann wrote down the name. "There any bad blood between you and this LaReue character? Unpaid bills? A financial dispute?"

"Not at all." She bristled, offended by the very suggestion. "If anything is amiss here, I suspect it is criminal negligence and carelessness on Mr. LaReue's part." Perhaps realizing how accusatory she sounded, she softened her tone. A weary sigh conveyed that she spoke more in sorrow than anger. "Please understand, gentlemen, it truly pains me to point a finger at another soul, let alone an individual with whom, up until now, I have had a most cordial and satisfactory business relationship. I believe we are placed on this Earth to understand our fellow travelers, not judge them, but, frankly, I can think of no other explanation for this dreadful turn of events. Mr. LaReue must have accidentally included the wrong snake in his last shipment. It's the only thing that makes any sense."

Ray found it the most plausible scenario as well, but knew better than to rush to judgment. He'd investigated more than a few cases where first impressions had proved misleading. "What about the masseuse?" he asked. "Heather Gilroy?"

"Oh, *her*," Madame Alexandra said disdainfully. "I can't believe that silly girl ran off to let me deal with this unpleasantness. Well, if she thinks she still has a job here, she is sorely mistaken."

So much for not judging others, Ray thought. "Did she say anything to you before she left?"

"Just that it wasn't her fault. That everything was proceeding normally, until the snake struck Ms. Segura."

Vartann jotted that down in his notebook. "So you didn't actually witness the attack?"

She winced at the word *attack*. "No. I arrived mere moments later, attracted by the commotion." She faltered, momentarily overcome by the memory. Tea sloshed over the brim of her shaking cup. She put it down on the desk to avoid spilling any more. "I arrived just in time to see Rita collapse onto the floor."

"And what happened next?" Vartann asked.

"Well, that's when Heather abandoned me. She panicked and ran out the door." Madame Alexandra shook her head, as though she still couldn't believe the missing woman could be so irresponsible.

"I called 9-1-1 and attempted to make Ms. Segura comfortable until the ambulance arrived." She looked anxiously at the two men. "Do you know if she is going to be all right? Have you heard anything?"

Ray had little to offer her. "We expect to hear more from the hospital shortly."

"Can you please let me know the moment you do?" The spa owner wrung her hands. "I cannot tell you how worried I am about poor Rita."

Ray considered the victim's prospects. Coral snake venom was nothing to take lightly, but, under ordinary circumstances, the prognosis was good provided the correct antivenin was administered in time. He was reluctant to comment on Rita Segura's medical condition, however, since he had not personally examined her or reviewed her treatment. He was here as a criminalist, not a physician.

"What can you tell us about Heather?" he asked. "Has she been working here long?"

"Not really," Madame Alexandra said. "Perhaps a month or two. I can't say I know her well, but she seemed competent enough. Until this morning, that is."

Vartann nodded. "Do you know of any reason why she might have had it in for Ms. Segura?"

Good question, Ray thought. After all, it was Heather Gilroy who had apparently placed the venomous snake on the victim. They had to consider the possibility that she had done so deliberately.

"Not at all," Madame Alexandra said. "I believe she may have personally tended to Rita before, but I am not aware of any animosity between them. As

I said, Ms. Segura was one of our most valued customers. A trifle demanding at times, but still . . ." She shook her head. "I can't imagine that anyone here would mean Rita harm."

"Well, we're going to need to talk to Heather anyway," Vartann said. "I assume you have contact info for both her and Mr. LaReue?"

"My assistant can help you with that." She got up from behind her desk and stepped out into the hall. Her fingers snapped imperiously. "Brian!"

A slight, middle-aged man emerged from an adjoining office. He hesitated at the sight of the uniformed police officers stationed in the hall, as though uncertain whether he would be allowed to respond to the summons. "Er, is it okay if I go over there?"

Vartann signaled the uni to let him through.

"This is Brian Yun, my assistant manager," she explained. "I am certain that he can provide you with whatever information you require." She sagged against the doorframe and dramatically placed the back of her hand against her brow. Fatigue showed upon her haggard countenance. "Now then, gentlemen, unless you have any further questions, I am sorely in need of some private meditation to recover from these harrowing trials."

"I think we're done now," Vartann said. "Although we may have more questions for you later." He turned to Yun and introduced himself and Ray. "Your boss said you might be able to help us."

"Of course." Yun was a short, potbellied man with a receding hairline, far less dramatic in appearance than his flamboyant employer. Wearing a plain white business shirt and a tie, he reminded Ray of his financial advisor. Worry lines creased a round, pink face with a weak chin. "You can expect our full cooperation." He dabbed at his brow with a linen handkerchief. "I'm still in shock over this whole thing. Poor Ms. Segura! I don't understand this at all."

"Were you here when it happened?" Vartann asked.

Yun shook his head. "No, thank goodness. I arrived a little after eight, to find the whole place in turmoil. The ambulance had already taken Ms. Segura away."

He guided them into his office, which was notably smaller than Madame Alexandra's. A cheap IKEA desk appeared meticulously tidy and well-organized. A framed photo of a white Persian cat rested atop the desk, next to a computer. An old-fashioned rolodex supplemented his hard drive. A small fridge hummed in the corner. "Can I offer either of you gentlemen a Snapple?" he asked. "It's my only vice."

"No, thank you," Ray said. There was only one extra seat in the office, so he remained standing while Vartann sat down across from Yun. A door closed in the adjacent room as Madame Alexandra sequestered herself. Ray wondered how Sara was faring in the Cleopatra Room. Had all the snakes been apprehended yet?

Yun positioned himself in front of his keyboard. "Very well. How can I help you?"

"We're going to need contact information for both Heather Gilroy and Chip LaReue," Vartann said. "As well as a complete inventory of all the snakes you've purchased from Mr. LaReue."

"No problem." Yun flipped through his rolodex and produced two cards, which he handed over to the detective. Then he tapped away at his keyboard, calling up the inventory data. "I hope Heather isn't in too much trouble. She's a sweet girl, really. I'm sure she just panicked. I really can't blame her. It must have been a frightful experience."

Snakebites tended to frighten people, Ray admitted. He still wished Heather had not run. "What's she like?"

"Nice girl," Yun insisted. "Saving up for college, I believe. Wants to be a physical therapist. A bit young and inexperienced, but she seemed to be fitting in. And she was comfortable handling the snakes, which was a definite plus. Believe me, it wasn't easy finding staffers who were willing to work with those creatures." He shuddered. "Understandably."

Ray noted his reaction. "Not fond of snakes?"

"More of a cat person myself," Yun confessed. He turned the framed photo on his desk around to face his visitors. He smiled weakly. "As you can probably tell."

Ray admired the photo, which depicted a plump white feline scowling into the camera. A sparkling rhinestone collar adorned the cat's neck. Large amber eyes glared balefully. The cat clearly did not like having her picture taken.

"A beautiful animal," Ray said. "Persian?"

Yun nodded. "My beloved Fala." He placed a hand over his heart. "Alas, she passed away a few weeks ago."

"I'm sorry for your loss," Ray said automatically. By now, the standard-issue condolence came readily to his lips. "So you don't actually handle the snakes yourself?"

"Thankfully, that's not part of my job description." Yun gestured around his office. Folders and ledgers were arranged neatly on the shelves. An in-box was overflowing. "I serve in a more administrative capacity. My job is to keep everything running smoothly, so that Madame can focus on maintaining the proper therapeutic atmosphere."

"I understand," Ray said. "Behind every successful boss, there's an able assistant making sure no balls get dropped."

Yun acknowledged the compliment. "I certainly like to think so." A printer beneath his desk spit out the inventory sheets they had requested. He reached down and retrieved them for Vartann, mustering a philosophical sigh as he did so. "They also serve who only push the paper."

"Beats playing with snakes, I guess." Vartann finished copying down the necessary addresses and phone numbers into his notebook. "What about Chip LaReue? You ever deal with him?"

"Naturally." Yun reclaimed his rolodex cards. "He came highly recommended when we first started searching around for someone to supply us with snakes." A pained expression came over his face. "I must say, I feel just horrible about this whole ghastly business. I can't help blaming myself a little."

"And why is that?" Ray asked.

Guilty eyes sought absolution. "The serpentine massages were my idea, you see."

"Is that so?" Vartann said. "Okay, I've got to ask. What made you think that would catch on?"

"I read about it in *Time* magazine," Yun divulged. "Then did some research online." He leaned forward, trying to explain his reasoning. "There's hundreds of spas and salons in Vegas. I figured we needed to offer something special, that no one else was offering. Madame agreed, at least until today." His face went pale and he sank back into his seat. "Oh Lord, you don't think she's going to blame me for this fiasco, do you?"

"That's between you and her." Vartann's tone made it clear that he had more crucial matters to worry about. "Getting back to LaReue, he have a grudge against this place? Any reason he might want to sabotage your business?"

Ray recalled that Vartann had asked Madame Alexandra the same question. She had denied any bad blood between her and her supplier, but perhaps Yun had a different take on things. Or might be more willing to air any dirty laundry?

"Not that I can think of," Yun said, echoing his boss's statement. "This is the first time we've ever had any problem with his snakes." He shrugged. "I suppose anyone can make a mistake, but what a tragedy that poor Ms. Segura had to suffer for it." He stared miserably at the other two men. "Are you going to be seeing her at the hospital?"

"Probably," Ray said.

If she survived. If not, he would be seeing her at the morgue.

"Well, when you do," Yun requested, "would you please tell her that everyone here is thinking of her, and that we're all terribly sorry for what happened." He started flipping through his rolodex again. "Perhaps I should arrange to have some flowers sent to the hospital." He looked to Ray and Vartann for guidance. "Would that be appropriate?"

"I have no idea," Ray said. Snakebite etiquette was not his forte.

6

UNLIKE HER FORMER roommate, Debra Lusky managed to exit the trailer without incident. Catherine wasn't sure what they had gotten out of the interview, except maybe that Jill had lousy taste in friends. She couldn't imagine how anyone could deliberately set up a friend to be frightened for her life.

If anyone tried to pull a stunt like that on me . . .

Then again, she recalled, a bunch of the guys at the lab, including Nick and Greg, had recently staged a mock "kidnapping" of Henry Andrews, the lab's toxicology whiz, as a birthday surprise. From what she'd heard of the prank, poor Henry had been utterly convinced that he had fallen into the hands of dangerous criminals—until the guys pulled off their ski masks. It seemed you could never underestimate how far some people would go to play a practical joke.

Just the same, she thought, *nobody had better volunteer me for* Shock Treatment. *Not if they know what's good for them.*

She watched Debra leave, then withdrew back into the trailer. Over by the makeup table, Brass was on the phone to someone. "What? Did you remind him that we happen to be investigating a possible homicide?" He scowled in irritation. "Never mind. I'll tell him myself."

He snapped the phone shut with more force than was strictly necessary.

"What's that all about?" she asked.

"Roger Park, the esteemed producer of this sterling example of television programming. Seems he would prefer to meet with us in the comfort of his own personal trailer."

Catherine guessed that was the two-story mobile leviathan she had noticed earlier. "I see. Well, we certainly wouldn't want to inconvenience him. After all, it's not like his brilliant show accidentally led to the death of one of his own employees."

"Sounds like a typical Hollywood type to me." Brass shrugged in resignation, as though it wasn't worth raising a fuss over. They had more important things to worry about than picking a fight with some self-important TV producer. "What the hell. I can use the exercise."

Catherine picked up her field kit. "Okay, let's go."

Leaving Pennington posted outside the makeup trailer, so that nobody would walk off with Jill's bloodstained garments, they crossed the parking lot to the deluxe trailer. Catherine craned her neck back to take in its full height. She had processed one-family dwellings that were smaller than this rolling penthouse. Its looming, silver-gray exterior

practically blotted out the sky. There were even outdoor awnings and a satellite dish.

Another uniformed officer met them at the entrance. "He's right this way."

The cop led them into a lavish reception area,
complete with black leather couches, cherry paneling,
hardwood floors, a fourteen-foot-high ceiling, and a
fully-equipped bar. A plasma-screen television was
bigger than the one in Archie's A/V lab. Track lighting ran across the ceiling. A second-floor balcony,
at the top of a spiral staircase, overlooked the reception area. An open bottle of Scotch waited atop the
bar. Catherine didn't blame Park for needing a drink,
not after what had happened, but she hoped that
he hadn't hit the bottle too hard. They needed him
sober. She glanced around, but did not see anyone.

"He was right here a minute ago," the uniform
insisted.

Movie posters and framed copies of *Variety* testified to the trailer's show-biz roots. Occupying a
prime position above the bar was a large canvass
poster for a movie titled *Zombie Heat.* The lurid art-
work depicted a hideous animated corpse posed
atop the burning husk of a torched LAPD patrol
car. The tattered remnants of a blue police uniform
hung upon the zombie's shriveled, mummified carcass. A ridiculously large bullet hole, blackened by
powder burns, was placed directly in the center
of his rotting forehead. Glazed white eyes peered
out from sunken sockets. A skull-like visage bared
jagged yellow teeth. Moldering green flesh was
stretched tightly over his bones.

"He'll stop at nothing for justice," a tagline promised. *"And brains."*

Catherine smirked at the poster. She had collected more than a few brains herself over the years—as evidence. Although hardly the avid pop-culture maven Greg was, even she had heard of *Zombie Heat.* The low-budget thriller had become a surprise sensation back in the spring. Lindsey had insisted on renting it, and Catherine had caught bits and pieces of it.

She hadn't been impressed.

A toilet flushed and Roger Park emerged from an adjacent bathroom. Catherine caught a glimpse of a marble countertop and gleaming silver faucets. At first, the elusive TV producer appeared to have lost his mind. Oblivious to Catherine and Brass, he paced back and forth across the office, gesticulating wildly while seemingly arguing with empty air.

"What? Are you kidding me? It's way too soon to be talking cancellation!" A Bluetooth earpiece explained his seeming psychosis. A glass of whiskey sloshed in his right hand. "I haven't even spoken with the local fuzz yet."

Brass cleared his throat. Park nodded at them, absently acknowledging their arrival, but carried on with his heated conversation. "All right, I can certainly see shutting down production for the time being, while we review our procedures, but let's not pull the plug until all the facts are in. I mean, it was just a freak accident. What were the odds?"

Brass held up his badge. He glowered at the distracted producer.

Park got the message. "Look I gotta go. We'll talk

later. We'll talk later." He smooched the air. "Love you." Switching off his earpiece, he finally greeted Catherine and Brass. "Sorry about that. Things are going crazy here."

"Having a bad morning?" Brass asked.

"The worst." Roger Park was a tanned smoothie wearing a light-colored blazer over a tight black T-shirt. Plastic surgery obscured his age. Frosted blond hair was tied back in a ponytail. A flashy gold watch glittered on his wrist. He popped an antacid tablet into his mouth, and washed it down with his Scotch. "Just wait until the lawyers get involved. I don't even want to think about the lawsuits. This is *The Crow* all over again."

Catherine got the reference. Actor Brandon Lee had been unintentionally shot to death during the filming of a supernatural action movie when a supposedly empty gun had proved to have a dummy bullet stuck in the barrel. As she recalled, the death was eventually ruled a tragic accident. No one had been charged, not even the poor actor who had pulled the trigger.

A good omen for Jill Wooten?

"Not exactly great publicity for your show," Brass said. "Or is it?"

"You think we did this for ratings?" Park scoffed at the idea, which was admittedly a bit farfetched. "How dumb do you think I am? Between you and me, this disaster has probably killed *Shock Treatment.*"

"Not to mention Matt Novak," Catherine reminded him.

"Right. Of course." Park remembered to assume

a more mournful tone. He nodded solemnly. "It's a horrible tragedy for all of us. Matt had been with the show since the beginning. He was like family."

Catherine wondered how much of the man's grief was genuine. "I'm sorry for your loss."

"Thank you." He looked them over, his gaze lingering on Catherine longer than she liked. "And you are?"

"Jim Brass, Homicide," the cop identified himself. "And this is Catherine Willows with the crime lab."

"Thank you for coming," he said, shaking their hands. A sweaty palm betrayed his anxiety and made Catherine wish she had kept her latex gloves on. She pulled her hand away after he held on to it a few beats too long. He gestured toward a long leather couch, which was big enough to hold an entire team of CSIs, plus maybe a lab rat or two. "Please, make yourselves comfortable."

"All right." She and Brass sat down on the couch. When Park wasn't looking, she wiped her palm off on a seat cushion.

He refilled his drink at the bar. "Can I get either of you something?"

"No, thank you," Brass said. "We just need some answers."

"Absolutely." Park turned on the charm as he sat down at the bar. "I can promise you our full cooperation with your investigation. I have nothing but the greatest respect and admiration for all law-enforcement personnel. I mean, look at *Zombie Heat*." He called their attention to the poster over the bar. "Beneath the blood and gore, it's the story of Officer Zombie, a heroic police officer whose dedication to fighting crime extends even beyond the grave. No wonder the public embraced it the way they did."

Catherine was impressed by how quickly Park had managed to turn a compliment into a plug for his own accomplishments. "Always nice to be compared to a brain-eating zombie."

"Well, that's just a metaphor," he insisted. "For the toll the job takes on hardworking crime fighters like yourselves. It eats away at you, get it? I came up with that myself." He raised his glass to his rotting brainchild. "I don't know if you've heard, but we're turning the movie into a TV show."

Zombie Heat: The Series? Catherine resisted an urge to roll her eyes. Between *Shock Treatment* and this new project, Roger Park was clearly a one-man cultural renaissance.

"Congratulations," she said politely. "I'll have to tell my daughter."

"You have a daughter?" He feigned disbelief. "Look at those cheekbones. I would never cast you as a mom."

"Thanks, I guess." Catherine wasn't sure whether to be amused or annoyed. Probably the latter.

Brass cut the charm offensive short. "Let's get started. Where were you when the shooting occurred?"

"With the rest of the crew, watching the scene from behind the flatscreen TV prop, which was actually a one-way mirror." A pained expression came over his face. "It all happened so fast. One minute, it was business as usual. Then . . . she shot Matt before we had a chance to stop her." He shook his head. "I still can't believe it. This has never happened before."

"That's almost hard to believe," Catherine said, "given the kind of stunts you pull." She had been thinking about this ever since Greg had first described the show to her. "How do you expect people to react when they think their lives are in actual jeopardy?"

Park defended his show. "Well, the actual shocks only last for a couple of minutes. We always come clean before things get out of hand. Just when it looks like there's no escape, the monster or somebody goes 'Surprise! You just got *Shock Treatment*!' You should see the look of relief on people's faces when they realize it's just a practical joke. They crack up, laughing—and are thrilled that they're going to be on TV."

Catherine didn't entirely buy the rosy picture Park was painting. "But nobody ever tried to fight back before? In self-defense?"

"We screen our victims very carefully," he insisted. "No one with a criminal record, a concealed weapons permit, or a history of mental illness. Plus, the sets for the pranks are thoroughly vetted to make sure they don't contain anything that might be turned into a weapon by a panicky victim. No beer bottles, letter openers, fireplace pokers, you name it. And the actors are all instructed to cut things short if it looks like the victims are about to go berserk. We just want to give people a momentary shock, that's all, then let them off the hook. Usually, they think it's a real hoot afterward."

"Except this time," Brass said.

"Clearly, Ms. Lusky misjudged her friend," he said, wasting no time before throwing Debra under the bus. "As part of the screening process, we inter-view all of our accomplices in advance. Debra as-sured us that Jill was not the violent type. I guess she was wrong about that, and Matt paid the price." He drowned his sorrows in another gulp of Scotch. "Like I said, a horrible, terrible accident."

"I don't know," Catherine persisted. "Seems to me this show was a lawsuit waiting to happen."

"Most of our victims are happy to sign a waiver in exchange for appearing on the show." Park smirked. "People will do almost anything to be on TV."

He had a point there. Catherine recalled some of the trashy reality shows she'd caught Lindsey watching on occasion. Wannabe celebrities making out in hot tubs with near strangers, eating bugs, tak-ing lie-detector tests, stripping for prizes, and God knows what else. She supposed Park was right. A lot of people would overlook being scared to death for a chance at fifteen minutes of fame. Probably even Lindsey and her friends.

"We also have insurance to cover any possible accidents or lawsuits," Park added. "Just a standard legal precaution. I never thought we'd actually need it."

"Better hope your premiums are paid up," Cath-erine said. She recalled the threatening calls Jill had received prior to her phony job interview. A crazy theory occurred to her. "Let me ask you something. Do you ever do anything to scare your victims in advance?"

Park seemed puzzled by the question. "I don't follow. What do you mean?"

"Jill Wooten was being terrorized by an anonymous caller," she revealed. "Did you and your people do that, to get her in the mood, so to speak? Make sure she was already on edge, so you'd be sure to get a good reaction from her?"

He shook his head. "That's a brilliant idea, actually. But, no, we don't plan that far ahead. We just rely on our accomplices to get the vic to the right place at the right time." His casual references to "accomplices" and "victims" made him sound more like a career criminal than a TV producer. "And, of course, if we had known Jill was really being harassed by a stalker, we would have called the whole thing off." He frowned. "I'm surprised Debra didn't mention that to us."

"She says she didn't know about it," Brass said. He moved on to another topic. "So whose bright idea was this whole 'wax museum' stunt?"

"That would be me," Park confessed. He didn't seem to be too broken up about it. "*Shock Treatment* is my baby. I've conceived and supervised probably ninety percent of our scenarios, including all of our most popular gags."

Catherine remembered Greg's enthusiastic recap earlier. "Like the flesh-eating disease episode?"

"Yep," Park bragged. "That was one of mine."

Lovely, she thought. She had seen necrotizing fasciitis in action before. It wasn't her idea of entertainment.

"Are you the sole producer?" Brass asked.

"No, I have a partner," Park admitted. "But she's pretty hands-off when it comes to the day-to-day running of the show. After all, she's got a lot more on her plate, you know?"

"Sorry, I don't know," Catherine replied.

Park blinked in surprise, taken aback that they didn't know what he meant. "My partner is Tricia Grantley." He waited in vain for them to catch on. "The studio exec?"

Catherine thought the name sounded vaguely familiar, but not much more than that. "Why don't you fill us in?"

"My bad," he apologized. "When you work in the industry, you sometimes forget that not everybody subscribes to *Variety*. Tricia is head of development at Lunara Pictures." Leaving the bar, he strolled over to the couch, where he pulled out his wallet and flipped it open. Inside was a photo of Park embracing a buxom African-American woman in a ruffled white dress. Park was wearing a tuxedo in the photo, his hair was still in a ponytail. "That's our wedding photo, taken here in Vegas five years ago."

Catherine recognized the deluxe wedding chapel at the Bellagio. Tricia Grantley clutched an enormous bouquet. Rose petals were strewn before the altar. Weddings at the elegant chapel could easily run $15,000 or more. She had once processed a triple homicide there. A jilted girlfriend had brought a shotgun to the reception.

"You make a lovely couple," she said.

"Thank you." He took his wallet back. "That was her I was talking to when you came in." A wince implied that the call had not gone well. "Needless to say, she's deeply concerned about today's unfortunate accident."

Catherine took a second look at the *Zombie Heat* poster. Noting that it was a Lunara production, she guessed that Tricia Grantley had greenlit her husband's film. Catherine hoped that Park's high-powered Hollywood connections wouldn't complicate their investigation. Vegas liked to portray itself as a studio-friendly town; all those movies and TV shows were good advertising and poured plenty of revenue into the local coffers. As did partying movie stars and their entourages. *All we need,* she fretted, *are some Hollywood high-rollers putting pressure on the mayor and the sheriff to wrap up this investigation quickly.*

"Did I hear that you're suspending production?" Brass asked.

"That's right," Park said. "While we conduct our own internal investigation into what went wrong, and wait for the official verdict as well." He stared morosely into his drink. "I just hope we're not gone for good. For our audience's sake, that is. I would hate to deprive our loyal fans of their favorite show."

"Of course," Catherine said sarcastically. She was sure Greg would appreciate Park's concern.

"In the meantime," Brass asked, "where are you staying in Vegas?" He glanced around the luxurious trailer. "Not here, I assume?"

He could do worse, Catherine thought. The mobile mansion rivaled plenty of top-dollar hotel suites. Assuming you didn't mind living in a parking lot.

"I have a penthouse suite at Caesars Palace," Park revealed, "when we're not on location. The rest of the cast and crew are booked into a motel north of the Strip."

It's good to be the producer, she thought.

"I'm going to need that address as well," Brass said. "You understand that nobody involved in this incident should leave Vegas until our investigation is completed. We may have more questions later on."

"No problem," Park said. "As it happens, we're going to be shooting the pilot for the *Zombie Heat* series here anyway." He grinned at the prospect. "Gotta love Vegas. It always makes great TV."

"Sure," Catherine said. "As long as nobody gets hurt."

"That's not going to happen again," Park insisted. "Once is more than enough." He took out a smartphone and checked his messages. "Speaking of which, I hate to rush you, but are we almost through here? I really need to deal with this crisis. Everybody and his brother wants a piece of me."

"Just a few more questions," Brass said. "Can you think of any reason why anyone would want to hurt Matt Novak?"

"Are you kidding? Everybody loved Matt. We're one big happy family here."

"What about away from the show?" Catherine asked. "Did he have any enemies?"

"Not that I know off. Matt was a single guy, with a couple of ex-wives, but no real drama." Confusion wrinkled his surgically-smooth countenance. "Why are you asking anyway? We know who shot him and why. That girl freaked and pulled a gun."

"We just need to examine every angle," Catherine explained. "Had you met Jill Wooten before?"

"No, just her friend." He helped himself to an-other antacid, as though his gut was not enjoying this interview. "I still haven't met her, really. She was pretty hysterical the last time I saw her. The paramedics took her away."

"What about her and Novak?" Brass asked. "Are you aware of any prior relationship between them?"

"She didn't even know who he was! He was wearing a hockey mask, remember?" A flicker of impatience eroded his easy manner. "Look, I un-derstand that you folks have to ask these kinds of questions, and I appreciate your diligence and com-mitment to the truth, but, honestly, there's no big mystery here. We shocked the wrong person and she killed Matt in what she thought was self-defense. You've got the footage. See for yourself."

"We'll do that," Brass promised. "But this loca-tion is locked down until we're done here."

"Naturally," Park agreed. "You have any idea how long that's likely to take?"

Catherine was used to being nagged by impatient landlords and business owners anxious to open up shop again. She had learned from experience to never let herself get pinned down. "That depends on what we find."

"That makes sense, I guess." He frowned, obvi-ously less than satisfied with her answer. She won-dered just how long the studio had leased this real estate for. "But, really, that's not going to take too long? I mean, it was just an accident, right?"

Probably, Catherine conceded. But right now they only knew one thing for sure.

Matt Novak was dead.

7

DESERT PALM HOSPITAL was starting to feel like Ray's home away from home away from home. Although several years had passed since he had actually worked full-time as a surgeon, he often found himself at Desert Palm processing a victim.

Like today.

Rita Segura was hooked up to a ventilator in the hospital's ICU. An IV was attached to her arm. Blinking apparatus monitored her vital signs, which appeared to be weak but stable. According to her attending physician, whom Ray had already spoken to, she had not regained consciousness since arriving at the hospital. Mechanical respiration was keeping her alive, while copious amounts of antivenin, as well as standard antibiotics, were doing the same. Her face was drawn and pale, her eyes closed, but Ray could tell that ordinarily she was an attractive woman. Her petite frame, and low body mass, helped explain why the venom had taken effect so quickly. Children and smaller individuals were typically more at risk from envenomation.

He reminded himself that, on an average, there were only about fifteen fatal snakebites in North America every year, mostly from rattlesnakes and other pit vipers. Nobody had been killed by a coral snake in years. There was every reason to hope that Rita would not become a statistic.

But she wasn't out of the woods yet.

An older gentleman was seated at her bedside. Engrossed in his vigil, he did not look up as Ray approached the bed. The CSI cleared his throat to avoid startling him.

"Excuse me," he said. "Mr. Segura?"

Rita's husband was in his sixties at least, with mussed silver hair and rumpled clothing. A wool sweater vest was unbuttoned. Sitting as close to the hospital bed as he could, he held on tightly to his wife's hand. Teary, red-rimmed eyes looked up at Ray. His cheeks were damp. "Yes?"

"My name is Ray Langston. I'm with the Las Vegas crime lab." He placed his field kit next to the bed. "I'm sorry to disturb you."

Marshall Segura pulled himself together. He wiped the tears from his eyes. "That's all right." He squinted at Ray. "Langston, you say? Aren't you the one who figured out what kind of snake had bitten Rita? The doctors here say you may have saved her life."

"It was a reasonable deduction," Ray said. "I'm just glad it proved useful."

Unfortunately, Desert Palm had not had the appropriate antivenin in stock, since coral snakes were hardly native to Nevada. It had been necessary to fly the antivenin in from Texas, causing a dangerous delay in Rita's treatment. Small wonder she hadn't regained consciousness yet. If only the doctors here could have administered the antivenin sooner.

"Well, you have my gratitude, young man." Segura turned his worried eyes back to his wife. "I hope you're not expecting to question Rita, though. I'm afraid she hasn't spoken since . . ."

He choked up, unable to complete the sentence.

"I understand," Ray said. In fact, Detective Vartann had declined to join the CSI on this call since Rita Segura was obviously in no condition to be interviewed just yet. "But I still need to examine her wound if you don't mind."

Segura nodded, his gaze never leaving Rita. "Go ahead. Do what you have to do."

"Thank you." Ray went around to the other side of the bed. He drew a curtain around them to provide a little more privacy. According to her chart, Rita had been bitten on the throat so Ray gently undid the top of her hospital gown and pulled it down to expose the base of her neck. A gauze bandage had been applied to the wound. He gently peeled it back.

A horseshoe pattern of tiny teeth marks confirmed that Rita had been attacked by a coral snake. A rattler or another pit viper, like copperheads and water moccasins, would have left two puncture marks instead. He was relieved to see minimal swelling around the site, which indicated that the antivenin and antibiotics were doing their job. The wounds had already scabbed over, but he hadn't been planning to measure their depth anyway. In-

stead he took out a tape measurer and carefully recorded the bite radius. He then took multiple photos
of the bite, placing a paper ruler against the uncon-
scious woman's throat for scale. The flash of the
camera did not rouse her.

"What are you doing that for?" Segura asked. His
tone was not confrontational, merely concerned.

"We need to identify the snake that bit her," Ray
explained. "Measuring the distance between the bite
marks may help us do that."

"I see." Segura averted his eyes from the ugly
wound. "Dammit, I always knew that snake thing
was a bad idea. I tried to talk her out of it." Revulsion twisted his face. "Disgusting creatures!"

"You don't like snakes?" Ray asked.

Segura snorted. "Who does?" His expression softened as he watched over his wife. "But she seemed
to enjoy it and I could never say no to her." His voice
grew hoarse with emotion. A handkerchief dabbed
at his eyes. "It's not right, I tell you. She's so young,
not like me. I'm not supposed to outlive her."

His grief struck Ray as genuine, but he couldn't
help noticing the extreme disparity in age between
the elderly man and Rita Segura, who was still in
her late twenties. The term "trophy wife" came to
mind, somewhat uncharitably. Was it possible there
were marital problems at play here, perhaps another
man? The victim's spouse was always a prime suspect in any possible homicide or attempted homicide. Too many dissatisfied husbands and wives, Ray
had discovered, came to consider "until death do
you part" an escape hatch instead of a vow. It was
enough to make one think twice about matrimony.

Maybe that's why so few CSIs take the plunge, he thought. *Aside from Grissom and Sara, of course.*

He replaced the bandage and pulled Rita's hospital gown back up. He walked around the bed to join Segura. Although Rita could not be interviewed yet, there was still her husband. "Do you mind if I ask you some questions?"

"No," Segura answered. "What do you need to know?"

Ray pulled up a chair. "Can you think of anyone who might want to harm your wife?"

"I know exactly who is responsible for this nightmare," Segura spat. Anger infused his voice, showing a harder side to the distraught old man. "The filthy animal she sent to prison."

Ray was surprised by his answer. This was more than he had been expecting. He felt like a prospector who had accidentally stumbled onto the mother lode. "What do you mean?"

"About a month ago," Segura said, "Rita received a summons for jury duty. I told her she should try to get out of it, but she insisted on doing her civic duty." He beamed at her proudly. "That's the kind of decent, upstanding woman she is."

"Very commendable." Ray was eager to get to the point. "So what happened?"

"She ended up serving on the trial of a vicious drug dealer. The jury even appointed her foreman. I went with her to the courthouse every day, just to provide her with moral support."

Or perhaps to keep a close watch on your alluring younger wife, Ray thought. He hated to be so cynical, but that was an occupational hazard. The job

trained you not to take people's testimony at face
value and to always look for ulterior motives.
Maybe this seemingly devoted old man also had a
jealous and suspicious streak?

"If only she hadn't gotten on that jury," Segura
sobbed, breaking into tears. "Maybe none of this
would have happened."

Was this just an act? Ray's gut told him that Marshall Segura was innocent, but he had been fooled
before . . . badly. Years ago, long before he became
a CSI, he had worked at a hospital much like this
one. A killer had also worked there, a self-appointed
"angel of death" who had put multiple patients out
of their misery before he was caught. The fact that
the killer had operated right under Ray's nose for so
long still haunted him, and had taught Ray a bitter
lesson: Murder often lurked right where you least
expected it.

Perhaps even in the heart of a weeping husband?

"Rita and the other jury members found the defendant guilty," Segura continued after he had composed
himself. "As well they should have. I'll never forget
the way that animal glared at Rita when the verdict
was read. She had nightmares about it for weeks." A
bony fist clenched at his side. "That criminal must be
responsible for this, or one of his scumbag friends!"

"I see," Ray said diplomatically. He wasn't entirely sure how an imprisoned drug dealer could arrange to have Rita attacked by a snake at a spa, or
even whether she was actually the intended victim,
but stranger things had happened. It was definitely
worth looking into. "Do you recall the name of the
defendant?"

"I'm afraid not. Sorry," Segura apologized. "But I'll tell you what I do remember. The no-good son of a bitch had a tattoo on his neck." He paused to make sure he had Ray's full attention. "A tattoo of a *snake*."

8

"MR. BOGGS, I presume?"

Their next witness flinched at the name. "Yeah, that was my character tonight. My real name's Hamilton, though. Bill Hamilton."

The makeup trailer being perfectly good for him, the middle-aged thespian occupied the same stool formerly graced by Jill Wooten and Debra Lusky. Catherine and Brass had relocated back to the dressing room after vacating Roger Park's roomier digs. Hamilton didn't seem to mind being interviewed here. Catherine guessed it was more comfortable than an iron maiden.

"Sorry to keep you waiting," she said. "Thank you for your patience."

"No problem," he rasped. "Believe me, I needed some time to recover."

He had the unglamourous, everyman features of a born character actor. He was short and pudgy, with thinning gray hair and a ruddy face. Stubble dotted his cheeks. Lurid red splotches stained his wrinkled business shirt. A blood spatter specialist, Catherine knew stage blood when she saw it. No way was it real; not only was it the wrong shade of red, but real blood would have turned brown by now.

Guess it fooled Jill Wooten, though.

Brass began by flipping open his notebook. "Sounds like you had a front-row seat for tonight's show."

"More like a supporting role," Hamilton grumped. He fished a pack of cigarettes from his shirt pocket, revealing the origin of his gravelly voice. Nicotine stained his fingertips. "Do you mind if I smoke? I'm still pretty rattled."

"Not in here," Catherine said. She didn't want to risk contaminating any evidence, let alone endure the secondhand fumes. "Sorry."

"Figures," he said sourly, putting the cancer sticks away. "Yeah, I saw the whole thing. Unfortunately."

"Tell us about it," Brass prompted.

He eyed the exit longingly, no doubt still hoping for a cigarette break. "I'm sure you've already heard the whole story."

"We need your version," Brass said. "For the record."

"Sure. I get it." He took a deep breath and began. "Everything was going according to the script at first. I was trussed up in the iron maiden, playing the part of the trapped club owner, when this week's vic tiptoed in, just like we planned. I put on my act, pretending to be scared shitless, ad-libbing beneath my gag. The girl fell for it, hook, line, and sinker. She looked absolutely petrified even before Matt charged in with the chainsaw." He sighed and shook his head. "Hell, you know what happened next."

Brass didn't force him to describe the shooting. "How many shots were fired?"

"One, I think." He sagged against the makeup table, momentarily overcome by the memory. "Oh man. I still can't believe that Matt is really dead. We've been doing this show for years now, and nothing like this has ever happened before."

"So they keep telling us," Catherine said.

"It's true," he insisted. "I swear to God, nobody's ever been hurt or injured before."

"Any close calls?" Brass asked.

Hamilton hesitated. "Well . . ."

This sounds promising, Catherine thought. "We'd appreciate anything you could tell us."

The actor wrestled briefly with his conscience. "Okay, once in a while, a vic freaks out and goes for the bad guy before he can reveal himself, but usually there's a supporting character or two, like me, who can jump in to restrain the vic before anybody gets hurt." He chuckled mordantly. "I remember this one time. A college quarterback went nuts and tackled Matt, knocked him flat on his butt. I had to break character and pull the guy off Matt. Things got pretty crazy there for a few moments, but it all turned out okay. I bought the guy a beer later on. It was no big deal."

"Unlike this time," Catherine observed.

"Well, I was bound and gagged, you know." He sounded like he had been replaying the incident over and over again in his mind. "There was nothing I could do to stop that girl once she pulled out her gun. I couldn't even call out to her, tell her it was just a gag. Not that she would have heard me, over the chainsaw." He reached automatically for a cigarette to steady his nerves, then remembered they were off-limits. "Looking back, we screwed up big time. We should have staged things differently."

"You think?" Brass said.

"Hey, it wasn't my idea," Hamilton protested. "I don't dream up these stunts. I just do what I'm told. Don't try to pin this on me!"

"Nobody's accusing you of anything," Catherine assured him, playing the good cop. There was nothing but sympathy in her voice. "Sounds like you've been with the show for awhile."

He relaxed a little. "Since the beginning, pretty much. I usually do the setup, play the worried school principal or park ranger or whoever, whatever it takes to set up the scenario. Nobody ever recognizes me or guesses that I'm an actor. I suppose I just have one of those faces. People accept me as an ordinary guy. Poor old Mister Boggs, trapped in the iron maiden. That's my forte. I don't often play the bear."

"The bear?" Catherine asked.

"That's what we call the monster of the week," he explained. "The Bigfoot, the serial killer, the crazy Satanist. The bear is usually an actor in costume, but sometimes it's just a prop. Like a ticking bomb or a phony spray of toxic waste. Once we even faked a terrorist attack."

Just good, clean fun, Catherine thought sarcastically. She had to work hard to keep her disgust in check. "Did Matt often play the bear?"

"Yeah. All the time. Park and Matt go way back. Matt was the stuntman on Park's first low-budget slasher flick, back in the day. They were old drinking buddies, although maybe less so these days, now that's Park's hit the big time and married to that big kahuna at Constellation. Tell you the truth, Park outgrew Matt, but still threw some work his way for old time's sake."

Catherine got the picture. "So Park was doing an old crony a favor, which ended up getting him killed."

"Yeah, how's that for a kicker?" Hamilton started to loosen up, becoming more gossipy. "Jesus, what a stupid way to go. I wouldn't wish that on anybody, not even Matt Novak."

Brass picked up on the put-down. "You had a problem with Novak?"

Hamilton shrugged, backpedaling a little. "It was no big deal. Matt just had a bit of an attitude lately. He'd started acting like a diva on the set, like he thought he was the star of the show or something."

"I take it that wasn't the case," Catherine said.

"Hardly," the actor scoffed. "If you ask me, he had the easy part. Anyone can put on a fright mask and say 'boo!' The hard part is convincing some poor vic of the reality of the situation, creating a context in which the shock makes sense. That's where I came in. I was the one that was really selling the scenarios. By the time I was done with them, the vics were already primed to jump out of their skins. I made it easy for Matt, not that he'd ever admit it."

Catherine detected a bit of professional rivalry. "He thought it was all about him, huh?"

"His ego was out of control," Hamilton said. "He thought he was a shoo-in for the lead in the new *Zombie Heat* series, even though he'd only played a bit part in the feature version."

"What happened to the original actor?" Catherine asked.

"That guy?" Hamilton snorted. "He and Park had a falling-out over the merchandising; the idiot wanted a cut on every toy and T-shirt using his image, even though he was buried under a ton of monster makeup at the time. Moron. He'll never work for Park again. Last I heard, he was in Bulgaria doing some straight-to-DVD schlock. But that didn't mean Matt was going to get the gig."

"Well, he's not getting the part now," Brass pointed out. "Unless he really can rise from the grave."

"Ain't that the truth." Hamilton fumbled for smokes again. "Unlucky bastard."

The actor was turning out to be a font of behind-the-scenes gossip. Catherine pressed him for more. "So how did Novak's new attitude go over on the set?"

"Honestly, I was surprised Park put up with it. Granted, they had a history, but friendships only go so far in this business. Like I said, Park had left Novak behind, career-wise. Matt should have been grateful for any crumbs his old buddy tossed at him. The last few months, though, he'd been mouthing off to Park on the set, making all sorts of 'artistic' suggestions, and generally behaving like a first-class pain in the ass. Park was letting him get away with murder, pardon the expression."

Catherine wondered why. The more she heard, the more she was starting to think there was something fishy about this "accident." The red flag was that menacing phone call Jill had received right before her bogus interview, the one that had convinced her to bring a gun to WaxWorkZ. Grissom had taught her to take "coincidences" like that with a mega-sized grain of salt. Her gut told her that someone had possibly orchestrated the shooting. But if it was a set-up, who was the target?

Novak or Jill . . . or both?

"About your shirt?" she asked. "That's not real blood, is it?"

Hamilton glanced down at his front and laughed. "No way. Just a little stage dressing."

Knew it, she thought.

Too bad the rest of this case wasn't as obvious.

9

"SNAKE EXPRESS," SARA called out. "Coming through."

Clerks and lab techs darted out of the way as she wheeled the vivarium down the sterile, aquamarine walls of the crime lab. The sealed glass container and its serpentine occupants rested atop a wheeled metal gurney. A borrowed set of tongs lay beside the vivarium. The tangle of snakes attracted a wide variety of reactions, ranging from acute fascination to shocked revulsion. Wendy Simms, the night shift's current DNA specialist, came away from her test tubes and cultures to watch the snakes roll past the glass walls of her laboratory. Henry Andrews, the toxicology expert, on the other hand, took one look at the gurney coming toward him and retreated back into his lab with unseemly haste. Sara found his reaction vaguely ironic, considering his speciality. *Then again*, she thought, *who knows more about how dangerous snake venom is than a toxicologist?*

"And where exactly are you going with that?"

David Hodges asked her. The trace specialist emerged from his lab. His ID badge was pinned to the lapel of his blue lab jacket. His lank brown hair was combed away from his forehead; Sara had once caught him applying dye to some gray streaks. As usual, he exuded an aura of self-satisfied snarkiness.

"The garage," Sara answered. "Unless maybe there's room in your lab?"

"I think not." He leaned over to inspect her scaly cargo. An indignant kingsnake hissed at him, proving it to be an excellent judge of character, as far as Sara was concerned; Hodges had a tendency to get on people's nerves. He tapped the glass. "Suspects, witnesses, or evidence?"

"All of the above, maybe." Sara looked up and down the bustling corridor. As far as she could tell, Ray had not gotten back from the hospital yet and the other CSIs all seemed to be out on calls. No surprise there; she imagined the *Shock Treatment* case was keeping Catherine and the guys busy. That left her on her own with the snakes, unless . . . She sized up Hodges, who seemed to be her best option at the moment. "Want to lend a hand with my friends here?"

"By all means." Hodges hurried ahead to open the door to the garage, which was located across the hall from the layout room. He puffed out his skinny little chest. "As I'm sure Grissom has told you, my usefulness extends far beyond the elusive subtleties of trace evidence." He cast her a sideways glance. "Speaking of which, I've been meaning to ask: how is Gil doing?"

Sara suppressed a smile. Hodges's man crush on

her husband was enough to make a less secure woman jealous. "He's fine," she answered honestly. "Holding down the fort in Paris."

Gil was lecturing at the Sorbonne, while they waited for a crucial research grant to come through. Their long-distance marriage puzzled some people, but was working for them so far. Sara was happier now, and more at peace, than she had ever been before. When she had first left the crime lab, a few years ago, it had been because all the violent death and tragedy had finally become too much for her; it had started to feel like her whole world revolved around bloodshed and homicide. These days, however, she found the grisly realities of the job easier to cope with now that she had a life outside the crime lab. A ring of pale skin on her fourth finger marked where her wedding band usually was. She never wore the ring at work, for both practical and emotional reasons. Besides the difficulties of pulling latex gloves over it, she didn't want her wedding band immersed in the viscera of a mutilated corpse. It belonged to her other life. With Gil.

It's all about maintaining a proper balance, she thought, *between the job and everything else*. She wondered if Hodges realized that. Did he have a life, or even, God forbid, a girl waiting for him at home?

Probably not, she guessed.

"Good to know," he said, sounding slightly disappointed. No doubt he had been hoping for a fuller report on his idol's continental activities. "Give him my regards the next time you talk to him."

"I'll do that," she lied. In fact, she and Gil spoke on the phone most every day, often for hours at a time. Oddly enough, the subject of David Hodges seldom came up.

"After you." He held open the door as she wheeled the gurney into the garage. The cavernous space, which was fitted better than most machine shops, was as good a place as any to store the snakes for the duration. It was secure, it was out of the way, and it was adequately heated and ventilated. She glanced around the garage, which held several workbenches, tool lockers, a transparent fuming chamber, decapitated mannequins (leftover from a vicious axe murder a few weeks ago), a fleet of impounded Harley-Davidson motorcycles, and, dominating the scene, a partially disassembled speedboat that had been fished from the bottom of Lake Mead. The boat, she knew, was linked to a quadruple homicide day shift had been working on for a week now. The choppers belonged to a biker gang suspected of torching a local bowling alley. Miscellaneous other artifacts and pieces of equipment were scattered around the room. An industrial-sized fan kept the atmosphere free of toxic fumes. In general, the garage housed the largest, most cumbersome pieces of evidence in need of processing. It was also the ideal location for the CSIs' bigger and messier experiments.

God help us, she thought, *if any of the snakes get loose*. The cluttered garage offered a profusion of nooks and crannies to hide in. *We'd never find them all again. . . .*

All the more reason to be careful with this living evidence. She and Hodges cleared off the top of a sturdy workbench, then each gripped one end of the vivarium with both hands. Sara did her best to ignore the agitated motions of the snakes, which hissed and snapped merely a few inches away from her face. Only a thin pane of glass separated her from the reptiles' fangs. A thick black milk snake glared at her. A forked tongue flicked at the glass.

"Ready?" she asked Hodges. "On my count, one, two . . . three!"

Grunting in effort, they heaved the vivarium off the gurney. The rectangular case, and its sinuous contents, was just as heavy as it looked, and the frantic activity of the snakes caused its center of gravity to shift erratically. Back at the spa, she had let Brookston and her partner load the vivarium into the Denali. Now it was up to her and Hodges to safely transfer the case to the counter. She didn't want to think about what would happen if they dropped it.

"You ever see that movie?" Hodges asked her, struggling to maintain his grip. *"Snakes on a Plane"?*

"At the moment, I'm more worried about snakes in a lab." Her muscles bulged, and she was grateful for every hour she had spent in the gym. The case tilted to one side, sending the snakes sliding over each other. "Let's save the movie chat for later."

"Fair enough."

Miraculously, they managed to heft the vivarium onto the counter without spilling the snakes all over the floor. Wiping her brow, Sara stepped back to admire the fruits of their labor. She had to admit that she could never have lifted the whole thing on her own.

"Thanks," she said sincerely. Despite his quirks,

Hodges often came through when it counted; she recalled that he had once saved Nick's life by figuring out that a buried coffin had been explosively booby-trapped. "So I guess you're not freaked out by snakes?"

"Hardly," he said, preening. "As a mammal, I make it a point not to cower before life-forms over whom I have a distinct evolutionary advantage. After all, if Commander Artemus Bishop can outwit the Serpent Empire of Saurian-Five, why should I be intimidated by a crate of squamous Ophidia."

"Saurian-Five?" Sara assumed that was some sort of *Astro Quest* reference. Hodges's devotion to that old cult television show was no secret around the lab; he had even been on hand to investigate a murder at a sci-fi convention once. Sara had seen a couple of episodes, but didn't quite get the appeal. "Well, in this case, the Serpent Empire definitely struck back."

Hodges regarded the snakes with renewed interest. He leaned up against the counter, his arms crossed atop his chest. "How so?"

She quickly brought him up to speed regarding the alleged snake attack at The Nile. "The challenge now is to figure out which of these wriggly willies is our biter."

The sheer number and variety of the enclosed snakes was daunting. She peered through the glass walls of the vivarium at over a dozen intertwined snakes, boasting all sorts of exotic colors and markings. It was like watching the world's most sinuous kaleidoscope. *For all we know*, she thought, *there could be more than one venomous snake in that tangle.*

Hodges inspected their suspects from a couple of angles. "I suppose a line-up is out of the question?"

"Not really an option," she agreed. "Even if our vic wasn't still in a coma and unable to identify her attacker." It was a shame that they hadn't been able to interview the missing masseuse yet; Heather Gilroy might know exactly which snake bit Rita Segura. "Ray thought the culprit was probably a coral snake."

"A reasonable supposition," Hodges said magnanimously, as though his own verdict was the final word. "The good professor is no Gil Grissom—who is?—but I've been impressed by his deductive acumen." He stroked his chin. "As I recall, there's a handy, if somewhat folksy, mnemonic device for distinguishing coral snakes from their less hazardous imitators. 'Red on black, friend of Jack; red on yellow, kill a fellow.'"

Sara was familiar with the rhyme. It referred to the sequence of the colored bands on the snake's hide. If a narrow yellow band touched a red band, the snake was best avoided.

"Actually, that's not one hundred percent accurate." She had used her smartphone to do a web search on the topic back at the spa. "There are species of coral snakes outside North America that break that rule. But, yes, it's fairly reliable here in the States."

"Of course," Hodges insisted a trifle defensively. "That's what I meant."

Sure you did, Sara thought. She squinted through the glass, looking for the right sequence of red and yellow bands. This was easier said than done; not only were there too many snakes to keep track of, but the tangled reptiles refused to keep still. It was often hard to tell where one snake ended and another began.

"I hate to say it," she concluded, "but I think we're going to have to sort through them one snake at a time." She gave Hodges an appraising look. "You up for that mission, Commander Bishop?"

"One by one?" Hodges looked less than enthused. His gaze swung toward the exit, as though he was having second thoughts about volunteering to help Sara out with the snakes. He started to back toward the door. "Actually, now that I think of it, there are these unidentified fiber samples that I really need to log in. . . ."

Sara played her trump card. "I'll be sure to tell Grissom just how invaluable you were."

"Really?" His mood perked up. "On second thought, I suppose those fibers aren't going anywhere."

Sucker, Sara thought. "Exactly. I'm sure they can wait a little while longer."

Halting his furtive retreat, Hodges considered the task at hand. He walked over to a cyanoacrylate fuming box located on a table nearby. The aquarium-sized case could be filled with Super Glue vapors to bring latent fingerprints into view. "You know, our reptilian adversaries might be a little easier to examine if we send them to the gas chamber first."

"Hodges!" A lifelong animal lover, Sara was appalled by the idea. "You can't be serious."

Granted, although she had avoided thinking

about it until now, they would probably have to euthanize the guilty snake once it was identified; that was standard procedure for dangerous animals that had demonstrably caused serious harm to human beings. Plus, they would need to subject the offending serpent to a complete postmortem, including an examination of its bite radius. But she was loathe to exterminate the whole batch just for convenience's sake.

"It was just a suggestion," Hodges said hurriedly, anxious to deflect Sara's wrath. He scooted away from the fuming box. "But I suppose we can always do things the hard way."

"More like the humane way," she clarified. "How would you like it if someone put you down just because one of your relatives bit someone?"

"Well, when you put it that way." He joined her by the vivarium. "Although, sadly, I can think of a few branches of my family tree where that's not such an unlikely scenario."

Tell me about it, Sara reflected ruefully. Her own turbulent family history was something she had spent years running away from. She pushed the painful memories aside in order to focus on the challenge before them. "We're going to need at least two more containers," she assessed. "Let's get this reptile rodeo under way."

It took several minutes to scrounge up two clear plastic bins. Sara punched holes in the lids to ventilate them and lined the bottoms with shredded faxes and lab reports. She set the bins up on opposite ends of the vivarium. *One for the dangerous snakes*, she thought, *and one for the innocent bystand-*

ers. She lifted the snake tongs, which she had borrowed from Tina Brewster, the Animal Control officer, from the edge of the gurney. The library in the break room had provided a hardcover guide to the snakes of North America. Color inserts provided plenty of visual reference for comparisons. Sara recognized the book. Grissom had donated it to the lab years ago. He had his own copy in Paris.

She offered the tongs to Hodges. "Care to do the honors?"

"Do I look like a snake wrangler to you?" Claiming a spiral notebook and pencil instead, he sat down on a stool at least a yard away from the snake-infested vivarium. "I think I'll just take inventory of our suspects."

"Suit yourself." Sara put on a pair of thick protective gloves, for safety's sake. Coral snakes had relatively short fangs; they had difficulty biting through heavy clothing. *Too bad Rita Segura was naked,* she thought. Sara approached the vivarium with the tongs, which could be operated with one hand, and slid open the lid with the other. "Keep an eye out for any slithery escape artists, okay?"

"I'm on the look-out," he promised.

"You'd better be."

She had to stand on a box to reach down into the seething mass of snakes. Deciding to start with an obviously harmless specimen, she gently used the tongs to grip a large king snake, with alternating black and gray bands, about a third of the way down its body; according to her research, you didn't want to apply the tongs to the snake's head or neck. Being careful not to squeeze too hard, she lifted the snake out of the case and took hold of its tail with her free hand as she had seen Brookston do. The helpful Animal Control officer had referred to the technique as "tailing" the snake. In theory, there was less chance of injuring the animal's spine if you supported it at both ends. Not at all slippery, the tail was easy to hold on to even with the gloves.

That's what makes this job interesting, she thought. *You learn something new every day.*

Somewhat awkwardly, she swung the snake over to one of the empty containers and dropped it inside. Keeping one eye on the transplanted serpent, she consulted the guidebook to make sure she knew what she had just handled. A color photo of a banded, bluish-gray serpent basking on a rock confirmed that it had indeed been an unmistakable specimen of *Lampropeltis alterna.*

"Gray-banded kingsnake," she called out.

Hodges jotted it down in his notebook. "Check."

Slowly, methodically, and more than a little gingerly, she transferred snake after snake to the "harmless" bin. The tongs were clumsy to use at first, but she soon got the hang of it. A portable clock/radio, tuned to a classical music station, helped to steady her nerves. She carefully identified each specimen as she added it to the holding tank.

"Albino corn snake."

"Check."

"Common garter snake."

"Check."

"Mexican milk snake."

"Check."

Five snakes in, she hit pay dirt. A long red snake,

with black and yellow bands, showed up amid the remaining serpents. Its blunt head and black snout matched the illustrations in the guidebook. Narrow yellow bands separated the broader red and black bands. Hodges's rhyme echoed in her brain.

"Red on yellow, kill a fellow . . ."

Her pulse quickened. "All right. I think we have our perp." She held her breath as, with an extra degree of caution, she fished the scaly suspect out of the vivarium and held it out for Hodges's inspection. "This look like a coral snake to you?"

"Whoa!" Hodges recoiled from the dangling snake, practically tumbling off his stool in his haste to get away from Sara's captive. He clutched his chest. "Not so close, okay?"

"You sure?" Sara teased. She reached out and firmly gripped the snake behind the head with her free hand, taking care to keep its jaws pointed away from her. Coral snake venom, she had learned, was twice as powerful as a rattler's. A loud popping noise, issuing from the snake's cloaca, indicated that it was upset. In nature, the snake made the noise to scare away predators. She offered Hodges a closer look at their suspect. "She's a real beauty."

"I can see it just fine from here, thank you." He hopped off the stool, retreating with the guidebook to a safe distance. "It does appear to be a coral snake." He kept a wary eye on the snake while comparing it to the photos. "The Texan coral snake, *Micrurus tener,* to be exact. Not native to Nevada, I might add."

Sara pondered that particular tidbit of info. "So how did it get here?"

"Just another tourist in search of a wild Vegas weekend?" He contemplated the writhing masses of snakes in the two containers. "Do snakes have bachelor parties?"

"Only if a mouse jumps out of a cake," Sara guessed. Before isolating the coral snake in a bin of its own, she took a closer look at their prime suspect. The snake was at least two feet long and about an inch wide. Round pupils met her gaze. To the casual eye, it did look much like the harmless milk snakes it was keeping company with. Sara could see how an unsuspecting masseuse might not notice the difference.

I still want to talk to Heather Gilroy, though.

She was admiring the snake's brightly colored scales when she spotted an irregularity along its length. Keeping a tight hold on the snake, she rotated it to get a better look.

"Check this out," she said to Hodges. "There appear to be some sort of scratch marks on its hide, about two-thirds of the way down its dorsal region. Make a note of that."

He scribbled in the notebook. "Unidentified scratches on its back. Got it." He eyed the snake suspiciously, as though it might slip from her grasp at any minute. Despite his earlier mockery of the Serpent Empire, he clearly wasn't going to relax until the venomous predator was safely locked up again. Commander Artemus Bishop would have been disappointed in him. "Anything else?" he rushed her. "Or are you done playing snake charmer?"

"Hard to say." Holding on to the squirming reptile was admittedly a challenge; it was difficult to conduct a thorough examination while simultaneously trying not to get bitten. "We'll have to get a closer look at those scratches later." She mentally ran through all the evidence the snake could possibly provide. "We're also going to need samples of its blood and venom for analysis." She twisted the snake to inspect its jaws. "Who knows? Maybe there's even some traces of the victim's DNA on these fangs?"

Hodges gave the snake's jaws a wide berth. "Don't expect me to swab those teeth. Or hold the snake while you do." He clearly considered that beyond his job description. "That's going to be easier said than done."

"I know," she said regretfully. There was really only one way to safely process the snake for evidence. *Damn.*

Hodges must have caught the sadness in her voice. His snarky manner gave way to an atypically gentle tone. "Sara, if you want, I'm sure Ray and I can put down that snake for you. A painless injection of barbiturates should do the trick."

"I'd appreciate that," she admitted, genuinely touched by Hodges's consideration. Given all the human carnage she had cleaned up after over the years, it had to seem funny that she'd be squeamish about euthanizing a deadly snake, but she'd always had a soft spot for animals. A vegetarian, she hadn't touched meat in years.

Not even snake meat.

Taking no chances, she relocated the coral snake to a tank of its own, apart from the other specimens. She doubled-checked to make sure the lid was sealed and secure. "In the meantime," she told Hodges, "we should finish our inventory, to make sure there's not another coral snake in the mix."

"No problem." He climbed back onto his stool. His pencil poised above the open notebook, he paused as though there was something else preying on his mind. He coughed to clear his throat. "Anyway, Sara . . ."

"Yes?" she asked.

"Does Grissom ever talk about me?"

10

NICK WAS ABOUT an hour into a new shift when Greg ambled into their shared office, clutching a manilla folder and a cup of coffee. The hip young CSI was wearing a gray T-shirt and dark slacks. Nick recalled the old days when Greg had sported spiked hair and an acid-stained lab coat. He'd matured a lot since then.

"What's up, pal?" Nick asked.

"Just some routine housekeeping." Greg flipped open the folder. "Ballistics confirms that the bullet that killed Matt Novak, the one we pried out of the wall at WaxWorkZ, came from Jill Wooten's gun."

"Good to know," Nick said. The news was not unexpected, but it paid to make sure all their ducks were in a row, just in case the matter ever went to trial. Meanwhile, Doc Robbins had already declared the COD to be a single gunshot wound to the chest. Traces of Novak's blood and tissue, identified by DNA, had been found on the deformed .38 caliber bullet they had found at the scene. "It looks like we know exactly how Novak died, and who pulled the trigger. It's the why that's still a little murky."

Catherine had shared her suspicions about the "accident" with the other CSIs. Nick wasn't sure what to think just yet. Had Jill really fired on Novak in a mistaken case of self-defense? Was this just a tasteless practical joke gone wrong? Or was there more to the picture than met the eye? Nick agreed with Catherine tha the fatal shooting deserved a closer look.

He sat in front of a laptop at his desk. The spacious office, conveniently located between the fingerprint and A/V labs, had once belonged to Gil Grissom, but was now shared by Nick, Greg, and Ray. An irradiated fetal pig, preserved in a tinted bottle of formaldehyde, occupied a shelf in memory of Grissom. Greg came up behind Nick and looked over his shoulder. "What you doing there?"

"Checking out your favorite show," Nick explained. "*Shock Treatment*, uncut."

Greg blushed slightly. "Hey, I never said it was my favorite show, just that I had watched it occasionally. You know me. I'm more of an indie film guy myself." He pulled a chair over and peered at the screen of the laptop, where Jill Wooten could be seen entering WaxWorkZ. "That the raw footage of the shooting?"

"Yep." Nick rubbed his eyes, which were already tired from staring at the screen nonstop. "We've got it from multiple angles."

For maybe the sixth time, he watched Jill creep apprehensively into the office behind the bar. The color footage fully captured her mounting fear and anxiety, which crossed over into full-blown terror when she discovered Bill Hamilton apparently trapped inside the iron maiden. Nick had personally examined the intimidating torture device, which had turned out to be a harmless replica. The rusty "metal" spikes lining its interior had actually been made of rubber, just like the teeth on the prop chainsaw. Hamilton had never really been in any danger, not that you could tell from his frantic, bug-eyed performance.

Jill sure didn't look like she knew it was a hoax. Panic was written all over her face. Nick turned down the volume before she screamed in horror. Matt Novak, in full chainsaw maniac mode, charged into the room and slammed the door shut behind him. He raised the whirring chainsaw high. Backing away fearfully, Jill reached into her purse and pulled out her Smith & Wesson. Novak toppled onto the floor.

A few minutes later, he was dead.

Nick hit Pause on the recording. He shook his head, appalled at what he had just seen. He turned toward Greg. "You're the expert. This how it usually goes?"

"Well, except for the shooting, yeah." Somewhat sheepishly, Greg described how the show was *supposed* to work. "Usually, just when this week's victim is convinced they're toast, the 'bear' comes clean. 'Surprise! You got *Shock Treatment*!' At which point, the victim's best friend or cousin or whatever emerges from hiding and everybody laughs it off."

"At least until they get home," Nick said. "Gotta

wonder what some of those victims really thought about getting set up by their so-called buddies."

"Oh, yeah," Greg said, smirking. "There was this one episode where the victim runs off and completely abandons his real-life girlfriend to be eaten by hillbilly cannibals without a backward glance. I mean, he got out of there so fast the hidden cameras could barely keep up with him. The girlfriend pretended to find it funny, but I always assumed that their relationship took a turn for the worse afterward."

Nick was inclined to agree. "Must be hard to see a guy the same way after he chooses to save his own skin over yours—even if the danger was only a hoax."

"That's what's kind of morbidly fascinating about the show," Greg said in a transparent attempt to rationalize his viewing habits. "You get to see how real people react under extremely bizarre conditions."

"Like we don't see that every night?"

"Er, good point." Greg steered the conversation back to the case. "From what I hear, Jill was definitely pissed off at her friend Debra for setting her up. Catherine said they nearly had an all-out catfight in the parking lot behind the club." His curved fingers clawed at the air. "Meow!"

"Can't say I blame Jill for losing her temper," Nick said. "That was one practical joke that really backfired. *If* it was really just an accident."

"Only one way to find out," Greg said, settling in for the long haul. "Let's see that footage again."

"Okay." Nick keyed it up back to the beginning

again. He wasn't looking forward to watching the tragedy play out one more time, but maybe a fresh pair of eyes would spot something he had missed. Besides, he couldn't really complain about having *too much* video coverage of the actual incident. Most of the time, they would kill to have this much evidence. *Too bad more of our cases don't take place on reality shows.*

They watched Jill fall for the prank again, with fatal results. Judging from the angle, this footage had been shot from behind the mock flatscreen TV on the wall. It gave them a perfect view of the whole deadly affair. The screen went blank shortly after Novak died, as someone belatedly remembered to turn off the cameras.

"You know," Greg said, after reviewing the footage, "is it just me, or does this particular scenario seem almost expressly designed to produce a messy outcome? Think about it. The hockey mask makes it hard for the 'slasher' to come clean, the noise from the chainsaw would drown out any hasty explanations, and the only other actor close enough to intervene is chained up inside an iron maiden. Throw in a gun, and it's a perfect recipe for an 'accidental' shooting. They couldn't have set things up better if they tried."

"Maybe someone did," Nick said. "Or maybe they just got sloppy." He mulled it over. "According to Catherine, the show's producer, Roger Park, personally put together this scenario and cast Novak as the slasher. You think he wanted Novak dead?"

"Who knows?" Greg leaned back in his chair. "It would be a pretty ingenious way to get rid of someone. You get someone else to pull the trigger for you, without them even being in on the scheme, so there's no way they can implicate you. And if the death is ruled accidental, you're in the clear."

"But why would Park sabotage his own show like that?" Nick asked. "Something like this is bound to shut them down for good, right?"

"Probably," Greg said. "Production has been suspended and the network has temporarily pulled the reruns from the air. On the other hand, take a look at this." He walked over to his own workstation and fired up his computer. A few clicks of a mouse took him onto the internet. "DVD sales have gone through the roof, and internet searches on the show are at an all-time high. This is more publicity than *Shock Treatment* has gotten in years."

"Well, I've certainly heard of the show now," Nick admitted, "where I hadn't before. I guess sudden death is always a headline grabber."

"Usually works that way," Greg said, "especially where Hollywood is concerned. Look at Brandon Lee, Heath Ledger, or even James Dean. Their final films got big publicity boosts from their untimely demises. If nothing else, *Shock Treatment* is going out with a bang."

Nick wasn't sure. "It still seems kind of short-sighted. What good does all that publicity do you if the show gets yanked off the air for good?"

"Maybe Park thought it was worth it?" Greg surfed the web, bopping from one show-biz news site to another, most of which he seemed to have saved as favorites. "From what I gather, *Shock Treatment*'s ratings had been sinking anyway. *Zombie Heat* is a much bigger deal these days. Park could probably afford to write off *Shock Treatment*. He's got bigger zombie fish to fry."

Nick took his word for it. Greg was probably the only CSI in the lab who read *Entertainment Weekly* cover to cover. He claimed that staying in touch with pop culture and music helped him out on the job. To be fair, it wasn't just an excuse. Last year Greg had helped them find a missing teenager by figuring out that her favorite underground band was in town. They had found her camped out on the sidewalk in front of the Ice House Lounge.

"Okay," Nick said. "So *Shock Treatment* was probably on its last legs. Why would he want to get Novak killed?"

"Catherine says that there had been friction on the set lately. That Novak had been acting like a jerk."

"Doesn't seem like reason enough to kill someone," Nick said. "Otherwise Hodges would be dead now."

Greg shrugged. "Since when do people need a good reason?"

Sadly, Nick knew what Greg meant. As a CSI, he'd seen people murdered for less. Just last week, a woman had been stabbed to death in a movie theater for talking too loud on a cell phone. And then there was that stand-up comic who poisoned another comedian because he didn't like his material. "Yeah, maybe. But this wasn't a case of someone simply losing their patience and whacking the guy. Why go to all this trouble to get rid of him if he was just a pain in the butt? Why not just fire him?"

"Good question," Greg said. "And how could Park have known that Jill Wooten would be armed?"

"Unless she was in on it?" Nick suggested.

Or maybe her crazy ex-boyfriend . . .

11

CATHERINE'S OFFICE WAS smaller than her job.

Ecklie had offered her Grissom's old office when she had taken over the night shift, but it just hadn't felt right, like she was living in someone else's house. Besides, she was comfortable here in her old corner office. Ferns and flowers counteracted the sometimes sterile feel of the crime lab. Ceramic plates and decorative glassware added a feminine touch. Framed photos of Lindsey, taken at various ages, reminded her that there was more to life than just blood spatter evidence. A brass name placard staked out her turf. A potted cactus needed watering. Blinds on the rear windows kept out the glare from the late-night traffic outside, while the clear glass wall facing her desk offered her a view of the corridor outside and the DNA lab across the hall. Subdued blue-green walls enclosed the rest of the office. Catherine routinely kept her door open to remain accessible to her people.

The autopsy report on Matt Novak was spread out on top of her desk. Aside from a pair of spooky "bloodshot" contact lenses, Doc Robbins had found nothing unexpected. The abrasion collar and smudging around the entry wound suggested that the fatal shot had been fired from slightly more than two feet away, as described by the witnesses. No additional ammo or wounds had been found during the postmortem. Novak had been killed by a single bullet from Jill Wooten's revolver. Just like everyone said.

But had she really thought she was in danger?

Brass rapped on her door. "Got a moment?"

"Come on in." Catherine looked up from the report. She took off her reading glasses. "What have you got?"

Brass looked tired from running down leads all day. Even though they were both technically on the night shift, practicality dictated that a lot of the footwork had to be conducted during daylight hours, when witnesses were up and about and shops and places were open for business. Squeezing in a few hours of sleep here and there could be a challenge. Catherine couldn't remember the last time she'd gotten a full eight hours. Maybe the last time she was in the hospital?

"I've been checking out Jill's story." He sank gratefully into a chair, resting his feet. "Turns out she did have a TRO out against her ex, who sounds like a real winner. Apparently he used to work as a trainer at her gym, but was fired for sexually harassing female customers. According to an affidavit Jill submitted over a year ago, he was not happy when she eventually ditched his sorry ass. He allegedly stalked her at her home and work, sent her hostile emails, and even tried breaking into her apartment one time."

Catherine disliked him already. She had a zero-tolerance policy when it came to abusive boyfriends and husbands. "No wonder Jill thinks he's responsible for those anonymous calls. He'd be my prime suspect, too. And her history with him definitely speaks to her state of mind at the time she fired the revolver."

"What about the gun?" Brass asked. "Any way the show could have known she might have it?"

Catherine shook her head. "The gun wasn't registered." Which meant that Jill had obtained the weapon illegally, perhaps because she hadn't wanted to wait for the mandatory 72-hour "cooling off" period. "No concealed weapons permit either."

In order to get a CCW permit in Clark County, a resident had to submit an application, complete an approved firearms course, get photographed and fingerprinted, pass a background check, and pay over a hundred dollars in fees. The process could take as long as six months, which was probably also longer than a frightened stalking victim was willing to wait.

"Figures," Brass muttered. "You run a trace on the gun?"

"Naturally, not that it did us much good." She pulled the printout from the file. "It was reported 'stolen' from a gun shop in Reno three years ago."

Both of them knew that "stolen" was often a euphemism for an illegal, under-the-table sale. Literally thousands of handguns and rifles were reported "lost" or "stolen" every year by less than reputable gun dealers. Many of those misplaced firearms ended up on the black market, rendering them more or less untraceable, which didn't exactly make Catherine's job any easier. Sometimes it seemed like it was easier to get a gun than a restraining order.

Wonder if Jill felt the same way? Especially this time around.

Even if Novak's death was chalked up to misadventure, Jill was still going to be in hot water for carrying an unregistered, concealed weapon without a permit. But her bad luck was possibly good news for the TV show and its lawyers.

"Sounds like Park was telling the truth in one respect," she observed. "Jill's gun would have slipped past their background check. No registration, no paper trail." She put away the report on the gun. "You got anything else for me?"

"Don't I always?" He reached under his jacket and pulled out a handheld digital recorder. "Jill gave us permission to lift those threatening phone calls off her voice mail. Phone records confirm that she got the last one a few hours before her job interview." He held up the gadget and clicked it on. "Get an earful."

A harsh, whispery voice, with a distinctly Southern twang, emanated from the recorder:

"Listen to me, you bitch! You better watch your back, 'cause I'm coming for you. Just when you least expect it, you're going to get what's coming to you . . . and then some! Don't even think you can get away from me. I'm going nuclear on you, baby. You're going to die screaming. . . ."

Brass clicked off the recorder. "That's just a sample. There's plenty more where that came from."

The temperature in the office seemed to have dropped several degrees. Catherine had been on the receiving end of her fair share of threats, but the vicious message still gave her a chill. If that really was Craig Gonch on the tape, she understood why Jill would want a restraining order—and a gun. "Well. I can't imagine why anyone would be jumpy after getting a call like that."

"Unless this has all been staged for our benefit," Brass speculated. "To make a premeditated murder look like a misunderstanding."

Catherine had thought of that, too. "But why would she want to kill Novak? As far as we know, they'd never met before."

"Well, that's the million-dollar question, isn't it?"

She took the recorder from Brass. She turned it over in her hands, wondering what Archie might be able to do with it.

"It would help if we knew for sure whose voice is on that tape."

Heather Gilroy's address led Sara to a low-budget apartment building across the street from a Choozy's Chicken franchise. She and Vartann compared notes on the case as they took the stairs to the fifth floor. The run-down building reminded Sara of her first apartment in San Francisco, right after college. Sadly, there was no elevator.

"This is my second time here," Vartann said. "We've been trying to get hold of Gilroy since yesterday, but so far she's in the wind." A long corridor, painted an institutional shade of beige, ran down the middle of two facing rows of apartments. Muffled noises escaped the thin walls. They counted down the doors to the right address. No light escaped the peephole. Sara didn't hear a TV or stereo blaring inside. Vartann knocked on the door. "Let's hope she's home this time."

Sara had come along to take Heather's fingerprints, as well any other evidence that might present itself. Before she could determine whether there were any suspicious prints on the vivarium, she had to be able to eliminate the masseuse's prints, which meant getting exemplars from Heather.

If we can find her, she thought.

As she let Vartann take point, she couldn't resist checking him out on the sly. Not for herself, but because she had gotten inklings that something might be developing between Vartann and Catherine, an impression that the other woman had cagily neither confirmed nor denied. Sara had worked with the laconic detective before, of course, but now she evaluated him from a different perspective.

Not bad, she concluded. Beneath his conservative dark suit, Vartann appeared to be in good shape. His lean, somewhat severe features had a certain appeal, if you liked tough guys. Catherine could, and had, done worse, especially if she was going to date a cop.

Vartann rapped harder on the door. He raised his voice. "LVPD. Open up."

No one came to the door. Sara listened closely, but did not hear anyone stirring inside. It was pushing eight p.m., a few hours before her next shift officially started, but sometimes you had to fudge the hours if you wanted to catch people at a sane hour. It was a weeknight, so hopefully Heather wouldn't be out tonight. Then again, Sara recalled, the runaway masseuse didn't have a job anymore.

A minute or two passed.

"Looks like we struck out again," Sara said.

"Yeah." Vartann took a break from knocking. "Sorry to waste your time dragging you out here."

"No problem." She wondered if Vartann was disappointed to be paired with her instead of Catherine. Or was it easier to concentrate on the case without any distracting sexual chemistry involved? Workplace romances could be tricky, as she knew better than most. On the other hand, she and Gil had worked out eventually. Maybe Catherine and Vartann had a shot, too.

Or was she getting ahead of herself?

Probably.

"If I didn't know better," Sara observed, "I'd think Heather Gilroy was avoiding us."

"Me, too." He scowled at the door. "Makes me wonder what she's got to hide."

A final emphatic knock proved equally futile. Alas, they did not have probable cause to force their way in, and Sara doubted they could get a warrant unless it could be proven categorically that Rita Segura had been bitten on purpose. They didn't even have grounds enough to put out a BOLO alert on Heather. All they had her on was fleeing the scene of a snakebite, which probably wasn't illegal. Sara prayed that Heather had not left town to avoid the heat.

Stymied for now, they turned back toward the stairs. Sara wasn't looking forward to lugging her gear back down five flights of stairs.

"Excuse me, are you looking for Heather?"

An unexpected voice, coming from the apartment across the hall, called them back. Sara turned around to see a curious neighbor standing in a doorway. The speaker was an overweight Caucasian woman, maybe retirement age, wearing a bright red Snuggie. The ridiculous garment made her look like she had her bathrobe on backward. It was not a good look—for anybody.

"Yes, we are." Sara felt a surge of hope. Maybe they had caught a lucky break. "Have you seen her lately?"

"Not since yesterday," the woman volunteered. "Which I admit has been something of a blessed relief."

Sara sensed the woman had something she wanted to get off her chest. "And why is that?"

"For the first time in weeks, I haven't had to endure that yappy little dog of hers. Usually, it's barking its head off all the time, enough to drive you absolutely crazy." She directed her grievance at Vartann. "You're with the police, you said? Surely that kind of disturbance can't be legal. Having a noisy dog like that when your neighbors are trying to sleep?"

"You have my sympathy," Vartann said in a noncommittal manner. He was clearly in no hurry to get sucked into a routine nuisance complaint. "And you are?"

"Camille Bozian," she answered. "5-D."

Sara realized that she was referring to her apartment number. Heather Gilroy lived in 5-E. "Do you have any idea where we might be able to find her?"

"Not in the slightest," Bozian said. "But wherever she is, she obviously took that irritating mutt with her. He always barks worst when she's not at home. Usually during the afternoon when I'm trying to get my beauty rest."

"When was the last time you saw her?" Vartann asked.

"Yesterday morning, I think." Bozian paused to replay the encounter in her mind. "I tried to catch her as she was rushing out to work, to speak to her about the dog again, but she said she was running late." The older woman clucked indignantly. "Five minutes later, the dog started yapping again. . . ."

First the dog, then the snakes. It sounded like Heather was having all sorts of animal control issues yesterday. Sara wondered where she might have taken refuge after the alarming incident at The Nile. "Do you know if she has a boyfriend?"

"Not that I know of," Bozian said. "Unless you count Jonas."

That sounds promising, Sara thought. "Who is Jonas?"

Bozian rolled her eyes. "The damn dog, who else?"

The audio/visual lab was one door down from Catherine's office. As usual, it took her eyes a moment to adjust to the dim lighting. Archie Johnson liked to keep the lights low to avoid any glare on the multiple screens and monitors crammed into the lab. The distinctive aroma of microwave popcorn, lingering in the air, gave the lab the feel of a one-man multiplex. The A/V center was one of the few labs in the complex where food was allowed, since there was no DNA or trace evidence to be contaminated, just pixels and electrons. Most of the lab rats had to confine their late-night snacks to the break room at the end of the hall.

Just as long as they keep the munchies away from Toxicology, Catherine thought.

His back to the door, Archie sat in front of an expensive array of high-tech computer monitors. An even larger plasma screen was halfway up the rear wall of the lab, directly facing the young gadget guru's workstation. Archie could transfer any image to the large screen with just a few strokes on his keyboard. Headphones were clapped over his ear, cutting him off from the everyday buzz of the lab. A glowing computer monitor displayed a spectrographic analysis of an audio recording. The timing, frequency, amplitude, and resonance of the sound were charted as fuzzy bands along an x–y axis, providing a permanent visual representation. A good analyst employed both his eyes and his ears.

She tapped him on the shoulder to get his attention. He took off the headphones and turned around to greet her. A slim young Asian man in a Hawaiian shirt, he was better-looking and less nerdy than most of his fellow lab rats. His athletic prowess and trim physique had recently earned him a cover shot on a professional surfing magazine. "Hi, boss. Didn't hear you come in."

"Sorry to interrupt." She nodded at the pulsating images on the screen. "That Jill Wooten's scary phone call?"

"In all its spectrographic glory," he confirmed. "Somebody sure didn't like her."

"And somebody else may have gotten shot because of it," Catherine said. "You think you can get anything out of that?"

"Maybe," he hedged. "The fact that the caller is using a creepy whisper is going to make a concrete identification tricky, but we might be able to establish a strong probability as to the identity of the caller, especially after I clean the recording up some more. And, of course, I'm still going to need an audio exemplar to compare it against."

"We're working on that," she promised him. "What about the source of the call? Any luck there?"

"Not really." Archie put away his headphones. "Phone records indicate that it came from a disposable cell phone."

Catherine was afraid of that. Disposable phones were now the medium of choice for obscene phone callers, career criminals, and the occasional terrorist. Finding the phone was going to be a real long shot. Chances were, the mystery caller had already trashed it.

Especially now that Novak was history.

12

SARA HAD NOT given up on finding Heather Gilroy yet. As she and Detective Vartann drove away from the apartment building, she called The Nile on her cell phone. At first nobody picked up and she feared that maybe the staff at the spa had called it a day, but, after several rings, she finally got a response.

"The Nile Spa and Salon," a male voice answered. "How may I assist you?"

"Mr. Yun?" Sara had met Brian Yun, the spa's assistant manager the other day, when she had provided him with a receipt for the snakes she had confiscated. "This is Sara Sidle from the crime lab. I'm glad I caught you."

A weary sigh was audible even over the phone. "Madame has me working late redoing our calendar. I'm afraid we've had several cancellations, after what happened to Ms. Segura." He sounded tired and under stress.

Sara wouldn't also be surprised to hear that The

Nile was receding and business wouldn't be coming back. Although the ill-fated snake massage had not yet attracted the sort of media frenzy that Catherine's *Shock Treatment* case was getting, Sara imagined the story was already spreading rapidly through Rita Segura's gossipy social circle. It was the kind of bizarre occurrence people couldn't resist talking about.

"I'm sorry to interrupt you," she said, "but I was hoping you could help us out. I don't suppose Heather Gilroy showed up for work today? We're still trying to track her down."

"I'm afraid not," Yun said. "In fact, Madame has already instructed me to mail Heather's final paycheck to her home address, along with a notice of termination, to discourage her from ever showing her face here again. Alas, poor Heather has been banished from The Nile."

"But you still have her personnel file, right?" Sara had another idea. "Can you tell me who is listed as her emergency contact?"

Yun hesitated. "I'm not sure. Isn't that information supposed to be confidential? It's only meant to be used in the event of a genuine emergency."

"Heather is missing," Sara pointed out, "and a key witness in what might be an attempted homicide. That sounds like an emergency to me."

"Homicide?" He reacted with shock. "But I thought this was just an accident."

Sara saw no need to update him on their investigation. "Homicide. Manslaughter. Negligence. Right now we can't rule anything out. And Heather Gilroy might be the only person who can help us clear things up."

"Oh," Yun relented. "I guess when you put it that way . . . hang on." He tapped away at his keyboard. "All right. I have that information for you now."

Sara gave Vartann a thumbs-up. She took out a notebook. "Thanks a lot. I really appreciate this." She copied down the address Yun read to her. "Trust me," she assured him, "you're doing the right thing."

"I hope so," he said glumly, sounding unconvinced. "For everyone's sake."

"Again?"

Greg groaned at the prospect of watching Matt Novak die one more time. He and Nick had already viewed the *Shock Treatment* footage at least a dozen times, twice for each angle. By now they knew every beat and nuance of the doomed actor's final moments.

Or did they?

Nick thought that maybe they were missing something. All of this footage, fortuitously dropped into their laps . . . there had to be a clue there that would shed some light on the proceedings. Maybe right in front of them.

"Yep," he drawled. "Only now we get to watch it on the big screen."

The two men had relocated to the A/V lab in order to view the footage on Archie's king-sized plasma screen. Archie himself was taking a break; he had said something about going out for a bite to eat before turning the lab over to the CSIs. Nick hoped that seeing the shooting video blown up on the largest screen in the lab would reveal something that had been too small to notice before. This was the next best thing to watching the incident in person.

"Yippee," Greg said unenthusiastically. He sat down at the keyboard next to Nick. "I can hardly wait."

Nick smirked. "I thought you were a fan."

"Not anymore." Greg rubbed his weary eyes. "From now on, I'm sticking to *America's Funniest Autopsy Videos*." He looked dubiously at Nick. "You expecting an alternate ending this time?"

"Not exactly," Nick said. "There's just something nagging me. Like it's right under my nose."

"A hunch?" Greg asked.

"Nah, more like a feeling. Like my subconscious has already noticed something, but the rest of my brain hasn't caught up yet."

"Ah," Greg said, understanding. "Cognitive jet lag. I hate that." He flexed his fingers and took hold of the mouse. "All right. Let's fire this puppy up and see if we can figure out what's bothering your itchy subconscious."

The footage was already loaded into the A/V lab network. Greg clicked on the file and selected the big screen. They started with a bird's-eye view of the shooting, taken by the camera hidden in the smoke alarm. They looked down as Novak and Jill, not quite larger than life, confronted each other once more in the back office of WaxWorkZ. Bill Hamilton, stuck in the iron maiden, was out of the shot. All that could be seen was the rusty dome of the maiden's forged metal cranium. Jill jumped as

Novak slammed the door behind him, trapping her in the office with his terrifying chainsaw.

The fateful encounter played out exactly as before. The chainsaw roared, its spinning rubber teeth a blur. Jill screamed. The muzzle flared. Matt Novak began his final death scene.

"Same thing," Greg said. "She shot him again." Working the keyboard and mouse, he attempted to restart the footage from the beginning. "One more time?"

"Hold on." Nick held up his hand. "Let it keep playing."

"You sure?" Greg asked. "The rest is just everybody milling around in panic, not sure what to do, until somebody remembers to turn off the cameras."

Nick remembered. They had played through the entire sequence at least once, watching the show's overwhelmed medic try in vain to stop Novak from expiring. "Maybe that's what's bothering me. Not during the shooting itself, but the aftermath. Go back to right after he was shot."

Greg rewound the clip to the moment in question. Novak was driven back by the impact of the bullet. He toppled backward onto the carpet. The chainsaw slipped from his fingers. He writhed upon the floor. Only moments from death, he clawed feebly at the air with one hand. His elevated arm trembled, as though he could barely hold it up. His masked face turned slightly to the left.

"Wait a sec." Nick squinted at the screen. He felt a surge of adrenalin, like a dog that had just caught a scent. "Freeze that."

Greg complied. "You got something?"

"Maybe." Nick leaned forward, peering at the screen, where Matt Novak was suspended in his death throes. He looked closely at the actor's masked countenance. It was hard to make out, but . . . "Can you zoom in on the hockey mask?"

Greg's fingers danced atop the keyboard. A grid pattern appeared on the frozen image and he selected the designated segment, which expanded to fill up the entire screen. The enlarged image was blurry and indistinct at first, but then the image-enhancement software kicked in. The panelized picture gradually resolved as contrasting colors and shadows sharpened their edges. Within minutes, a relatively clear image of the chainsaw slasher's mask took over the screen. Nick stared at the image, stroking his chin thoughtfully.

"Hmm," he murmured.

"What is it?" Greg inquired. "C'mon, dude. Give."

Nick didn't keep him in suspense. "Look at his eyes, and the turn of his head. Is it just me or is he glaring at that phony TV screen? Not at the woman who just shot him, but at the camera crew hiding behind the concealed one-way mirror."

"Maybe. It's hard to tell from this angle," Greg said uncertainly. "Hang on. Let me try something."

He quickly called up a view from another camera, the one on the other side of the mirror. Fast-forwarding to the same moment, he froze the image just as Novak turned his face toward the camera. Then he enlarged the picture again.

This time there could be no mistake. From behind the featureless white hockey mask, Novak's eyes glared furiously into the camera. "Bloodshot" contact lenses masked the actor's actual brown irises, but failed to conceal the murderous intensity of his narrowed eyes. If looks could kill, Novak's dying gaze would have filled up the coroner's wagon.

"Wow," Greg murmured. "He is seriously pissed."

"But not at Jill," Nick pointed out again. "Not at the woman who just shot him. But at somebody—or somebodies—on the other side of that mirror."

Greg scratched his chin. "You think maybe he blamed the show for the accident?"

"Possibly." Nick was doubtful. "But he had been with the show for years. He was part of the gag. Why would he look angry when it backfired? I mean, I can see him being shocked, or scared, or even despairing, but angry enough that he ignores his killer to give the camera crew the stink-eye instead?"

Inspiration lit up Greg's own eyes. "Maybe that's not all he was doing." Manipulating the image via the keyboard, he pulled back on the image until most of Novak's body was revealed. "Look at his hand. The one in the air."

Nick could tell that Greg was on to something. He stared at the gloved hand, which appeared to be grasping at the air, just like before. His brow furrowed. "What about it?"

"You'll see." Greg zoomed in on the hand and enlarged it. They waited for the enhanced image to fully resolve. "Wait for it."

A large hand, stuffed inside a blood-smeared work glove, filled the screen.

"Check out the finger," Greg chortled. "And I do mean *the* finger."

Nick couldn't believe his eyes. "What the hell?"

On the screen, Novak's middle finger was extended slightly above the others.

"You see that?" Greg pointed at the screen. "He's actually trying to give them the bird."

"Maybe," Nick allowed. He was going to want to check it out from a few more angles to be sure, but, yeah, it sure looked like Novak was making a feeble attempt at flipping someone off—with his dying breath, no less. "Talk about having an attitude problem. He sure wasn't going into the light quietly, that's for sure." He pondered the actor's last moments. "It's almost like he realized that he had been set up."

"But by whom?" Greg asked.

"Not by Jill Wooten, it looks like." Novak's anger had been directed elsewhere. "Or at least Novak sure didn't seem to think so."

Greg considered the possibilities. "So who was on the other side of that mirror?"

"Good question." Nick flipped through the file. "At least a half dozen people. Roger Park, the camera crew, the medic, the sound guy, Debra Lusky." He leafed through the statements of the various witnesses. "Novak could have been glaring at any or all of them."

The indignant finger hung upon the screen. One last defiant gesture, caught forever by the hidden cameras. Nick felt like they owed it to Matt Novak to find out why he had left this world so angry.

Who had the dying actor blamed for his death?

Frank and Mimi Gilroy lived in a suburban ranch home at the end of a well-lit cul-de-sac in a nice, middle-class neighborhood that Sara didn't recall ever visiting before. A fading brown lawn was already dreading winter. Shrubs and a small rose garden defied the arid desert climate, and rugged hills rose in the distance. Wicker furniture occupied the front porch. GILROY was printed in block letters on the mailbox at the curb.

"This looks like the place," she said.

Heather's employment records listed her parents as her emergency contacts. Sara hoped that, if nothing else, the elder Gilroys might know where their daughter could be located.

It was worth a shot.

Vartann parked at the curb. At ten-thirty on a weeknight, the neighborhood was already quiet. The phosphor glow of a TV set radiated through the front window. It looked like the Gilroys were still up. They got out of the car and headed for the door. Sara wore a plain black jacket instead of her gear to avoid alarming the neighbors. As far as she knew, this wasn't a crime scene.

"Crap!" Vartann blurted as he took a shortcut across the lawn. He glanced down at his feet.

Sara paused in her tracks. "What is it?"

"Ugh." Lifting his right foot, he glared in disgust at the sole. "Watch your step. Some dog's been using this yard as a toilet."

Sara decided to stick to the paved front walk. She recalled that Heather's dog was also missing, but was reluctant to read too much into a random piece of poop. Plenty of people had dogs, maybe even Heather's family.

"Thanks for the warning." She couldn't resist

teasing him a bit. "Didn't anyone tell you not to step in the evidence?"

"Is that what this is?" He extended his soiled sole toward her. A fecal odor confirmed the nature of the specimen without benefit of advanced forensic technology. "You're free to bag it if you like."

Sara made a face. "I'll pass, thank you."

He scraped his shoe off on the grass as best he could, then joined her on the front porch. As before, she stepped back and let him ring the doorbell. A chime sounded inside, followed almost immediately by some high-pitched yapping.

She and Vartann exchanged a look. He lifted an eyebrow. "Didn't that neighbor say something about a yappy dog?"

"Could be a family tradition," Sara pointed out. She still didn't want to jump to conclusions. "Lots of folks get the same breed over and over."

"Good point," Vartann conceded. "One of my uncles has had seven bulldogs, all named Marlene."

Marlene? Before Sara could inquire further, the door was opened by an older white man wearing a button-down sweater and slacks. Receding gray hair was combed back neatly. He peered warily at his visitors through a pair of bifocals. "Yes?"

"Frank Gilroy?" Vartann asked.

"Yes," the man confirmed. "Can I help you?"

Vartann held up his badge. "Detective Vartann, LVPD. This is Sara Sidle from the crime lab. We're looking for your daughter, Heather."

Frank tensed visibly. "She doesn't live here."

That's not exactly what we asked, Sara noted. She found it interesting that Heather's father didn't ask why the police were looking for her. Which implied that he had been in touch with her, and was familiar with her recent difficulties.

"We know that," Vartann said. "But do you know where we can find her?"

" 'Fraid not." Frank did not invite them in.

A station wagon was parked in the driveway. According to the DMV, Heather drove a used lime-green Yaris. Sara hadn't spotted any vehicles matching that description yet, but Gilroy's garage door was closed. It was possible the Yaris was hiding nearby.

"We're not looking to arrest Heather," she explained. "We just need to ask her some questions about that incident at her job yesterday. You know about that, right?"

Frank faltered, uncertain how to respond. He tugged at his collar. "Um, I'm not sure."

"It would be better for Heather if she talked with us," Sara advised him, playing good cop. She tried to peer past him into the house, but he blocked her view. "Avoiding us gives the wrong impression."

Her words appeared to give him pause. He started to glance back over his shoulder, but caught himself. "I'll tell her that . . . if I see her."

Frantic yapping continued to punctuate the conversation. What was Heather's dog's name again? Sara smiled slyly as a sneaky ploy popped into her mind.

"Jonas!" she called out. "Here, Jonas!"

The unseen dog barked excitedly. Running paws raced toward the door. A female voice shouted in alarm. "Jonas . . . no!"

The command came too late. A wiry white-and-brown terrier darted out the door, past Frank, who grabbed unsuccessfully for the hyper canine. Sara knelt down just in time for a furry little torpedo to pile onto her lap. Yipping loudly, the terrier started licking Sara's face enthusiastically enough to remove several layers of epithelials. A metal tag hung on the dog's collar. Doing her best to avoid being licked to death, she managed to get a look at the tag. Engraved letters read JONAS.

Sara stood up, much to the terrier's frustration. She confronted Frank. "Care to explain why your daughter's dog is here, Mr. Gilroy?"

"I . . . I . . ." At a loss for words, Frank gripped the door more for support than to bar the way. He stared at the telltale canine with a stricken expression that reminded Sara of any number of crestfallen felons who suddenly found themselves faced with a murder weapon they thought they had disposed of. He swallowed hard. "I can explain this. . . ."

Sara doubted that.

"It's okay, Dad." Heather Gilroy appeared behind her father. Sara recognized the blond masseuse from her driver's license photo. She was dressed casually, in a violet jogging suit. Taking mercy on her father, she slid past him onto the porch. "I can handle this."

Frank seemed to realize the jig was up. His shoulders sagged in defeat. "You sure, honey?"

"My problem," she insisted. "Let me deal with it." She scooped up Jonas, who had been circling Sara's ankles, trying to get her attention. Heather gave the terrier a gentle bop on the nose. "Bad dog."

Her father retired to the foyer, but kept a close watch over the proceedings. Sara glimpsed an older woman spying on them from the living room. Heather's mother, no doubt. The woman was wringing her hands anxiously.

Heather shooed Jonas inside, then pulled the door shut to get a little more privacy. "Please," she entreated. "Don't blame my folks for any of this. They were just trying to protect me."

"I understand." Sara got the impression that Heather was ready to talk. She decided to make it easy on her. "Why don't we sit down?"

It was a bit nippy out, but not freezing yet, so there was no need to move indoors. Heather deposited herself in a white wingback chair, while Sara and Vartann claimed a matching wicker couch. The porch lights made observing Heather no problem. She looked nervous, but resigned. Despite her history, she didn't seem like a flight risk. "You know," she said. "It's almost a relief to get this over with. I've been a nervous wreck since . . ."

"Why don't you tell us about it," Vartann suggested. "In your own words."

"Not much to tell, really." She smiled weakly. "It was just an ordinary Monday morning at The Nile, except that Ms. Segura ended up taking Madame Alexandra's place in the Cleopatra Room. I put the snakes on the client, just like I've done plenty of times before. But then that striped snake bit her— and wouldn't let go." Her bottom lip trembled. "I had to yank the damn thing off her!"

That sounds right, Sara thought. According to her research, coral snakes tended to hang on to their victims, in order to inject a full load of venom. "What then?"

"Well, Rita was pretty freaked out, no surprise. So was I, to be honest. But at first the bite didn't seem that bad. Then she started getting woozy and collapsed onto the floor." A guilty look came over Heather's face. "That's when I cleared the hell out of there."

Vartann regarded her sternly. "Why did you run?"

"I don't know. I just panicked." Unsure what to do with her hands, she picked at a loose strand of wicker on her armrest. "She looked like she was dying. I was afraid I was going to get arrested or sued or something." She looked anxiously at Sara and Vartann. "Am I?"

"Not tonight," Sara said. "We're still conducting our investigation."

Heather didn't look terribly reassured. "Oh."

"Do you know any reason why anyone would want to hurt Ms. Segura?" Vartann asked.

"On purpose?" Heather seemed surprised by the question, as though that possibility had not even occurred to her before. "Why would anyone want to do that?"

"That's what we're trying to figure out," Sara said. "Did Rita have any enemies, maybe somebody with access to the snakes?"

"How would I know?" Heather threw up her hands. "I barely knew the woman."

"What about Madame Alexandra?" Vartann asked. "She was the one who was supposed to get the snake massage that morning, right?"

"Yes. Every Monday, before we opened. I was getting the room ready when Ms. Segura showed up."

That fit with what they had heard before. Sara spelled it out for her. "Could somebody have meant for Madame Alexandra to be bitten instead?"

"I can't think why," Heather said. "But, you know, she's just my boss. I don't know anything about her personal life."

Come to think of it, Sara thought. *Neither do we.*

She still had to get Heather's fingerprints and DNA, but first she had another question. "Do you know the difference between a coral snake and a milk snake?"

"Not really," Heather confessed. "Madame Alexandra told me they weren't poisonous, and that was enough for me. The serpentine massages were popular, so she had us all doing them. That doesn't mean we knew anything about the snakes." She looked sick to her stomach. "I guess that was a mistake, huh?"

"Looks like it," Sara said.

13

"You don't look like a cop."

J. T. Aldridge did not strike Ray Langston as the scary criminal mastermind Marshall Segura had pictured. He was a skinny, unimposing white guy in his late twenties with multiple priors for selling pot on street corners. An orange prison jumpsuit seemed slightly too large for his scrawny frame. A buzz cut kept his short brown hair under control. Confused blue eyes looked Ray over, a trifle suspiciously, but without the shark-like deadness Ray had come to associate with stone-cold killers. About the only thing that fit Segura's description was the angry snake tattooed atop Aldridge's jugular. Its jaws were open, poised to strike. Crimson teardrops dripped from its exposed fangs. *A rattler,* Ray noted. *Not a coral snake.*

"I'm not," he said. "I'm a doctor. With the crime lab."

High State Desert Prison was only about twenty-

five miles northeast of Vegas. Ray was glad that
he hadn't needed to drive all day to interview the
convicted drug dealer; in fact, it had taken longer
to arrange this visit with the Department of Correc-
tions. According to court records, Aldridge had been
found guilty by a jury headed by Rita Segura. Motive enough to have someone plant a coral snake at
The Nile?

Ray was here to find out.

"A doctor?" Aldridge perked up. "Like a medical
doctor?"

"That's right."

Ray sat opposite the convict in a private interview room. Painted concrete walls and barred windows made the interrogation rooms back at the
police station seem homey by comparison. A stony-
faced prison guard, his beefy arms crossed atop a
barrel chest, watched over the encounter from a dis-
creet distance. Ray actually found the guard more
intimidating than Aldridge, even though the inmate
was the one handcuffed to his chair. A billy club
rested against the guard's hip.

"Cool." Aldridge leaned forward. He lowered his
voice to a conspiratorial whisper. "You think maybe
you could write me a prescription for some, you
know, medical marijuana? I need it for my nerves."
He held his free hand so Ray could see it shake. "I
have a problem with, what do you call it, anxiety."

"I'm not really here in a medical capacity," Ray
hedged. "But perhaps we can talk about that later."
Nevada was one of fourteen states that had legalized
the medicinal use of cannabis, but it was typically
used to relieve the symptoms of patients suffering

from AIDS, cancer, or glaucoma. He doubted that Aldridge qualified for a permit, but didn't want to deny him just yet. He still needed the convict's co-operation. "Right now I want to talk to you about your trial."

Aldridge snorted. "That wasn't a trial. That was a joke. My stupid public defender was just going through the motions. He couldn't even get my name right. The whole thing was a big misunderstanding. A case of, you know, mistaken identity? I was just in the wrong place at the wrong time."

"I see." Ray took Aldridge's claims with a grain of salt. Convicts who freely admitted their guilt were about as rare as slot machines that paid out jackpots on a regular basis; according to most prisoners, every conviction was an appalling miscarriage of justice. Ray got straight to the point. "Do you remember the jury that convicted you?"

"Not really." Aldridge drew back from the table, going on guard. He eyed Ray warily. "How come?"

"One of the jury members was attacked," Ray divulged. He was reluctant to mention Rita Segura by name, just in case Aldridge was unfamiliar with her identity.

"And you think I did it?" The inmate acted incredulous. He gestured at the austere concrete walls surrounding them. "Look around, man. I've got the perfect alibi."

"You could have arranged to have someone on the outside do it," Ray observed. Like Heather Gilroy, perhaps. "A witness at the trial claims you glared at the jury when the verdict was read."

"I was pissed, man, that's all. Doesn't mean I'm

out to get them, or that I even remember what they looked like. They were just twelve dumb sheep who fell for the prosecution's bullshit." Flushing with anger, he raised his voice enough to get a cautionary look from the guard, who took one step forward. Aldridge dialed it down, but still tried hard to convince Ray. "If I wanted to get back at anybody, it would be that hard-ass judge for throwing the book at me, or the narcs who busted me, or that scumbag who fingered me to get himself a better deal. Trust me, if I was out for revenge, the damn jury would be at the bottom of my list. A whole lot of other people are responsible for me being in here."

Ray was inclined to believe him. Aldridge was just a small-time pot dealer with no violent crimes on his record. He didn't seem the type to hatch an elaborate revenge scheme from behind bars. Still, Ray's gaze was drawn back to the coiled serpent on the convict's neck.

"Nice tattoo," he commented.

"You like it?" Aldridge said proudly. "I'm going to get a bigger one on my back."

"Another snake?"

"Nah, I'm thinking of a flaming skull this time. Or maybe a dragon." He cast a furtive look at the guard before lowering his voice once more. "So, anyway, about that prescription?"

"Don't count on it," Ray said.

14

"OKAY, THE CHUPACABRAS clip is a must," Park said. "But what do you think of the necrophilia bit? Would that be inappropriate in a tribute reel?"

Three days after the shooting, WaxWorkZ remained a closed crime scene, but the TV crew had been allowed back into the trailers in the parking lot. Catherine and Greg found Roger Park in a private editing bay in his trailer, looking over the shoulder of a scruffy guy wearing a baseball cap and a military-surplus jacket. On the screen of an expensive-looking monitor, a scaly, green-skinned monster, sporting large red eyes and yellow tusks, burst out of a cage, startling a teenage girl in a zoo uniform. Was that Matt Novak playing the monster? Catherine suspected as much.

"Mr. Park?" an assistant interrupted. "These people are here to see you."

The producer looked up from his work. "Ms. Willows. Catherine. What a pleasure to see you again."

Thankfully, he didn't offer a sweaty palm again. "Thank you. This is my colleague, Greg Sanders." She resisted the temptation to introduce Greg as the show's biggest fan. "I hope we're not interrupting you."

"Not at all," he said amiably. "We're just putting together a salute to 'The Best of Matt Novak' for a special episode—or maybe just a bonus feature on the DVD. That's yet to be determined." He shrugged. "It seemed like the least we could do."

"I'm sure it's how he'd like to be remembered," Catherine said with a straight face. She didn't mention that Novak had been giving the camera the finger right before he died. "Any decision yet on the future of the show?"

"I wish!" Park rolled his eyes. "*Shock Treatment* is still in limbo, pending the results of an internal review." He fished a roll of Tums from his pocket and chomped down on one. "So, may I ask how your own investigation is proceeding?"

"We're making progress," she replied, "but I'm not at liberty to discuss the details."

"Of course. I should have realized." Park didn't press the issue. "So what brings you here today?"

She got straight to the point. "We need to search your trailer."

"This trailer?" He reacted in surprise. "Why is that?"

Catherine was hoping to find the disposable cell phone that had been used to threaten Jill Wooten, or anything else that might link the show to her or

Craig Gonch. "We're just being thorough," she said vaguely. "In light of new evidence, I want to give the set and the trailers a closer look."

"But the shooting took place in the club," he protested. "Not here."

Catherine didn't back down. "Like I said, we're being thorough."

"I don't know." Park frowned, his cooperative facade slipping. "Do you have a warrant?"

"Do we need one?" Catherine asked. Whether the trailers in the parking lot could be legally considered part of the crime scene was a gray area. She was willing to make a case for the search to a judge, but she was hoping she wouldn't have to. "You promised us your full cooperation, remember?"

Park looked like he was regretting his words. "It just seems like overkill."

"Let us worry about that," Catherine said. "Better safe than sorry."

"Do it for Matt's sake," Greg added, speaking up for the first time. He nodded at the tusked monster on the video screen, who was currently chasing the terrified zoo employee around a cage. "Besides, the sooner we wrap up our investigation, the sooner you might be back on the air."

Park sighed. "Fine. Go ahead. We have nothing to hide." His oozy charm reasserted itself. "I don't mean to be difficult. It just seems like a waste of time." He gestured toward the editing equipment. "Any chance we can keep working while you're here? I promise to keep out of the way."

"Sorry." She wondered if he really just wanted to keep an eye on their investigation. "I'm afraid I'm going to have to ask you to clear out until we're finished."

"I see." An almost subliminal scowl came and went upon his face. "In the meantime, before we go, do you think we'll be able to move these trailers soon? We start shooting on the *Zombie Heat* pilot this weekend. Just outside the city."

As before, Catherine refused to let herself get pinned to any specific deadline. She had no intention of rushing her investigation to accommodate Park's shooting schedule. "Like I explained the other day, that depends on what we find."

"I know, I know," he said impatiently. "But any more delays will cost us money."

She had heard the same complaint from countless casino owners, shopkeepers, and long-distance truckers. She gave Park the same answer she always did.

"I appreciate your situation. We'll do our best not to inconvenience you any longer than necessary."

Park knew better than to push her any harder. "All right. I understand. I wasn't bullshitting you the other day when I said that I have tremendous respect for people in your line of work." He moved away from the editing bay. "You know, we're going to need an expert consultant on the *Zombie Heat* show, to make sure we get all the police stuff right." He looked over Catherine and Greg with a speculative eye. "Maybe one of you might be interested?"

Greg stepped forward, a little too quickly. "Seriously?"

"Thanks for the offer," Catherine said quickly, shutting that pipe dream down before it got too far. "But our investigation is our only priority right now." She gave Greg a pointed glance. "And we can't have any conflicts of interest."

Greg got the message. "Absolutely," he agreed hastily. "We're all about just doing our job here."

That's more like it, Catherine thought, grateful that Hodges was nowhere around. The vainglorious lab rat would have been practically salivating over the producer's offer. She still remembered the time that *Hard Crime,* a cable documentary series, had followed them around on a case. Hodges had shamelessly played to the cameras, trying to milk his fifteen minutes of fame for all it was worth. She, on the other hand, had let out a sigh of relief when the intrusive TV crew had finally moved on to some other poor, unsuspecting police department. Park's proposition had no appeal to her.

If I had wanted the spotlight, I would have stuck with stripping.

"Sorry," Park said. "I didn't think of the conflict of interest thing. I was just speaking hypothetically."

"Well, hypothetically, no thanks." She wondered about Park's motives. Had his offer been some sort of veiled bribe or attempt to curry favor? Or was everything just about producing his shows with him? He wouldn't be the first big shot wheeler and dealer she'd met who had a one-track mind where his business was concerned. Her own father had been like that. "Now, if you don't mind, we'd like to get to work."

Greg herded Park and the editor guy out of the trailer, then locked the door so he and Catherine wouldn't be disturbed. Finally getting the place to themselves, they started their search with a quick walk-through of the entire mobile palace, which proved to be even more opulent than she had imagined. Besides the reception area and editing bay, she counted at least four entertainment centers, three computers, two bathrooms, a fully equipped kitchen with marble floors and a walk-in pantry, a pinball machine, a pool table, and a master bedroom that put her own digs to shame. All that was missing was a swimming pool, sauna, and eighteen-hole golf course.

Maybe that's on the roof, she thought.

"Whoa," Greg said, taking in the lavish setting. "I will never make fun of trailer parks again." He kept his hands in his pockets to avoid contaminating any possible evidence. "How much you think a trailer like this costs?"

"One point nine million," she said. "I looked it up." Having scoped out the layout, she settled on a plan of attack. "Why don't we start at opposite ends and work toward the middle?"

"Whatever you say, boss." He started toward the back, then paused and turned back to her. He lowered his head sheepishly. "Say, Catherine?"

"Yes?"

"You know, right, that I wasn't really interested in that consulting gig?" He seemed embarrassed by his gaffe before. "I was just being polite."

"Uh-huh." She had heard more believable excuses from mass murderers. She knew that Greg had creative ambitions beyond the crime lab. In his spare time, he was even writing a book on the history of crime in Las Vegas. She decided to chalk the incident off to a momentary lapse. "Just don't get too polite, okay?"

"I hear you, loud and clear." Smirking, he took a moment to admire the *Zombie Heat* poster over the bar. "Still, you've got to admit, it did sound kind of cool."

She grinned back at him. "I'll stick with real dead people, thank you very much."

Getting to work, she pulled on some latex gloves. Her eyes scanned the furnished reception area as she weighed their odds of finding anything useful. Locating the guilty cell phone was a long shot. It was probably history by now. But maybe they could find something else that linked the production to the threats against Jill, just in case her ex-boyfriend wasn't responsible. Catherine still found the "coincidental" timing of the anonymous calls more than a little suspicious. She couldn't help suspecting that there had to be some sort of connection between the calls and what happened later.

She was also hoping to find a motive for arranging Matt Novak's death, aside from the fact that he'd had delusions of grandeur on the set. Nick had shown her screen shots of Novak's final moments and she had agreed with him that the dying man's furious reaction didn't exactly jibe with an accidental shooting. She sensed that there was more to the story. Something about this shooting just didn't smell right, and over the years Catherine had learned to trust her instincts.

Now then, she mused. *If I was a missing cell phone, where would I be?*

She thought back to all the times she had helped

Lindsey track down her phone, which had a re-
markable ability to go astray whenever it wasn't
near-surgically attached to the girl's ear. Catherine
winced at the memory of their last phone bill, then
started probing all the obvious places. She checked
the drawers and cupboards. She flipped over the seat
cushions. She searched the bar. After about thirty
minutes, however, she had found nothing more incriminating than a couple of spare bottles of Tums
and a marked-up script titled *Zombie Heat:* "Pilot."

The latter was labeled CONFIDENTIAL, NOT TO BE CIR-
CULATED. Park's name was printed on every page of
the script to ensure that its provenance could be
traced should a copy turn up where it didn't belong.
Catherine guessed that its contents would probably
be a hot ticket on the internet.

She wasn't even tempted to take a peek.

Moving on to the bedroom, she wondered why
Park even bothered to book a suite at Caesars. The
king-sized bed was large enough to host a three-
some with room to spare. A polished cherrywood
cabinet held a deluxe entertainment system. Shut-
tered windows kept out the daylight. Before turning on the overhead lights, she swept the room with
her flashlight. She often found that an oblique beam
brought stray objects into view by creating visible
shadows. It was a good way to pick up details she
might have overlooked otherwise.

The beam turned up nothing on the bed and carpet, but when she ran it across the high ceiling, she
noticed a glint of light near the smoke detector. Her
mind raced back to the hidden cameras in Wax-
WorkZ. In particular, the one in the ceiling.

"Well, well," she said aloud. "What have we here?"

Greg poked his head in. "You find something?"

"Maybe," she said. "Not the mystery cell phone, but get a load of this." She climbed onto the bed to get a closer look. The beam from her flashlight bounced off what appeared to be a pin-sized camera lens, hidden in the shadow of the smoke detector. "It looks like Park's predilection for hidden camera hijinks extends to his private life."

Greg chuckled, turning his own beam on the camera. "Perhaps he's planning an X-rated spin-off?"

"You still interested in a consulting gig?" she teased him. "I wonder if Park's bed partners knew about the camera?" She took it for granted that the camera wasn't aimed at the bed for security purposes. "Not to mention his high-powered Hollywood executive wife?"

"Tricia Grantley, right?" Greg sounded impressed. "She's made the *Entertainment Weekly* 'Power List' for five years running."

Figures he knows that, Catherine thought. She glanced down at the high-quality mink blankets beneath her feet. She didn't want to think about how much discarded DNA she was standing on. "Not that his personal life is any of our business, I guess. Unless he was sleeping with Jill Wooten and so far there's absolutely no evidence to support that."

She was tempted to confiscate the bed sheets, but couldn't figure out a way to justify it. Not on the basis of a vague feeling. She didn't even have a working hypothesis at present, just a sense that they were still missing a few key pieces of the puzzle.

We're stumbling around in the dark here. Like one of the victims on Park's show.

She hopped off the bed, hoping that Greg had turned up more than just a kinky spy-cam. "You find anything yet?"

"Not really." He poked around at the foot of the bed, then bent to pick something up with a pair of sterile tweezers. "I just keep finding these tiny little rubber bands tucked away in the corners." He held the tiny elastic band, which was maybe .3 centimeters in diameter, up for her inspection. "Not sure what they're for. Maybe some sort of TV thing?"

Catherine chuckled. "Clearly you haven't subsidized enough orthodontists in your life. Those are dental elastics, to be worn with braces." She remembered them well from Lindsey's adolescence. "Trust me, those things get everywhere. I'm still finding them behind the bathroom sink and under the couch."

She had noticed a few elastics beneath the seat cushions in the trailer's reception area as well, but hadn't thought anything of it until now. "Funny, I don't remember seeing anyone with braces among the crew. And Park didn't mention any kids."

"Maybe his shiny incisors got straightened at some point?" Greg suggested. "Along with the obvious plastic surgery."

"Probably. Or maybe those elastics belonged to someone else." She thought it over. "What the hell. Bag it."

They didn't have a search warrant, but, in a pinch, she could always argue that the production trailer was part of the crime scene. It would be a stretch, but the tiny elastic was a lot easier to confiscate than, say, the sheets. More important, Park had already given them permission to search the trailer.

"Okay." Greg popped it into a small brown-paper bindle. "How come?"

Catherine shrugged. "Just covering the bases."

A phone rang beneath her jacket. It wasn't the phone she was looking for, but she answered it anyway. Caller ID flashed BRASS.

"Excuse me," she told Greg, stepping away to take the call. "Willows here. What you got, Jim?"

A short conversation later, she put away the phone.

"That was Brass," she told Greg. "He's tracked down Craig Gonch's current address."

Jill Wooten's stalker ex-boyfriend had a lot of explaining to do.

The sooner, the better.

15

"YOU EVER PERFORM an autopsy on a snake before?"

"Necropsy," Albert Robbins corrected Ray. "A postmortem examination of a human being is an autopsy. With an animal, it's a necropsy."

"You're right," Ray recalled. He blamed the lapse on loss of sleep. He and Sara had been working long hours working the snakebite case. "I stand corrected."

Doc Robbins shrugged. Blue surgical scrubs protected the stout, middle-aged medical examiner from the inherent messiness of death. A metal crutch provided his prosthetic legs with additional support. His trim white beard gave him an avuncular appearance. "Just a semantic distinction. To answer your question, this is indeed a first. Although remind me to tell you sometime about the night a living rat burst from the abdomen of a drowning victim. Next to that, a dead snake is nothing."

The euthanized coral snake was stretched out

atop the stainless steel operating table in the center of the morgue. Built to accommodate human cadavers, the table easily held the snake, which Ray estimated to be approximately twenty-four inches in length. Lidless eyes stared glassily into oblivion. The snake's round pupils were fixed and unmoving.

Robbins began the examination by dictating into a handheld digital recorder. "The specimen appears to be an adult coral snake, of the species *Micrurus tener*." He clicked off the recorder long enough to fix Ray in his sights. "I believe I am looking at the cause of death."

"Guilty as charged," Ray confessed, at home in his own blue scrubs. With Hodges's assistance, he had put the snake down with a fatal injection of barbiturates. His voice held a tinge of regret. It was a shame that the animal had to be destroyed, but it had already nearly killed one person and there was no way they could have examined the snake without risking getting bitten themselves. Nobody at the crime lab was an experienced snake handler.

"Then what exactly are we looking for?" Robbins asked.

"Anything that can tell us where it came from, or who might have handled it recently." Ray indicated the scratch marks on the snake's back. "What do you make of these?"

Robbins peered at the scratches beneath the bright overhead lights. Prompt refrigeration had left the snake's exterior well-preserved. He spoke again into his recorder. "Subject has four shallow lacerations on its dorsal region, ranging in length from one to two inches. The wounds are partially healed over, indicating that they occurred perimortem. No indication of infection or necrosis. The wounds are parallel to each other, and approximately a quarter of an inch apart." He clicked off the recorder. "Any chance it got these scratches when you captured it?"

"Possible," Ray answered, "but unlikely. The Animal Control team seemed to know what they were doing, and Sara didn't report any similar injuries on any of the other snakes." The rest of The Nile's serpentine masseuses were still residing in the garage. Ray made a mental note to inspect them for scratches, as well as to examine the tongs Sara had used to transport them. He doubted that he would find anything illuminating, however. Sara would have mentioned if one of the other snakes had been injured in her care.

He bent over the table to inspect the wounds. Even though the snake was well and truly dead, he found himself instinctively avoiding its fangs. The lacerations sliced diagonally across the snake's colored bands, leaving the torn scales ragged along their edges. "The parallel spacing makes me think either a claw or bite mark. Maybe it got into a fight with another snake?"

Coral snakes actually feed on smaller snakes. Maybe it had tried to make a meal of one of Madame Alexandra's nonvenomous specimens? According to his research, coral snakes were reclusive by nature. He wondered how one would react to being crowded in with serpents of other species. *It was probably already in a bad mood*, Ray thought, *before it was dropped onto Rita Segura.*

"Hard to say," Robbins said. "I'm a coroner, not a

vet, you know. I don't deal with a lot of snake-on-snake violence." He sounded a trifle impatient. No doubt he had human victims to attend to. "Still, I'll take blood and venom samples, and have David do a full histological work-up. Could be good practice for him."

Sara entered through a pair of swinging double doors, briefly letting some warmer air into the artificially cool environment of the morgue, which was typically kept at a crisp forty-five degrees. She had also changed into scrubs, as much to avoid contaminating the evidence as to protect herself from infection. "Just spoke with Heather Gilroy again," she reported. "She claims she's never heard of J. T. Aldridge."

The two CSIs had already compared notes on their respective interviews. If there was a connection between the jailed drug dealer and the woman who had actually placed the coral snake on Rita Segura, they had yet to find it. Ray had checked the inmate records before departing the penitentiary. J. T. Aldridge had not received any correspondence from Heather, nor visits from anyone matching her description.

Which doesn't mean they couldn't have used a go-between, he reminded himself. "So what's your gut feeling about Heather?"

"Well you've actually met Heather. I haven't. I'm just trying to get a better sense of the players here. Do you like her for this?"

"Honestly, no," Sara admitted. "I've been wrong before, of course. But I don't believe she sicced the coral snake on Rita on purpose. The fact that she panicked and ran actually argues in her favor. I think she was genuinely shocked when Rita collapsed after that bite."

"Unless she was simply surprised by how fast Rita reacted to the venom," Ray speculated. "Coral snake venom often takes several hours to take effect. Heather may have figured she'd be nowhere around when Rita stopped breathing."

He wondered if maybe Heather had designs on Rita's wealthy, older husband. Had the masseuse ever met Marshall Segura? Were they already involved? There was nothing to indicate a clandestine affair so far, but Heather wouldn't be the first ambitious golddigger to want to get a rich man's wife out of the way. He recalled a case last year when a real estate tycoon's mistress had tried to dispose of the missus by planting a bomb under the hood of her limo. The careless girlfriend had blown herself up instead.

"Maybe." Sara sounded dubious. "But if Heather wasn't involved, that would imply that someone else introduced the coral snake to the vivarium, either by accident or design. Heather admitted that she was no snake expert. Overworked and undertrained, she might not have even noticed if there was an extra snake in the tank."

"What about the prints on the vivarium?" Ray asked. "Anything suspicious?"

Sara shook her head. "That was a dead end. All I found were Heather's prints and some belonging to the other masseuses. None that shouldn't be there." She watched as Doc Robbins placed the snake in the hanging scale he usually employed to weigh various human organs. "Of course, it's possible that who-ever added our friend here was wearing gloves."

"And according to Brian Yun, the Cleopatra Room was usually kept unlocked." Ray had noted the spa's lax security during his visit there. "It wouldn't have been too hard for someone else to smuggle a snake in there."

"So what would the motive be?" Doc Robbins asked. He pulled his surgical mask into place before beginning his dissection of the snake. A gleaming scalpel deftly opened the specimen's abdomen, ex-posing its coelomic cavity. Bodily fluids spilled onto the table, which was equipped with a built-in drain. "Random terrorism, like the Tylenol poisonings?"

"Or one of Madame Alexandra's competitors," Sara speculated, "trying to sabotage her business?"

Ray saw where she was going. He recalled that Rita Segura had arrived at The Nile without warning, taking Madame Alexandra's place in the Cleopatra Room.

"Maybe it didn't matter who got bitten, as long as *somebody* did."

Or had the spa owner been the intended target all along?

16

"Turn right at next intersection," a robotic voice instructed. *"One mile to destination."*

A GPS unit guided them toward Craig Gonch's reported address. Catherine had been on the job long enough that she remembered when they'd had only maps, directions, and their own knowledge of the city to find their way around Vegas. Having been born and raised in Sin City, she was pretty good at navigating its streets and back alleys, but she didn't mind an electronic backup once in a while. The sooner they reached a crime scene or witness, the better chance they had of solving the case. She had once taken a wrong turn on her way to a 409 outside Boulder City. By the time she'd figured out her mistake, a sudden downpour had washed away vital evidence.

They had never caught the killer.

Never again, she thought, recalling the incident. *GPS is our friend.*

She rode shotgun in Brass's unmarked Taurus. He had picked her up in front of WaxWorkZ not long after sunset. She felt bad about leaving Greg to finish up searching the TV trailers by himself, but she wanted to check out Craig Gonch for herself, to see if the alleged stalker was really the kind of guy who would anonymously threaten Jill Wooten over the phone. Her field kit rode in the back seat of the sedan. She wanted to get fingerprints from Gonch. Not to mention a voice sample.

"You have arrived at your destination."

Gonch lived in a low-rent neighborhood only a few blocks away from "G-string Row," a notorious stretch of strip joints and hot bed motels within sight of the Sahara. The apartment building where he reputedly hung his hat was basically a glorified motel as well, renting by the week. Two floors of apartments, their numbered front doors exposed to the elements, faced a trash-strewn parking lot. A yellowed plastic sign out front proudly advertised COLOR TV. Catherine guessed that it had been there since the Kennedy Administration, which was probably the last time anyone had fixed the potholes in the blacktop. The ice machine near the manager's office was out of order. Broken glass crunched beneath the Taurus's wheels.

Brass parked the car and switched off the GPS unit. "Looks like Gonch has fallen on hard times since he got bounced from his job at the gym."

"You think?" Catherine said dryly.

She had been in worse neighborhoods, on a regular basis, but Gonch's current surroundings left a lot to be desired. Shifty-looking customers loitered in the parking lot, but Catherine didn't see anyone fitting Gonch's description. A few of the locals scurried away at the sight of the unfamiliar Taurus, while others glared at the new arrivals with an interest that bordered on threatening. Catherine checked to make sure her sidearm was accessible. She liked to think that she wasn't nearly as trigger-happy as Jill Wooten, but if someone came at her with a chainsaw, all bets were off.

"I can see why you had trouble locating Gonch," she commented. "I doubt anyone living here really has a permanent address."

"Let's hope he hasn't relocated again," Brass said. "Or we've visited this scenic location for nothing."

He put away the GPS and locked it in the glove compartment. This was not the sort of milieu where you wanted to leave an expensive piece of electronics out in the open. They got out of the car and looked around. A chilly wind, blowing across the parking lot from a living, breathing collection of mug shots hanging out under a streetlight, smelled of both marijuana and tobacco. Everything about Brass must have screamed "cop," since the party quickly dispersed into the night. Catherine wasn't sad to see them go. Unlike *Shock Treatment*, they didn't need an audience.

They took a short flight of steps up to the outdoor walkway connecting the top-level apartments. The paint on the wooden doors was peeling. Cigarette butts and used bubble gum were practically ground into the cement. Every other overhead lightbulb was flickering or needed to be replaced. Going from Roger Park's $1.9 million luxury trailer to this dump was enough to give Catherine the bends. She was starting to think Greg got the better end of the deal.

Brass stopped in front of the second door from the end. "This is it."

A tarnished metal "9" hung lopsided on the door. A rubber mat said GO AWAY instead of WELCOME.

Ha-ha, Catherine thought, unamused. *Sorry. Can't oblige.*

"Sounds like he's at home," Brass observed.

Light seeped through the window curtain and around the edge of the door. A TV was playing inside. She put down her field kit, just in case she needed her hands free, and held back while Brass walked up to the door. He knocked decisively.

Catherine heard someone move on the other side of the thin walls. The TV set turned off abruptly. The curtains parted slightly, then closed again. Whoever was inside seemed in no hurry to answer the door.

Too bad we're not going to take no for answer.

Brass held his badge up to the peephole in the door. "LVPD. Open up."

The badge did the trick. After a brief pause, the door swung open, just a crack. A chain lock kept it from opening all the way. An apprehensive female voice escaped the apartment.

"Yes?"

The speaker, a young woman, was obviously not Craig Gonch. Through the narrow gap, Catherine glimpsed a pretty girl with curly brown hair, wearing a man's football jersey two sizes too big for her. She looked to be in her early twenties, around Jill Wooten's age, or maybe even younger. The partially closed door hid most of her face. Only one brown eye was visible. It regarded Brass with obvious trepidation.

"LVPD," he repeated, lowering his badge. "We're looking for Craig Gonch. Is he here?"

"Why?" she asked uncertainly. She did not seem inclined to unchain the door and ask them in. Her cyclopean gaze darted from Brass to Catherine and back again. "Is something wrong?"

"We just need to ask him some questions," Brass said. He took hold of the door to keep her from closing it. Leaning forward, he tried to peer past her into the apartment. "He at home?"

"Questions?" the girl echoed. "What about?"

"That's between us and Mr. Gonch," Brass said gruffly, losing patience with the girl's delaying tactics. He stuck his foot in the door, invading her personal space a few more inches. "Would you mind opening the door, Ms. . . . ?"

"Ruvasso," the girl supplied. "Gabriella Ruvasso."

"Thanks." Brass didn't budge. "Now then, the door?"

She swallowed hard. "Okay."

He let go of the door so that she could close it enough to give the taut chain a little slack. Catherine half-expected her to slam it shut, but Gabriella just undid the chain as requested. The door finally swung open all the way, revealing the girl in her entirety. The numbered purple jersey hung halfway to her knees. Bare feet with painted toenails shuffled nervously. Long chestnut hair hung over the right side of her face, Veronica Lake–style, although it was unlikely the young woman had ever heard of the long-dead actress and her trademark peekaboo tresses. Gabriella's slender fingers toyed with the hanging locks, but did not brush them away from her face. A suspicion formed within Catherine's mind.

Wanna bet she's hiding something?

"That's better." Brass stepped inside before Gabriella could change her mind. Catherine followed him into a cluttered apartment that consisted of a bedroom, a kitchen nook, and a bathroom in the back. The sheets were unmade. Dishes were piled in the sink. Dirty laundry littered the floor. A half-eaten TV dinner rested on a tray on the bed. A cigarette was stubbed out in an ashtray. Smoke rose from the ashes.

The lack of housekeeping was not the first thing Catherine noticed. Instead her gaze was drawn to the horror movie posters tacked up on the walls. *Dawn of the Dead. Friday the 13th.* One poster in particular caught her attention. It was for *The Texas Chainsaw Massacre.* The original, not the remake. *Who will survive,* the movie's tagline asked luridly, *and what will be left of them?*

She and Brass exchanged a look.

Just another weird coincidence, or . . . ?

"Anyway," he pressed Gabriella. "Is Craig around?"

Unless he was hiding in a closet or under the bed, he obviously wasn't in the small apartment. But perhaps he had just stepped out for a minute?

"No." She shook her head. "Not right now."

The sideways motion disturbed her hair. Catherine caught a glimpse of purple. Gabriella saw her looking and hastily rearranged her hair to conceal it.

Catherine recalled the restraining order against Gonch. "Something wrong with your eye?"

"N-no," she stammered. She backed away, lowering her gaze to avoid meeting Catherine's eyes. "I'm fine."

"Are you sure?" Catherine stepped forward and, before the girl could protest, gently brushed the hair away, exposing a blackened eye, swollen nearly shut. The deep purple coloration of the bruising suggested that the injury was fairly recent. " 'Cause it looks to me like somebody has used you for a punching bag."

Bastard, she thought. *No wonder Jill's scared of him.*

"Did Craig do that to you?" Brass asked bluntly.

"No! No!" she insisted, hiding the ugly shiner with her hand. "It was a stupid accident. I . . . fell down the stairs."

"Onto your eye?"

Catherine didn't believe it for a second. She had heard lame excuses like this as far back as her stripper days, from countless abused wives, daughters, and girlfriends. It was almost enough to make her wish that Craig Gonch *had* been wearing the hockey mask when Jill opened fire the other day. From the looks of things, he had it coming.

"Yeah," Gabriella fibbed. She mustered a transparently bogus smile. "Clumsy, huh?"

"Well, we're still going to need to talk to Craig," Brass said. "You know where he is?"

"Um . . ." She stalled, no doubt terrified of upsetting Gonch by squealing on him. "I'm not sure."

Brass gave her a stern look. "Ms. Ruvasso, I'm losing patience."

"You won't tell him I told you?"

"That won't be necessary," Catherine assured her.

Gabriella wrung her hands together, caught in a bind. Catherine regreted putting her on the spot like this, but protecting Gonch was only going to hurt Gabriella in the long run. They were probably doing her a favor, especially if they ended up putting Gonch away for a while.

"Okay," the girl relented. She lowered her voice, looking around nervously as though afraid someone might see her talking to the police. "He's at work."

"That's more like it." Brass pulled out a notebook and pen. "And where would that be?"

The layout room, which was located across the hall from the garage, was an ideal spot to sift through the evidence. The spacious light table provided plenty of room to spread everything out, which was why Nick preferred it to the more modest expanse of his own desk. Crime photos, documenting various ongoing cases, plastered the walls. One wall currently featured a gallery of screen captures from the *Shock Treatment* footage, while an adjacent wall, which had been staked out by Ray and Sara for their own case, was occupied by enlarged photos of snakes, fangs, and a nasty-looking bite wound.

Greg wandered over to inspect the reptilian mug shots. "Snakes," he quipped, doing his best Harrison Ford impression. "Why did it have to be snakes?"

"Beats me," Nick said. Despite his involvement with the Matt Novak case, he was aware of the bizarre snake massage incident Sara and Ray were investigating. It had been hard to miss the influx of live serpents into the lab. Frankly, he didn't feel too bad about not pulling that case. "At least none of our suspects have scales and fangs."

"You haven't seen the chupacabra episode," Greg said. Leaving the snake board behind, he went back to the light table as the two men got down to the business at hand. Matt Novak's personal effects and clothing, taken off his body, were laid atop the illuminated glass surface. A hair and fiber specialist, Nick always gave such items special attention. You never knew what sort of evidence people were carrying around on their person, often without even knowing it. Warrick, he recalled, had once apprehended a child murderer thanks to dog hairs found on the vic's sweater.

Warrick. . . .

Thinking of his deceased friend and colleague elicited a familiar pang. Warrick had been gone for two years now, murdered by a corrupt undersheriff, but the memory still stung. It was a reminder that their job could be a dangerous one. The night shift had lost at least two CSIs to violence since Nick had joined the team. That was two too many.

Shaking off the melancholy ruminations, he surveyed Matt Novak's final costume: a plastic hockey mask, novelty contact lenses, a flannel shirt, denim overalls stained with both real and fake blood, work gloves, underwear, socks, and combat boots. Matching bullet holes, in the front and back of the shirt, testified to his COD. For the first time in the history of *Shock Treatment*, Nick gathered, someone had not been firing blanks.

In addition to the clothing, David Phillips had

also found a concealed miniature microphone, no doubt intended to pick up any ferocious bellows or growls. Novak's pockets had contained a key chain, a roll of Life Savers, and a handful of small change. A quick count revealed that he had died with exactly forty-nine cents on his person.

Not even enough for a candy bar.

Interviews with his coworkers had constructed a rough biographical portrait of the dead man. Divorced with no children, Novak had lived alone in a bungalow in Los Angeles. Along with the rest of the crew, he'd been booked into a low-budget motel north of the Strip for the duration of the Vegas shoot. A search of Novak's shared hotel room, which Nick had conducted while Greg and Catherine were exploring Roger Park's trailer, had found nothing suspicious. If necessary, the CSIs could ask their counterparts in L.A. to conduct a search of Novak's permanent residence, but so far the evidence didn't appear to justify imposing on them. Nor did it seem worth a road trip on Nick's part. The shooting had taken place in Vegas. Chances were, all the evidence was here.

Greg sorted through the smaller items. Latex gloves protected them from contamination. "You say this stuff was actually on him when he was shot?"

"Yep," Nick replied. "All his belongings from a locker in the dressing room trailer are over there." He cocked his thumb at a labeled cardboard box sitting at the other end of the table. "His regular clothes, his wallet, cell phone, room key, etcetera." Archie had already confirmed that the phone was not the one used to terrorize Jill Wooten. "Everything he was going to need when he was through playing boogeyman for the evening."

"Doesn't sound too promising," Greg said.

"Probably not," Nick agreed. "One funny thing, though. He seemed to be in the market for a new sports car . . . and not a cheap one. He had brochures for Porsches, Lamborghinis, BMWs. Real high-end, pricy stuff. I'm not sure how much saying 'boo' on cable pays, but I'm guessing he was shopping out of his price range. Like he had come into some serious money, or was expecting to."

"Well, Catherine did say he thought he was a shoo-in to be the new lead in *Officer Zombie*," Greg recalled. "Maybe he was counting his chickens early? Or just window shopping."

"I suppose." Nick shrugged. "It might not mean anything, but I thought I'd mention it."

"Hey, you never know," Greg said. "It's like you always told me. Sometimes it's the little things, that don't seem worth noticing, that break a case wide open." He looked over the mundane residue of Matt Novak's last night on earth. "Makes sense . . . except why did he hang onto his keys? Wouldn't he leave that in the locker with the rest of his stuff? I mean, I doubt he was planning to drive back to his motel room dressed as a chainsaw maniac."

"Good point," Nick said. He picked up the keychain, which was a miniature replica of an Academy Award. Only a couple of metal keys were attached to the ring. "Especially since his car and apartment are back in L.A. Why was he carrying these keys at all?"

Greg scratched his head. "Maybe it's some sort of lucky charm?"

"Could be," Nick admitted. Back when he had played college football for Texas A&M, he had known plenty of players with personal totems and rituals of their own. There had been this one guy who always ate a raw onion before a big game, and another guy who kept a photo of a bulldozer taped to the inside of his helmet. It was possible that Novak's key chain had possessed special significance to him. Actors were supposed to be superstitious. "If so, it sure didn't bring him much luck the other night."

Greg snorted. "You can say that again."

Nick took a closer look at the tiny plastic Oscar. *Talk about wishful thinking,* he thought. According to the Internet Movie Database, Novak's acting credits weren't exactly award-worthy, unless they had started handing out Oscars for scaring innocent reality show victims. Noting a seam in the plastic, he realized there was a removable cap on one end. He pulled it off to reveal a metallic USB connector protruding from the base of the ersatz Oscar.

"Hey, take a look. It's actually a flash drive."

"Okay, now *that's* interesting." Greg regarded the portable storage device with budding excitement. "What data could be so important that Novak would want to carry it with him everywhere, even when he was impersonating a chainsaw killer?"

"Let's find out," Nick said. "Go get your laptop."

Wasting no time, Greg returned a moment later with his work laptop. Nick felt a tremor of anticipation, like they were definitely on to something. He plugged the drive into the computer's USB port. On the screen, a solitary file showed up in the G drive.

Nick tried to open the file. A dialogue box asked for his password.

"Damn," he muttered. "The data's encrypted."

He should have known it wouldn't be that easy.

"Let me try," Greg volunteered.

Nick stepped aside to let Greg take a whack at it. The younger CSI tried several passwords, including "Oscar" and "bear," but nothing worked. An attempt to do an end run around the encryption ended in failure.

"No dice," Greg said finally, conceding defeat. "I think this calls for some seriously high-powered hacking mojo."

Nick knew what he meant. "Let's go see Archie."

17

THE STRIP WAS hopping.

Despite a nip in the air, the sidewalks of Las Vegas Boulevard were as packed as ever. Neon lit up the night. Palm trees swayed above the legendary street that pretty much defined Vegas as far as the rest of the world was concerned. Taxis, tour busses, and ritzy stretch limos crept through bumper-to-bumper traffic, giving the vehicles' occupants plenty of time to take in the sights.

And there was a lot to see. The gaudy grandeur of Sin City seemed to have warped time and space itself, placing a gleaming Egyptian pyramid next door to a shining medieval castle, complete with a drawbridge, spires, and turrets. A ten-story-tall sphinx gazed out over the anachronistic scenery. Emerald laser beams fired from his eyes, causing a man-made lake to boil. According to legend, the sphinx slew all who could not solve its riddles. Some days, Catherine felt like there was a sphinx

looking over her shoulder—every hour seemed to
bring more riddles than answers.

Brass's Taurus cruised north past the hotels, casinos, and resorts. Rubbernecking drivers brought
traffic to a crawl. The Taurus's windows were rolled
up to keep out both the cold and the exhaust. Rid-
ing shotgun next to Brass, Catherine scanned the
bustling sidewalks, on the lookout for Craig Gonch.
A printout of his driver's license photo rested in her
lap. The photo showed a ruggedly handsome young
man with a square chin, wavy brown hair, and blue
eyes. Gonch actually managed to look hot in a DMV
photo; Catherine couldn't blame Jill or Gabriella for
falling for him. A raffish smile offered no hint that
he was a potential stalker-slash-abuser.

They never do, she thought. If there was one thing
she had learned, as a CSI and as a woman, it was
that faces lied. Unlike evidence.

A life-sized replica of the Statue of Liberty saluted
them at the corner of Tropicana. A roller-coaster
looped above a glittering facsimile of the Manhattan
skyline. A jaded native of Vegas, Catherine easily
tuned out the distracting spectacle to focus on the
faces on the sidewalk, but without much luck. So
far Gonch was nowhere to be seen. She started to
wonder if Gabriella had steered them in the wrong
direction, or had perhaps tipped Gonch off that they
were looking for him. For all they knew, he could
have already ducked out of sight.

C'mon, girl, Catherine thought. *Don't let us down.*

They had left Gabriella with both Brass's business card and a number for a domestic-abuse hot-
line. Probably a wasted effort on both counts, but at

least they had made the effort. Who knows? Maybe it would make a difference somewhere down the road. Gabriella was still young enough to write Gonch off to experience. Catherine thanked God that none of Lindsey's boyfriends had ever hit her. At least as far as she knew.

The traffic inched along. Stuck behind a slow-moving Deuce bus making frequent stops, they slowly left the south end of the Strip behind. Lady Liberty shrunk out of sight in the rear-view mirror. A giant neon Coca-Cola bottle reminded Catherine that she hadn't eaten for hours. Her stomach rumbled.

"I figure we go as far as the Sahara," Brass suggested. "Then turn around and head back down the other side of the street."

"Sounds like a plan," she agreed. Beyond the Sahara casino, the big-ticket attractions gave way to a less touristy stretch of older motels, bars, and wedding chapels. They were unlikely to find Gonch working that far up the boulevard, if he was even in the vicinity. If what Gabriella had told them was true, he was going to be where the heavy pedestrian traffic was.

In the meantime, they had several more blocks to go before they had to try to turn around. The Venetian mega-resort loomed ahead on the right, further adding to the Strip's giddy sense of geographical dislocation. No expense had been spared to re-create the postcard-pretty charm and glory of Venice, Italy. Spotlights showed off its ornate marble towers and facade. Singing gondoliers, many of them imported straight from the genuine article, serenaded boatloads of huddled tourists as they paddled their sleek black gondolas around a sparkling blue lagoon. A paved walkway, flanked by towering white pillars, bridged the pool, connecting the sidewalk to the colonnaded entrance of the Doge's Palace. Men and women swarmed across the bridge, eager to simulate a European vacation, or perhaps just get a little shopping or gambling in. Security guards in imitation Venetian police uniforms were on hand just in case the party got too rowdy. A multistory hotel rose between the bridge and another palace, which housed the Vegas branch of Madame Tussaud's.

Great, Catherine thought. *Another wax museum.*

Three nights had passed since the *Shock Treatment* shooting and they still couldn't say for sure whether it had been an accident or not. She wondered if maybe they were wasting their time. Suppose the shooting was just what it had first appeared to be: an unfortunate collision between a sadistic prank and a scared young woman with a gun?

"Say, Jim," she began, even as she continued to scrutinize the faces outside on the Strip. "What's your current take on this whole . . . hang on!"

A strapping figure caught her attention. The man, whose chiseled features bore an unmistakable resemblance to the photo on her lap, was handing out flyers on the sidewalk in front of the Venetian. A snug black sweatshirt, advertising a bar named Headlights, showed off his buff physique. Tight jeans and comfortable sneakers were well-suited to traipsing up and down the length of the Strip. He thrust his handbills at every passing pedestrian, not taking no for an answer. The flyers were a lurid shade of pink.

Looks like our boy, Catherine thought. According to Gabriella, Craig Gonch now spent his nights drumming up business for the topless place where they met. Not exactly the most promising of careers, but a buck was a buck. Catherine guessed that the gym had paid better. *Too bad he couldn't keep his hands off the clientele.*

She rolled down the passenger-side window for a better view. Keen blue eyes compared the flyer guy's scruffy good looks to the driver's license photo.

It was a match.

"Over there on the right," she alerted Brass. "You see him?"

"Roger that." He took his eyes off the road long enough to ID Gonch as well. "Nice. Good eyes, Willows."

"Tell it to my optometrist."

Horns blared behind him as he abruptly pulled over to the curb and hit the brakes. Catherine was already unbuckled and out of the door before Brass killed the ignition. She wasn't about to let Gonch out of her sight. It would be too easy to lose him again in the neon-charged activity of the Strip. The cold night air came as a jolt after the car's heated interior. She was glad she had put on a jacket earlier.

Wonder if Gonch has his cell phone on him?

Intent on giving away his flyers, Gonch paid no attention to the parked Taurus. Catherine heard him pushing his spiel on men, women, and families alike. "Hottest girls in town!" he promised. A southern accent carried echoes of the menacing phone call Jill Wooten had recorded. "Open all night, 24/7!"

"Is there a buffet?" a vacationing senior citizen asked.

Brass quickly joined her on the sidewalk. They closed in on Gonch. Catherine let Brass approach from the south, while she circled north to head him off if necessary. Curious passersby parted to let Brass through as he held up his badge.

"Craig Gonch?" he called out. "LVPD."

Gonch stiffened in alarm. Catherine knew he was going to rabbit even before he hurled an armload of glossy pink flyers in Brass's face, then bolted from the cop.

"Damn!" Brass swore, batting the tossed handbills away from his face. They fluttered to the ground, littering the pavement with lewd come-ons and snapshots of barely covered silicone. He trampled the flyers beneath his feet as he took off in pursuit. "Give it up, Gonch!" he shouted at the fleeing suspect before calling for backup on his phone. "Suspect is heading north on Las Vegas Boulevard toward Spring Mountain Road!"

Gonch barreled through the crowd. Startled tourists threw themselves backward against the guardrail between the sidewalk and the lagoon. An overweight sightseer, wearing the requisite baseball cap and fanny pack, didn't get out of the way fast enough and Gonch shoved him aside. The unlucky tourist tumbled onto the ground, spilling the better part of a Big Gulp onto the concrete. "Hey, what's your problem?" he hollered indignantly. "Douchebag!"

Catherine shared the sentiment. Gonch was rapidly moving up her shit list. He was making this way harder than it had to be.

"That's far enough, buster." She moved to block his escape. She unzipped her fleece jacket to reveal the sidearm on her hip. Her hand rested on the grip of the weapon. "Down on the ground . . . now."

Gonch froze, trapped between Brass and Catherine. She saw Brass coming up behind the fugitive, his scowling face flushed with anger and/or exertion. Huffing and puffing, he looked more than ready to give Gonch the third-degree right there in front of the Venetian. His ragged breathing made Catherine think Brass needed to log in a few more hours at the gym. *Too bad we didn't drag Nick along,* she thought. The brawny ex-quarterback was better suited to tackling runaway suspects, as he had proven on more than one occasion. Gonch was lucky not to be on the receiving end of one of Nick's takedowns.

"Don't make me repeat myself," she warned.

Gonch looked about frantically, searching for a way out. Any hopes Catherine might have had that he was ready to surrender were dashed when he abandoned the sidewalk for the bridge over the lagoon. He made tracks toward the Venetian. She guessed that he was hoping to lose himself in the crowds swarming the resort's myriad shops and restaurants. Gonch wove through the people on the bridge, apparently gambling that neither Brass nor Catherine would open fire in such a densely populated area.

A pretty safe bet, she admitted. Her gun remained in its holster.

No way was he going to get away, though. Chasing after him, she called out to the security guards posted at the opposite end of the bridge.

"LVPD! Stop that man!"

To her relief, the costumed guards surged onto the bridge. Gonch skidded to a halt, once again stuck with nowhere to run. Catherine and Brass sprinted toward him. "This jerk had better be guilty," Brass panted. "Of something."

A low railing ran along both sides of the bridge, which arched gracefully over the lagoon. A slightly off-key rendition of "O Sole Mio" wafted up from a gondola passing under the archway. Gonch ran to the rail. He peered over the edge.

Oh, for God's sake, Catherine thought. *Don't tell me he's actually going to . . .*

Sure enough, he vaulted over the railing. Gravity seized him and he plunged into a half-full gondola just as it emerged from beneath the shadow of the bridge. Watching from above, Catherine honestly couldn't tell if Gonch had deliberately landed in the gondola or if he had been aiming for the water instead. Either way, the desperate leap for liberty proved a bust. His crash landing capsized the gondola, spilling all concerned into the lagoon, which, thankfully, was a mere four feet deep. A huge splash pelted her face with water droplets. A teenage couple, who only seconds before had been enjoying a romantic boat ride, shrieked as they abruptly found themselves dumped into what was effectively an oversized wading pool. Scrambling to his feet, the soaked gondolier swung his oar at Gonch while swearing furiously in Italian. The wooden pole missed Gonch's head by a fraction of an inch. He stumbled backward, losing his balance and splashing back down into the pool. Spectators on the shore and bridge hooted and jeered at the free entertainment. The tranquil lagoon was suddenly the hottest show on the Strip.

Catherine just shook her head.

I need a vacation. . . .

Brass joined her at the rail. "Is it just me," he sighed wearily, "or are these punks getting dumber every year?"

"You do the math." Catherine wiped the spray from her face. "Half the population is of below average intelligence."

"Don't I know it," Brass said.

They let the Venetian guards do the soggy work of pulling the irate gondolier off Gonch. The guards waded into the lagoon to retrieve the drenched fugitive, who appeared to have finally had the wind knocked out of him. None too gently, they dragged him to the sidewalk. Sirens and flashing lights heralded the arrival of a couple of LVPD patrol cars, responding to Brass's summons. The wet guards turned Gonch over to the cops, then checked on the upset teenagers, who were complaining loudly about getting dunked. Catherine expected the couple would get some vouchers and other freebies from the Venetian.

"Guess we go read Mr. Gonch his rights," Brass said. He took a few moments to catch his breath before trudging away from the rail. "Let's hope this fishing expedition pays off."

Catherine eyed their dripping quarry. "Well, if not, we can always throw him back into the lagoon."

"I don't suppose I can get a towel?"

Gonch shivered in an interrogation room at police headquarters, just up the block from the crime lab. He had exchanged his sodden street clothes for orange jailhouse attire, but his hair was still damp. A sullen expression marred his good looks.

"Forget it," Catherine said without a trace of sympathy. She and Brass sat opposite Gonch on the other side of a glass-covered metal table. Stark gray walls, devoid of color or warmth, cut them off from the world outside. A horizontal mirror hid a one-way window. A closed-circuit TV camera recorded the proceedings. Just like a *Shock Treatment* set, actually, but without the deception. This was as real as it got.

Gonch's antics at the Venetian had turned his interview into an interrogation. Seeing to his comfort was not only the least of Catherine's concerns, it was pretty much the opposite of what she and Brass were going for. They wanted to sweat the truth out of him.

"Next time," she advised, "maybe you'll think twice about going for a moonlight swim instead of cooperating with the police."

"Screw you."

Getting dumped into a cold lagoon on a chilly winter night had not done wonders for his mood. A surly tone hinted at his true character.

"See, that's the kind of attitude that gets you into trouble." Brass commenced the questioning. "So why did you run anyway?"

"I dunno."

"You don't know?" Brass was openly skeptical. "You saying you pulled all that for no reason?"

Gonch's brow furrowed. You could practically see

the wheels turning inside his thick skull as he tried to come up with a semi-plausible explanation for his behavior back on the Strip. "The guards at the Venetian don't like me soliciting in front of their place. I thought maybe they'd called you." He snorted indignantly. "Like they own the sidewalk or something."

"So you jumped off a bridge into a gondola just to avoid being told to move it along?" Brass shook his head. "Sorry. I'm not buying that."

Catherine had a better theory. "Your attempted getaway wouldn't have anything to do with the shiner you gave your girlfriend, Gabriella Ruvasso, would it?"

"She walked into a door." He eyed Catherine suspiciously. "Why? Did she tell you something different?"

"Yeah, actually," Brass said. "She said she fell down the stairs."

"Stairs. Door. Whatever." He leaned back in the chair, smirking. "It was an accident. I don't remember the details."

"Yeah, sure." Brass remained unconvinced. "Well, do you recall making any threatening calls to your ex, Jill Wooten?"

"Jill?" Gonch appeared genuinely startled by the question. Sitting up straight, he gave Brass and Catherine a wary look. "Is *that* what this is all about? I haven't talked to that skank for months. She's old news."

Catherine wasn't sure she believed him. "You sure about that?" An open file rested on the table-top in front of her. She leafed through the enclosed documents. "According to these records, it definitely sounds like you were stalking her before. Harassing her at work and at home. Leaving angry notes on her door." She tapped a xeroxed copy of a police report. "Says here you even tried to force your way into her apartment once."

"I only wanted to talk to her, that's all," he muttered. "It was no big deal. Jill made it sound a whole lot worse than it was, just to get back at me." A sneer twisted his lips. "Jealous bitch."

"Oh yeah," Brass said. Sarcasm dripped from his voice. "You sound like you're totally over her now."

"I am!" Gonch insisted. "It's just that you reminded me of all that old garbage. Brought back some crappy memories, you know?" He scoffed at the file in front of Catherine. "I swear, I haven't even thought of Jill in forever. Why should I? I've got a new girl now."

"Yes," Catherine said archly. "We've met."

Gonch either ignored her frosty tone or missed it altogether. "So you've seen how smoking she is, right? Way hotter than Jill."

"She's pretty all right," Catherine granted him. "Aside from the black eye."

"I told you, that was an accident." He scowled at Catherine, like he wanted to give her a dose of the same medicine. "The point is, why would I still be hung up on my ex when I've got action like that waiting for me at home?" A smug expression replaced the scowl. He tipped his chair back, all cocky attitude again. "I've traded up."

To a woman who lets you smack her around, Catherine thought, eager to wipe the smirk from his face.

"I don't know. You wouldn't be the first guy who didn't know when to let go, even when he was already seeing someone else."

Just a few months ago, in fact, a happily remarried insurance salesman had tracked down and stabbed his first wife on what would have been their twenty-fifth wedding anniversary. In that case, the first cut had indeed been the deepest. Catherine was willing to believe that Gonch was still carrying a chainsaw-sized chip on his shoulder where Jill was concerned. Maybe enough to be a contributing factor in her death.

Somebody had to have made those phone calls.

"I'm telling you, I'm over her!" He got agitated enough to rattle his handcuffs. "Gabby is hotter, better in bed, and, frankly, less of a pain in the ass." He leaned back and crossed his arms atop his chest. "If you want to know the truth, Jill could really be a buzzkill sometimes. I don't know why I put up with her as long as I did . . . except for the sex, I guess."

And they say chivalry is dead, Catherine thought.

"Hey!" A lightbulb finally went off above Gonch's soggy scalp. "Is this about Jill shooting that guy? On that TV show?"

Brass leaned forward. "You heard about that?"

"Sure! It was all over the news." He snickered derisively. "I can't believe they actually punked her like that. Idiot. I always knew her boobs were bigger than her brains."

Catherine wondered if Gonch had really only just now remembered the *Shock Treatment* incident. *Maybe that was actually why he ran from us,* she thought, *and not just the fact that he's been hitting his new squeeze.*

"You ever watch that show?" Brass asked.

It dawned on Gonch that he might be in trouble for more than just running from the police. "Sometimes," he said cautiously. "But why are you asking me about that? I heard what happened. Jill thought she was blowing away some psycho with a chainsaw."

"Actually, she thought it might be you," Catherine divulged. "And she pulled the trigger anyway."

"No shit?" Gonch looked offended, taken aback by the notion that one of his past or present punching bags might actually fight back. "Wow. I guess I got off easy then. Who knew she was that crazy?"

Catherine wasn't interested in discussing Jill's mental health. She wanted to know how crazy Gonch was. "You like horror movies, don't you?"

"Sure. That's not a crime, is it?" He snorted again. "That's another way Gabby beats out Jill. She doesn't mind a good slasher flick. Jill always hated that stuff. Like I said, she could be a real drag sometimes."

Catherine found it interesting that Gonch knew Jill's weak spot. "Too easily scared?"

"Maybe." He shrugged. "Not my problem anymore."

Brass took another tack. "You own a cell phone, Mr. Gonch?"

"You know I do," he groused. "Your boys took it off me. Am I going to get it back?"

"Not right away," she told him. "We're going to have to take a look at it."

Maybe Archie could link it to the threatening calls, assuming its immersion in the lagoon hadn't damaged it too badly. *Probably a long shot*, she thought, *but it pays to be thorough.*

"What for?" Gonch complained. "So I have a cell phone. Big whoop. Who doesn't these days?"

"We'll ask the questions, Mr. Gonch," Brass said firmly. He consulted his notebook. "What were you doing at approximately 7:45 on Sunday night?"

Catherine recognized the time. According to Jill's phone records, that was when she had received the most recent of the anonymous calls, just a few hours before her scheduled job interview . . . the call that may have driven Jill to homicide.

"I dunno. At home, I guess. With Gabby."

"You make any calls that night?"

"Maybe. I can't remember." He tried to figure out where Brass was going with this. "But I didn't call Jill, no way. Check my phone records if you don't believe me."

"We'll do that," Catherine said, although she wasn't sure how much that was going to prove. The problem with cell phones was that they rendered alibis kind of academic in cases like this. If Gonch was behind the calls, he could have made them from almost anywhere. All he needed was just a few private moments when nobody was looking. Even if he really had spent the evening with Gabriella, he could have easily slipped away for the moment to call Jill on a disposable cell phone.

She mentally compared his voice and accent to the threatening call, but, like Jill herself, she couldn't say for sure that Gonch had been the voice on the phone. It sounded like him, sort of, or maybe just like someone trying to imitate his accent. A more scientific analysis was required before she could reach any definite conclusions, which was where the crime lab came in.

Gonch squirmed impatiently. "Look, are we almost done here?"

"Oh, you're not going anywhere soon," Brass said. "Not after that ruckus at the Venetian." In a very real sense, Gonch had done them a favor by getting himself in trouble; as a result, he was in no position to walk away. "Your soggy ass is ours."

"But right now all we want is your voice." Catherine produced Gonch's cell phone and dialed Archie at the A/V lab. When running a voiceprint comparison, it was always best to re-create the original sample as much as possible. In an ideal world, that would involve using the actual phone used by the mystery caller. They couldn't be sure that was this phone—in fact, it probably wasn't—but it was worth a shot. In any event, they wanted the sample transmitted via a cell phone.

"My voice?" Gonch parroted.

"That's right." She placed the phone to her ear.

Archie picked up at the other end. "Catherine?"

"We're ready to roll," she informed him. "You recording this call?"

"I am now," he said.

"Okay, stay on the line." She put on her reading glasses and took out a transcript of the latest call. "I'm going to read something to you," she explained to Gonch, "and I want you to repeat it after me, word for word."

In theory, an exact word-to-word match would make it much easier for Archie to run a voiceprint comparison despite the caller's whispery attempt to distort his voice. Just to play it safe, she would have to get Gonch to whisper another sample later on. The more versions Archie had to work with, the better his chances of making a solid identification.

Gonch balked. "And if I don't?"

"Then you'd better hope your smoking new girlfriend feels like bailing you out sometime soon." Brass gave Gonch a hard, cold look. "Me, I'd let you rot for awhile. Maybe give you some time to think about the way you treat women."

Gonch started to sweat. "I don't know what Jill told you, but you are not going to pin her problems on me. I had nothing to do with that TV show mess."

Catherine handed him the phone. "Prove it."

He reached for the transcript in her hand. "Okay. Give it to me. I can read it myself."

"Forget it," Catherine said. "That's not how it works." Studies had shown that the best voice samples were obtained by having the subject repeat phrases spoken by the examiner rather than letting him or her read it directly from a transcript. For some reason, you got more natural intonations that way. "And don't try to do anything funny with your voice. Just speak naturally."

Proper procedure dictated that she get at least three workable samples of Gonch mimicking the anonymous call. She was fully prepared to put him through as many recitations as it took to get Archie some decent exemplars to work with, including a whispered version. Despite their name, "voiceprints" were nowhere near as reliable as fingerprints, but an expert analyst could often narrow a pool of suspects down to just a few probable candidates.

"Okay, okay," he muttered. "Whatever it takes to get you off my back."

"Then repeat after me." She put on her reading glasses and glanced down at the transcript. "Listen to me, you bitch. . . ."

Gonch flared up again. "I never said that!"

"That's up to the lab to decide," she stated calmly. "If you cooperate."

Brass looked at his watch. "You got all night, Gonch? 'Cause we're not going anywhere until this gets done."

"One more time," Catherine said. "Listen to me, you bitch. . . . "

Gonch mumbled under his breath. "Listen to me, you bitch."

"Louder and more clearly, please."

He glared murderously at Catherine. "Listen to me, *you bitch*."

"That's better," she said with a smirk. "Much more convincing." She moved on to the next line. "You better watch your back."

Gonch fumed in his chair, but got with the program.

"You better watch your back. . . ."

18

"VISITORS ARE BY appointment only," Chip LaReue drawled. "But I suppose I can make an exception in your case."

The LaReue Reptile Farm was located along a dirt road on the outskirts of town. A chain-link fence, topped with razor wire, enclosed the complex, which consisted of a large barnlike structure adjacent to a smaller adobe residence. A pick-up truck was parked out front. The professional snake dealer had been strolling toward the barn when Ray and Sara had arrived in the Denali shortly after sunrise. He'd changed course to meet them in the middle of the driveway. The morning sun beat down on them. It was already looking to be a warm day.

Ray put away his ID. "You don't seem surprised to see us, Mr. LaReue."

"Heard about that trouble at the spa," LaReue said. A thick Cajun accent suggested that he was hardly native to Las Vegas. "Figured you'd come calling eventually. Surprised it took so long."

Chip LaReue had the leathery, sunbaked complexion of someone who spent plenty of time outdoors. A safari jacket, equipped with plenty of bulging pouches, hung upon his compact, wiry frame. Strands of stringy brown hair poked out from beneath a faded tan baseball cap. A toothpick dangled at the corner of his mouth, below a drooping handlebar mustache. Lean and laconic, he appeared unintimidated by the CSIs. His hands were tucked into heavy work gloves.

"We've been busy," Sara said dryly. "Tracking down everyone connected to that snakebite."

"Bad business that," LaReue commented. "Snakes have a bad enough rep, without that sort of nonsense making it worse. Just makes snake conservation all that harder." He snorted in disgust. "People don't realize that snakes have more to fear from us than we do from them."

"How's that?" Ray asked.

"No big secret," LaReue said. "We encroach on their habitats, then go apeshit when we see them around. People kill snakes all the time, out of fear or spite or superstition. Snakes only attack people when they're disturbed." He shook his head. "To be honest, I thought that snake massage thing was a dumb idea, but I figured, what the heck, a sale is a sale." A grimace twisted his sandpapery features. "Serves me right for not listening to my gut."

"Who do you usually sell to?" Sara asked.

"Private collectors, zoos, research labs, pharmaceutical companies." He didn't bother to explain why such institutions needed the reptiles. "The massage thing was a new angle, but it seemed harmless at the time. Especially since they didn't want any hot snakes."

Ray guessed he didn't mean stolen. "Hot?"

"Venomous," LaReue clarified. "You need a special license to deal in poisonous snakes."

Sara briefly wondered if Grissom had such a license. "And how does one get one of those?"

"Varies from state to state," LaReue said. "Here in Nevada, you need to demonstrate that you know how to properly handle and house the snakes." He did not come off as evasive or defensive. "All my paperwork is in order if you want to see it."

"Maybe later," Ray said. "Right now we'd like to talk to you about the snakes you sold to The Nile."

"Fine with me. I've got nothing to hide." He glanced at his wristwatch. "You arrived just at feeding time, though. Mind if we walk while we talk?"

Ray glanced at Sara, who shrugged in assent. "Why not?" he agreed. "I admit I'm curious to check out your operation."

"Didn't figure you for the squeamish types." LaReue looked them over appraisingly. "Guess you couldn't be, considering your profession."

He led them into the barn. Hanging plastic sheets kept in the damp atmosphere, which was generated by an industrial strength humidifier chugging away in one corner. Well-constructed wooden shelves supported rows of snake cages with sliding glass doors. Each shelf held three to four cages, depending on the size of their inhabitants. Shredded newspaper lined the floors of the cages. Electric heating

pads controlled the temperature. An incubator occupied another corner; snake eggs, neatly arranged
in open plastic boxes, could be glimpsed through a
glass plate in the door. A refrigerator possibly held
supplies of antivenin. Ray was impressed at how
clean, organized, and well-maintained the set-up
was, almost like the crime lab.

A sizable variety of snakes was on display as well.
Scanning the shelves, Ray identified rattlers, mambas, boa constrictors, pythons, kingsnakes, water
snakes, racers, and even an Indian cobra. The sheer
diversity of colors, sizes, and markings rivaled the
garish carpets favored by Vegas casinos, and were
much more pleasing to the eye. Ray would have
liked to have browsed the display at leisure.

"Nice collection," he said, impressed.

"Thanks," LaReue replied. "Can't stock every breed
of snake. That would take a space the size of a jet
hangar. But I've got most of the popular varieties."

"Including coral snakes?" Sara asked.

"A few," he admitted. "But the snake that bit that
rich lady wasn't one of mine."

Sara didn't take his word for it. "How do you
know that?"

"Check the inventory," he challenged her. He
ambled over to a counter and pulled out a drawer.
Inside was a tray of dead white mice. He took out
the tray and walked over to the first wall of cages.
"There should be a record of every snake I delivered
to The Nile. None of them hot."

"We did that," Ray divulged. He and Sara had
compared Hodges's inventory of the confiscated
snakes against the purchase orders Brian Yun had

provided. They had matched up perfectly—except for one anomaly. "There was an extra snake in The Nile's vivarium. A western coral snake."

"Well, it didn't come from me," LaReue insisted. He slid open the glass door on the first cage and casually tossed a lifeless mouse carcass inside. Not waiting to see if the cage's cold-blooded occupant accepted the offering, he closed the door and moved onto the next case. "All my coral snakes are accounted for."

"Are you sure of that?" Sara asked, playing devil's advocate. "All these snakes wriggling around. Couldn't an extra snake end up in a shipment by mistake?"

LaReue shook his head. "No way." He nodded at a separate set of shelves farther down the wall. Ray noted that the doors on those cages were equipped with showcase locks for extra security. "I keep the hot snakes in their own section, safely locked up. Don't see how a coral snake could have snuck in with the kingsnakes, unless it had taken lessons from Houdini. And, believe me, when I'm handling the hot snakes, I pay close attention to what I'm doing."

Ray could believe it. "Ever been bitten?"

"You bet." LaReue put the tray down on top of the incubator and peeled off his left glove. The top half of his index finger was missing. "Got sloppy with a Mojave rattler once. Had to watch my finger rot away to the joint." He pulled the glove back on. "Won't make that mistake again."

He went back to feeding the snakes. A hungry green boa eagerly swallowed the mouse, which gradually made its way down the snake's digestive tract. You could track its progress by the lump it formed beneath the boa's hide. Ray was grateful that LaReue didn't provide his merchandise with live food. The CSI had a strong stomach, as LaReue had surmised, but that would have been a little disquieting, as he suspected Sara would agree. "Where do you get the mice?"

"I have my own breeding colony in the back room," LaReue explained. "All perfectly humane." He left the boa to finish digesting its meal. "'Course, not every species eats rodents. I feed mealworms and crickets to the insectivorous breeds, and goldfish to the water snakes."

"And other snakes to the corals?" Ray asked.

"Yep. Little blind snakes, mostly. With maybe a shovel-nosed snake once in a while, just for variety."

LaReue definitely seemed to know his snakes. It was hard to imagine that he could have shipped The Nile a coral snake by accident. "We're going to need to review your records," Ray said nonetheless. "To make certain there are no discrepancies."

"Knock yourself out." LaReue didn't ask for a warrant. "I'll xerox everything after I finish up here. But I can tell you now, you're not going to find anything out of order. I run a tight ship."

"So it appears." Ray considered another possibility. "Suppose one did want to get a coral snake, possibly under the table? Are there any less reputable snake dealers out there?"

For the first time, LaReue looked uncomfortable. He turned his back on the CSIs, the better to concentrate on feeding his snakes. "I wouldn't know anything about that."

"Why do I find that hard to believe?" Sara asked.

"I don't know," LaReue said tersely. "You tell me."

"I think what my colleague is saying," Ray said, "it's that you strike us as a man who is very familiar with his field. Hard to imagine that you wouldn't know who the other players are."

LaReue shrugged, his back still to his visitors. "I mind my own business."

"Mr. LaReue," Ray said firmly, "I'm going to ask you to put that tray down and give us your full attention." They had tried being polite, but LaReue was clearly playing his cards close to his vest. Ray's voice took on a sterner tone, the same one he had once used when lecturing to an inattentive classroom. "We really need to get some answers here."

The snake dealer turned around slowly. Irritation showed upon his grizzled face. "Look, I'm trying to be cooperative." He placed the tray down on a nearby counter, perhaps a little harder than necessary. The dead mice bounced upon the metal. "I want to get this cleared up as much as anyone. My reputation's on the line."

"Then don't hold out on us now," Sara advised him. "Or maybe your name might end up leaked to the press. Not exactly good publicity for your business . . . especially if Ms. Segura doesn't survive."

The last Ray had heard, the snakebite victim had yet to regain consciousness. Artificial means were still being employed to keep her breathing.

LaReue's face hardened. "You threatening me?"

"Who, me?" Sara professed innocence. "I'm just saying that the longer this case drags on, the harder it's going to be to keep your name out of this."

Ray tried a softer approach. "All we want is to find out where that hot snake came from. You said it yourself: incidents like this reflect badly on your industry. If there's a bad apple, you owe it to yourself to expose him."

A long minute passed as LaReue mulled the matter over. Ray wondered what was behind the man's reticence. Professional loyalty to a fellow dealer, or fear of retribution?

Who was he protecting? And why?

"All right," LaReue said finally. "There is this one guy. I have no idea if he has anything to do with this whole mess, but if you were looking to get your hands on a hot snake, without leaving any sort of paper trail behind, he's the guy you'd want to talk to."

Now we're getting somewhere, Ray thought. "What's his name?"

"Fang," the snake dealer said. "Fang Santana." He frowned, like he already regretted spilling the beans. "Just don't tell him I sent you."

19

"Gee," Archie said. "Guess I should have sold tickets."

Catherine chuckled dryly. "You know us, we're suckers for a good spectrographic voice analysis."

The CSIs crowded into the dimly lit A/V lab. Catherine stood directly behind Archie's workstation, while Nick and Greg looked over her shoulder. Glowing sonograms coursed across the lab tech's monitor.

"Seriously," she added. "The media is breathing down our necks on this case, which means Ecklie is, too." She suppressed a yawn; this was her second double shift in a row. "Anything you can do to throw some light on the particulars would make all our lives easier."

Another day had passed since she and Brass had interrogated Craig Gonch. She had managed to squeeze in a few hours of sleep this afternoon only to find Conrad Ecklie waiting for her when she reported back to work in the evening. His new responsibilities as undersheriff had not mellowed her prickly, autocratic boss; if anything, he was even more concerned with politics and public relations than before. Still, she conceded, at least he wasn't a murderous S.O.B. like the previous undersheriff. The one who had killed Warrick.

Ecklie only wanted results, not blood. As he had made abundantly clear.

"Where are we on the Matt Novak case?" he had demanded, barging into her office without asking. As ever, his saturnine features were less than supportive. A dark, conservative suit made him look more like an undertaker than a crime scene investigator. "Everybody from CNN to Access Hollywood is demanding an update, and City Hall wants to know if we're going to press charges."

"Tell them to increase our budget," Catherine had said. "You know we've been short-handed since Riley left. And Sara and Ray are tied up with another case."

"Yes, I heard. The snake thing." He plopped down into a chair. "Look, Catherine, I don't need to remind you that the city has put a lot of time and effort into encouraging movie and TV crews to shoot in Vegas. It's good for the economy and for tourism. So I really need to know: is this going to get ugly or not?"

She gestured at the bulging file on her desk. "We're making progress."

A veteran criminalist himself, Ecklie knew just how little that empty phrase could mean. "That's not good enough," he said. "We can't keep the press and Hollywood hanging. You need to wrap this up, one way or another."

"You want it fast," she asked, "or do you want the truth?"

"I want the truth . . . fast." Rising to his feet, he shook

his head in disappointment. "You know, Catherine, I always thought you had a better grasp on how the system really worked than your predecessor. Right now, though, you're reminding me an awful lot of Grissom."

Catherine shrugged. "I'll take that as a compliment."

"Don't," he said curtly. "Get me an answer, ASAP."

"Understood," Archie said, bringing her back to the present. "I just hope you're expectations aren't too high. Voice analysis is not an exact science. There are no sure things, especially not if the caller is making an effort to disguise his voice."

"Caveats duly noted," she said. "What have you got for us?"

"Well, first off, Craig Gonch may have an alibi."

"Huh," she reacted. "How do you have an alibi for a phone call?"

"By calling someone else at the same time." Archie pulled up Gonch's phone records, which were displayed in grid format upon his monitor. He pointed to a highlighted line on the screen. "Gonch was on the phone to another number at the same time that Jill Wooten received her scary mystery call."

Catherine didn't recognize the number on the screen. "On the phone to whom?"

"Headlights," Archie said. "It's a topless place."

"So I've heard," Catherine said. "Okay, we're going to need to verify that. See if anyone at the bar remembers taking Gonch's call. We have to make sure it was really him using his phone and not his girlfriend or someone else."

"Maybe he was using two lines at once," Greg suggested. He pantomimed holding a phone to each ear. "Or even two phones."

"Unlikely," Catherine said. "Who makes harassing calls to an ex while simultaneously on the phone to work?"

Greg wasn't ready to give up on his crazy theory just yet. "Someone who wants to set up an alibi?"

"For a crank phone call?" Catherine shook her head. "I've met Craig Gonch. Frankly, he didn't seem that clever."

Nick moved on to the main event. "What about the voice analysis?"

"The news isn't exactly encouraging there either," Archie warned them. Dispatching the phone records back to electronic limbo, he called up another program on his computer. A pair of spectrograms appeared on the monitor, one atop the other. Each horizontal display charted the speech samples' frequency and amplitude, producing a graphic representation that resembled an EKG or seismic readout. A thorough voice analysis entailed both a visual and aural comparison of two samples, recorded under as similar circumstances as logistically possible. In a match, two identical spectrograms could be superimposed on each other.

But not this time. The dual waveforms oscillated across the screen, visibly out of synch.

Catherine frowned. "Okay, I'm no expert here, but even I can see that our two samples don't remotely match each other."

"That would be my conclusion as well," Archie said. "Granted, the whisper effect introduces an extra margin of error, but, honestly, I don't think Gonch is your guy. And there's something else, too: the more I listen to it, the phonier the southern accent in the original recording sounds. It's like someone's doing a bad impression of Gonch."

"Really?" Catherine asked. "What makes you think that?"

"Well, for one thing, Gonch mispronounced 'nuclear' when you took the sample. He said, 'I'm going nuke-u-lar on you, baby,' like he was George Bush or something." Archie did a pretty good imitation of Gonch's surly tone as well. "Okay, that's a very common mistake, but here's the thing: the mystery caller got it right."

"So it wasn't Craig Gonch," Catherine concluded. "But who?"

"Somebody who knew about Gonch's predilection for slasher movies?" Nick speculated. "Think about it. Jill has a stalker ex-boyfriend with a thing for horror films, she's on the receiving end of some scary phone calls, *and* she gets targeted for *Shock Treatment.*" He stepped back from the monitor. "Either that's a perfect storm of creepy coincidences, or someone knew exactly what they were doing."

Catherine leaned toward the latter explanation. "Debra Lusky? She was Jill's ex-roommate. She would have known about Gonch, and she's the one who set Jill up to get shocked on the show."

"Makes sense," Greg said. "But why would she want to get Matt Novak killed? She didn't even know him."

"As far as we know," Catherine stressed. "Although I suppose it's possible she didn't care about Novak at all. Maybe she just wanted to get Jill in trouble."

"That seems a bit extreme," Nick said. "Why risk

killing an innocent person just to put your friend in a difficult legal position? And what would be her motive for tricking Jill into shooting someone anyway?"

Good question, Catherine thought. Grissom had usually hedged away from speculating too much about motives, lest it compromise their scientific objectivity. He had believed that if you concentrated on the physical evidence, determined the where and the when and the how, the why would sort itself out eventually. Catherine had never quite agreed with him in that respect. In her experience, people rarely committed murder without a reason. Figuring out that reason, by calculating the human variables involved, was sometimes the best way to make sense of the evidence.

"You think maybe Debra and Jill planned this whole thing together?" Greg suggested. "That Jill was in on the scheme from the beginning?"

"That's possible, I suppose," Catherine said. Jill had struck her as genuinely shook up the other night, right after the shooting, but maybe the struggling model was a better actress than anyone had realized. "But to what purpose? To frame her ex for some nasty calls?" Catherine found that hard to believe. "Sounds far-fetched to me."

Greg shrugged. "Hey, after working this job, I'm not sure anything is too far-fetched anymore."

He has a point, Catherine thought. Just in the last few years alone, she and her team had run across a dead girl with three different blood types in her veins, a homicide at a sci-fi convention, a baked corpse with a dead racoon stuck to its face, human ribs served up with barbecue sauce, a modern-day headhunter, and a psychopathic surgeon who liked to turn human organs into twisted pieces of art. After all that, was it really that hard to imagine that Jill and Debra had somehow staged this whole thing?

Maybe not?

"Perhaps they did it for the notoriety," Greg theorized. "Have you seen the papers? Jill is all over them. She was an unemployed model, right? Assuming the death is ruled an accident, all this publicity could be the best thing that ever happened to her."

Catherine thought it over. "You know, Debra did say she was hoping to boost Jill's career."

"Well, she sure did that all right," Nick said. "With a bang."

Catherine felt that sphinx sneaking up on her again, bringing more riddles than answers. "Anyway, thanks for the assist, Archie." She turned toward the door. "If nothing else, you've eliminated Craig Gonch as a suspect. Looks like he had nothing to do with this."

"Hang on," Archie said, calling them back. "I'm not done yet."

"Is that so?" Catherine was encouraged by Archie's cocky tone. "Okay, don't keep us in suspense. Show us the goods."

"Believe me, I saved the best for last." He shut down the voice analysis program and opened up another file. "This is the data I downloaded from Matt Novak's flash drive. It took me a while to crack the encryption, but I think it was worth it." He grinned in anticipation. "Warning: some of this footage may not be appropriate for younger viewers."

He wasn't kidding. Catherine's eyes widened at the X-rated action that started playing on the monitor. Photographed from above, a nude white male was grinding away at the woman beneath him, who, bizarrely enough, appeared to be wearing a rubber "Zombie Heat" mask, complete with molded maggots and glimpses of exposed bone. The shriveled green-gray skin stretched over the mask's skull-like visage contrasted with the smooth pink skin generously on display below the woman's neck as she pretended to snap at the man heaving atop her. There was no audio, but Catherine's imagination could easily provide a soundtrack of grunts and moans, with maybe a monstrous growl thrown in to go along with the Halloween mask. Distracted by the sheer weirdness of the scene, it took her a second to recognize the location.

"That's Roger Park's trailer."

She recalled the miniature spy-camera she had found hidden above the TV producer's bed. Owing to the camera angle, the man's face could not be seen, but a familiar blond ponytail, not to mention the locale, gave her a pretty good idea of who was co-starring in this particular video. From the looks of things, Park's fetish for horror movies extended to his private life.

Talk about too hot for TV, she thought. *Now if we can just get a good look at his face.*

As if on cue, the couple rolled over in bed, so that the woman ended up on top. "Busted," Catherine muttered as the camera caught the flushed, sweaty features of Roger Park. It was the first time she had ever seen him without his Bluetooth on his ear. More than ever, she was glad that she had turned down that consulting gig.

"Who is that? Park?" Nick asked. He had yet to meet the producer.

"In living color," Catherine said.

"Or unliving," Greg quipped.

"I don't know," Nick said. "They both look pretty animated to me."

On the screen, the woman started inching down Park's body, heading south.

"Um," Greg said. "If she wants to eat his brains, she's going in the wrong direction."

Catherine begged to differ. "Not where most guys are concerned. Okay . . . I think we get the gist of it."

Eventually, a CSI was going to have to review the footage in its entirety, but at the moment she was inclined to delegate that chore to someone else. As a criminalist in 21st century Las Vegas, she had already seen more than enough sex tapes to last a lifetime. Even if this one was slightly more outré than most.

"Okay, that was just freaky," Nick said as Archie hit the Pause key, freezing the image on the screen. "And not in a good way."

Greg shrugged, affecting a seen-it-all attitude. "I don't know. Some people like cosplay, you know?" He smirked at the screen.

"Way too much information," Catherine said. She quickly turned the discussion back to the evidence. "What's the story, Archie? She ever take that mask off?"

"I'm afraid not," he replied. "And, yeah, I

watched the whole thing, for which I deserve a day off." He leaned back in his seat. "What do you think? Not exactly a smoking gun, but I thought you guys might be interested."

"You thought right." Catherine gazed at the frozen footage, which Matt Novak had been carrying on his keychain right up to the moment of his death. "Looks like prime blackmail material to me."

Nick nodded in agreement. "Isn't Park married to some big-time Hollywood executive?"

"Tricia Grantley," Catherine confirmed. She had looked up Park's A-list spouse after their last visit to his luxury trailer. "She heads the studio that bankrolls his movies and TV shows."

Nick pointed at the zombie girl. "You think that's her?"

"Not a chance." Catherine had seen Park's wedding photo. "Ms. Grantley is a zaftig African-American woman." She contemplated the masked white girl on the screen. "Wrong skin color. Wrong body type."

"In that case," Greg said, "does Park's wife know about his extramarital grave-robbing?"

"I doubt it," Catherine replied. The *why* of Matt Novak's shooting seemed to be coming into focus at last. "No wonder Novak had been lording it around the set lately, and acting like he was a shoo-in to star in Park's new TV series. He figured he had Park wrapped around his finger."

"Or dangling on his keychain, to be precise," Nick added.

Greg grinned in amusement. "How's that for irony? He who lives by the hidden camera, gets

screwed by the hidden camera." The producer's pre-
dicament was obvious to all concerned. "Park had a
big problem."

"Which definitely gives him an incentive to get
Novak killed," Catherine realized. "All he needed
was the right scenario and a properly armed and
jumpy patsy. Like Jill Wooten."

"But why Jill?" Greg asked. "How did he find just
the right unwitting accomplice for his scheme? Unless she was actually in on it all along?"

"That's what we need to find out," Catherine
said. She looked at the masked zombie girl again. "It
might help if we knew who she was."

Nick ran through the possibilities. "Jill Wooten? Debra Lusky? Some anonymous casting couch
cutie?"

Catherine squinted at the screen. "I don't think
that's Jill's body. She's taller and curvier. Hard to say
for sure, though, what with the odd angles and all."

Unfortunately, the rubber mask covered the top
of the woman's head, including her hair. Catherine
found herself wishing that the makeup in *Zombie
Heat* hadn't been so extensive.

"What about Debra Lusky?" Nick asked.

"Possibly," Catherine said. "The woman in the
video seems to be about the right size and weight."
She thought back to her interview with Jill's former roommate, remembering a rather plain young
woman who paled in comparison to her more glamorous friend. "Again, I can't be positive. Needless to
say, Debra was wearing a good deal more clothing
the night I met her, and she didn't have a naked
producer on top of her at the time." She tapped Ar-

chie on the shoulder. "You see any tattoos? Scars? Any other distinguishing marks."

"Not that I recall," he said. "But I can go through the footage more carefully if you like. Try to zoom in on some of the better shots of her."

"Thanks." Catherine appreciated his initiative. "Take it frame-by-frame if you have to." A question occurred to her. "Just how long is the footage anyway?"

"Approximately twelve minutes," Archie sighed. "Give or take a bit of kinky role-playing."

That was a lot of frames, she realized, and Archie probably had some other cases backed up. She made an executive decision. "Greg, you take over examining the footage."

"Me?" His face fell. Greg looked less than enthused at the prospect of poring over the entire tape in mind-numbing detail. Not that she could blame him; twelve minutes of slow-motion, freeze-framed zombie sex sounded like a surefire recipe for eyestrain, not to mention a certain loss of appetite. "What did I ever do to you?"

Nick snickered and slapped Greg on the back. "Have fun, pal."

Despite his brief attitude, Greg knew better than to try to weasel out of the assignment. Catherine was the supervisor now. She called the shots.

"Keep me posted," she told him. Exiting the lab, she took one last look at the macabre tryst on the screen. "I want to know who that horny zombie is."

Nick chuckled as he followed her out the door. "I can't believe you actually just said that."

"Neither can I," she said.

20

FANG WAS NOT his real name.

Ted Santana lived in a trailer park outside Henderson, an industrial town a few miles southeast of the glitz and glamor of Sin City. The low-rent ambience of the park could not have been more different from the upscale environs of The Nile. Rusty mobile homes, in varying states of repair, squatted along both sides of blacktop roads. Drying laundry hung on clotheslines. Barbecue grills, toys, and cheap plastic playground equipment littered the patchy brown lawns. Weeds and potholes infested the pavement. Santana's neighbors eyed Sara and Vartann with myriad combinations of curiosity and suspicion. Laughing toddlers splashed in a blue plastic wading pool, oblivious to the strangers' arrival. A chained mutt growled at Sara, who remembered investigating a murder-suicide here a few years back. She doubted that Rita Segura had ever set foot in the vicinity.

"There he is," Vartann said, leading the way. The park's manager, not wanting trouble, had told them where to find Fang Santana. It was mid-afternoon and the temperature had climbed into the mid-fifties. Sara was starting to forget what sleep felt like.

Their target was already in the system, due to a prior conviction for selling dangerous reptiles over the internet, but he would have been easy to spot even if Sara hadn't already eyeballed his mug shots. The black-market snake dealer was a walking advertisement for his wares. His shaved cranium had a distinctly serpentine cast to it. A snakeskin vest exposed a smooth, hairless chest. A curved fang hung like a pendant from his neck. Bony rattles were strung around his wrist as a bracelet. A bad case of eczema made his skin dry and scaly. Torn jeans and alligator boots completed his ensemble. Frown lines made him look older than his thirty-plus years. Old bite marks scarred his bare arms.

Talk about overkill, Sara thought, getting a nasty vibe from the guy. *No wonder LaReue didn't want to get on his bad side.*

Santana was seated on the steps outside his trailer, entertaining a couple of teenage girls who were way too young for him. The girls acted both repelled and fascinated by the banded milk snake Santana was handling for their amusement. They squealed in delighted horror as he extended the snake's narrow head toward them. A forked tongue flicked in and out of its jaws.

"Go ahead," Santana urged the teens. "Touch it. You know you want to."

Ick, Sara thought. *Looks like we got here just in time.*

Intent on his performance, he didn't notice Sara and Vartann until they were practically in front of him. The detective's shadow fell over him. "Mr. Santana?"

"Who wants to know?" He glared up at the new arrivals, annoyed at the interruption. Novelty contact lenses gave him yellow eyes with slitted pupils. A lisp impeded his speech.

Vartann produced his badge. "LVPD. We'd like to ask you some questions."

The girls evaporated at the sight of the badge. Santana scowled at their departure. He rose angrily to his feet. "What's this all about?"

"Coral snakes," Sara said. "You sold any lately?"

"Without a license?" Santana feigned shock at the very notion. "Why, that would be illegal!" He leered at Sara, undressing her with his eyes. "And you are?"

"Sara Sidle," she replied coldly. "I'm with the crime lab."

"Pleased to meet you, Sssara Sssidle." He drew out the sibilants in her name. A forked tongue flicked into view, revealing the source of his lisp. His breath reeked. "Want to play Eve and the Serpent sometime? Maybe take a bite of my apple?"

"No thanks." She found his bisected tongue more repulsive than shocking. She knew of several tattoo parlors in the city that performed the procedure, which involved a red-hot wire and an excess of bad judgment. "Too wormy for me."

He shrugged. Lifting the snake to his lips, he kissed it on the mouth. "Don't know what you're missing, babe."

"That's enough," Vartann growled. "Save the sideshow act for the jailbait." He got in Santana's face, standing at least three inches taller than the alleged snake dealer. "You dealing in hot snakes again?"

"Like I'd really tell you if I was," Santana hissed, not backing down. "I've checked in with my probation officer this month, right on schedule. You've got no right to hassle me."

Vartann rapped the corrugated metal wall of Santana's trailer. "And if I checked out your digs here, I wouldn't find any illegal reptiles?"

"You got a warrant?"

That would certainly make life easier, Sara thought. Unfortunately, even with Santana's record, there was no way a judge was going to issue a warrant based on a vague tip from an unproven informant. Chip LaReue hadn't even known for sure if Santana knew anything about the Nile incident.

"You're a convicted felon on probation," Vartann reminded him. "All I need is probable cause." He peered at the brightly colored snake coiled around Santana's arm. "Hey, Sidle. That look like a coral snake to you?"

Sara played along. "Could be."

"What? Are you kidding me?" Santana protested. "It's a harmless milk snake, perfectly legal." He held out the snake for their inspection. "Look at the bands. You know how it goes, 'red on black, pat it on the back.' "

"I don't know," Sara hedged. "That only applies to North America. For all we know, that could be some exotic coral snake from overseas or south of the border." She called Vartann's attention to the carefree children in the wading pool. "Lots of kids in this park. A loose snake could pose a major threat to innocent lives. If there's even a chance our friend here is in possession of dangerous reptiles, seems to me that's grounds for immediate action."

To be honest, she wasn't sure that argument would hold up in court, but Santana was already on probation. All they needed now was an excuse to turn up the heat . . . and see just how cold-blooded Santana actually was.

"Works for me." Vartann pulled his best cop face on Santana. "So what's it going to be? We going to do this the easy way or not?" He tapped his jacket pocket. "Just for the record, I have your probation officer on speed-dial."

If he'd been a cobra, Santana would have been spitting poison by now. Deprived of that option, he had no choice but to give ground. "Fine," he snarled. "It's no skin off my nose." He stepped aside to give them access to the trailer's front door. He held onto his pet snake like it was a security blanket. "See for yourself. I'm clean."

"Maybe later," Sara said. "First, I think we'll check out your *other* trailer."

Santana's cocky attitude wilted a little. "Other?"

"C'mon, Ted," she said, rubbing in his real name a little. "You think we didn't check with the park's management first? We know you're paying rent on *two* spaces." She savored his obvious discomfort as she confronted him with the fruits of their homework. "You trying to hoodwink your probation officer, in case she drops by for an unannounced visit, or are you just afraid to sleep under the same roof as your venomous contraband?"

"You don't know what you're talking about," he blustered, but she could tell that they had him on the ropes. He nervously toyed with the milk snake. "You can't do this!"

"Watch us," Vartann said.

The detective stayed close to Santana as they escorted him across the park to a second trailer three lots away. A rusty old Shasta travel trailer rested in the middle of an untended lawn. Its white aluminum exterior looked like it hadn't been washed since the Clinton Administration. Cardboard was taped up over the windows. A KEEP OUT sign discouraged nosy neighbors. A sheet was draped over a box by the steps. Sharp little squeaks escaped the sheet. Sara yanked the sheet away to reveal a cage full of live mice, resting atop a plastic milk carton. The mice scurried away from the disturbance.

"Dinner for some scaly friends?" she guessed.

Santana glowered balefully. "No law against keeping mice."

"Maybe." Vartann took hold of the suspect's arm, in case he tried to make a break for it. "But let's see what else you're keeping."

By now, a small crowd had gathered to watch the proceedings. "Wonder what your neighbors would think if they knew you might be keeping poisonous snakes this close to their kids?" Sara didn't bother keeping her voice low. Angry mutters emerged from the crowd. "If I were you, I wouldn't count on them to back you up."

She tried the door, only to find it locked. Vartann frisked Santana for the key and handed it to Sara. Leaving the detective (and the surly residents) to keep watch over Santana, she entered the trailer. The cardboard over the windows kept out the daylight, so she resorted to a flashlight. The beam from the flash swept over the cramped, shadowy interior.

It was obvious at a glance that nothing human lived in the extra trailer. The furnishings had been gutted to make room for a wall of metal racks supporting rows of large, plastic containers. The bins were piled on the racks all the way up to the fiberglass and particle board ceiling. Coiled snakes slithered inside the bins, which had been labeled by a magic marker. Sara scanned the labels, which were practically a who's who of hot reptiles: sidewinders, green mambas, Gila monsters, cobras, rattlers . . . and coral snakes.

In no hurry to check out the contents of the bins herself, Sara decided to take the labels at their word. Emerging back into the sunlight, she gave Vartann a thumbs-up. "Notify Animal Control that we have a situation here," she informed him. "Multiple situations, in fact."

Santana looked around anxiously, as if contemplating an escape attempt, only to find himself surrounded by a sea of hostile faces. Even if he managed to break free from Vartann's grip, he wasn't going to get far. In fact, judging from his irate neighbors, he was probably better off in police custody.

I think this is one snake we can handle ourselves, she thought.

She carefully locked the trailer door before

rejoining Vartann. She took the milk snake off Santana's hands while Vartann cuffed him and read
him his rights. "Theodore Santana, you're under arrest for possession of illegal venomous reptiles, possibly with intent to sell."

Assuming a judge didn't throw the evidence out,
he was looking at up to five years in prison and
fines of up to $250,000 for each charge against him.
At the very least, he was in clear violation of his
probation.

"Not to mention accessory to an attempted homicide," Sara added.

"What the hell?" Santana said. "Where you'd get
that from?"

Sara played a hunch. "We can run the DNA on
those coral snakes. If they're related to this other
snake we confiscated recently, one that attacked a
woman near Summerlin a few days ago, you could
be in even bigger trouble than you already are."

"Holy crap," Santana swore. He was shaking so
hard his bracelet rattled. Slitted eyes pleaded for
mercy. "Hey, maybe we can make a deal or something?"

Vartann smirked at Sara. This was going just the
way they wanted. "No promises," he told Santana,
"but any cooperation at this point will count in your
favor." He got down to brass tacks. "You sell a coral
snake to anyone recently?"

Santana wavered. "Maybe," he said weakly. "I
can't remember."

"Time's running out," Vartann warned. "Give us
a name."

Santana caved. "Never got his name. Just his money. He wanted a coral snake, no questions asked. Said he'd heard I was the guy who could hook him up."

"And did you?" Sara asked.

"Sure," he confessed. "But I swear, I didn't know what he wanted it for. I figured he was just a collector or something. How was I supposed to know about that crazy shit at the spa?"

Obviously, Santana had been keeping up with current events. Sara imagined the story was spreading pretty quickly through the reptile trade. A smarter perp might have disposed of the evidence by now, but obviously Santana had been too cocky—or greedy—to get rid of his scaly wares.

"Describe him," Vartann ordered.

"Okay, okay." Santana closed his eyes to concentrate. "He was this prissy little dude. Tubby. Losing his hair. Kind of straight-laced." A sneer conveyed his scorn. "Not the kind of guy who looked like he was into hot snakes, but his money was good. Said it was a gift for a friend."

Some friend, Sara thought. But it was looking like Heather Gilroy, not to mention Chip LaReue, were off the hook. "Give us more. Height? Age? Race?"

"In his forties maybe," Santana said. "White. Shorter than me. Nervous, like he couldn't wait to get out of here. Kind of spooked by the snake, too, which was weird." Santana was throwing out everything he could think of now in hopes of finding a get-out-of-jail-free card. "I offered him a beer, but he turned up his nose at it. Asked for an iced tea instead. Like I had any of that stuff around."

A bell went off in Sara's head. "Is it just me," she whispered to Vartann, "or does that sound like Brian Yun?" The Nile's overworked assistant manager fit Santana's description to a tee.

"I was just thinking that," Vartann said. His ordinarily saturnine face showed unusual animation. "Brian Yun drinks iced tea. He offered Langston and I some Snapples."

Makes sense, Sara thought. Yun sometimes worked late at The Nile. He could have easily slipped the coral snake into the vivarium when no one was around, then sat back and waited for all hell to break loose in the morning. *But why?*

They still needed a motive—and some conclusive evidence. They could hardly convict Yun on the testimony of a snake like Santana.

"We need more proof," she told Vartann. "But it's a start."

The detective nodded. He took Santana by the arm and dragged him back toward the car. Raucous neighbors, including the two trailer-park Lolitas he had been chatting up before, jeered his departure. Santana ducked his head, just in case somebody threw something at him. "So now what?" he whined. "You going to put in a good word for me or what?"

"We're going to show you some pictures first," Vartann said. He called for back-up to secure the trailer until Animal Control showed up. "Then we'll talk."

One way or another, Sara figured, Santana

wasn't going to be selling any more snakes out of his mobile home for awhile. He was going to be lucky to stay out of a cage himself.

She recalled his sleazy come-ons earlier. "So much for the Serpent," she told him. "How about *them* apples?"

21

"THANK YOU FOR coming in, Ms. Wooten."

Brass and Catherine greeted Jill in his office at police headquarters. The clean, professional environment was less intimidating than the interrogation suites down the hall. Framed commendations and medals hung upon the walls. A painted blue bookcase loomed behind a tidy desk. An American flag hung on a pole in one corner. A bronze statuette of Blind Justice occupied a position of honor on the desktop. A gray vinyl couch rested against the western wall. The door was closed to keep out the hubbub in the halls. The personable atmosphere often helped to put nervous witnesses at ease, making it easier to get them to open up. Brass hoped the office would have the same effect on Jill Wooten. A box of tissues waited atop the desk, in case she broke down again.

"No problem. Trust me, I want to get this whole mess straightened out more than anyone." Jill occupied a comfortable chair across from Brass. Five days later, she did not appear quite as shell-shocked as she had been on the night of the shooting, but she was still visibly under strain. Dark circles under her eyes hinted that she had not been sleeping well. A loose white cardigan and mid-length green dress were less sexy than the outfit she had worn to her interview at WaxWorkZ. She looked like she was dressed for jury duty, not a hostess job. "Besides, you said you might be able to help me out on the gun charges."

"I can't make any promises," he said. "But your cooperation will definitely be taken into account."

Jill nodded. "I guess that's the best I can hope for, under the circumstances. I know I should have gotten the gun registered and all, but it just seemed easier and faster to skip all the paperwork and checks. I was scared of Craig, you know? I didn't feel safe."

"We've met Mr. Gonch," Catherine told her. She sat next to Jill, in one of the guest chairs. "We understand."

"But you know," Jill said defensively, "I tried to be a responsible gun owner. I kept it locked up under my bed. In a metal lockbox."

"Except for the night in question," Brass observed.

"Yeah," she admitted glumly. She braced herself to go over the traumatic experience one more time. "What else do you need to know?"

"We're still looking into the events leading up to the shooting," Brass began. Jill flinched at the word *shooting*, and he felt another twinge of sympathy for the poor girl. Not a day went by that he didn't think of Officer Martin Bell. He suspected that Jill would never forget Matt Novak's dying moments, even if it really had been a case of mistaken self-defense.

"Events?" she asked. "Like what?"

Brass clamped down on his emotions. He couldn't permit himself to identify with Jill too much, not while she was still a suspect in a possible case of premeditated murder. "You know, how you ended up on the show, those suspicious phone calls, etcetera."

"But I told you," Jill said, "I'm pretty sure Craig made those phone calls."

"Actually, it looks like Mr. Gonch is in the clear," Brass informed her. The manager at Headlights had confirmed that Gonch had been on the phone to him at the same time that Jill had received that last call. Seems Gonch had been trying to scrounge up some more work handing out flyers on the Strip, and had pestered the manager about it for nearly twenty minutes. "We looked into it, and it appears he didn't make those calls to you."

He didn't mention Gonch's new girlfriend.

"Really?" Jill appeared puzzled by the revelation. "Are you sure?"

Catherine backed Brass up. "The evidence suggests that Craig had nothing to do with it."

"But . . . who else could it be?"

"That's what we're trying to find out." Brass pushed the interview in another direction. "What about Roger Park, the producer of the TV show? Did you have any contact with him prior to the other night?"

After thinking it over, they had decided to post-pone interrogating Park for the time being. Until they had a better case against him, it was probably best not to let the producer know he was under sus-picion. Tipping their hand too early would just en-courage him to lawyer up.

"No," Jill insisted. "I'd never met any of those people before. I thought I was going to a job inter-view, remember? Not an audition."

"Are you certain?" Catherine asked gently, woman to woman. "If there was something going on between you and Park, we really need to know about it."

Brass regretted having to go down this road, es-pecially if Jill really was an innocent pawn in all of this, but the question needed to be asked. *An aspir-ing model, a sleazy Hollywood producer*, he mused. *I'd be slipping if I didn't check to see if those pieces fit together.*

"Are you kidding? How can you even think that?" Her voice grew shrill. "I didn't even know Park's name until I heard it on the news later on. I keep tell-ing you, I didn't know anything about that goddamn show. That was all Debra's idea. She's the one who got me into this mess, that sneaky, two-faced cow."

It was obvious that Jill was still holding a grudge against her former roommate. Brass wanted to know just how deep the bad blood between them ran. "And why would she do a thing like that?"

"Because she's a jealous little bitch," Jill said bit-terly. She shook her head in disgust. "Damn it, I knew it was a mistake letting her back into my life."

"I don't understand," Catherine said. "I thought you were friends." *Like sisters*, Debra had said.

"Maybe at first," Jill conceded. "Back when we started out as roommates. But things went sour pretty fast."

"What was the problem?" Catherine asked.

"Honestly, I think she just couldn't get over the fact that guys always liked me better. I mean, you've met her, right? She's cute enough, I guess, in a nerdy sort of way, but when we were out together, I naturally got more attention than her." She shrugged. "It wasn't my fault. I wasn't deliberately trying to upstage her or anything, but you know how guys are. A girl like Debra's not going to be their first choice. And I think it really got to her after a while."

Brass could see it. Jill was a statuesque redheaded model. Debra was a brainy type who wrote ad copy for a living. He could guess which woman had her pick of the guys.

"So what happened?" he prompted.

"It just got to be too much," Jill said. "We had a big falling-out and I asked her to find someplace else to live. We didn't see each other at all for nearly a year. Then, a few weeks ago, she friended me on Facebook. Stupid me, I figured why not? I thought she was ready to make up." Her face and voice hardened. "I should have known better than to trust her again. She's still the same backstabbing jerk she always was, even with her phony new smile."

Catherine's eyes widened slightly. She leaned in toward Jill. "New smile?"

"Yeah. Deb used to have some seriously crooked teeth, before she got them fixed." Jill snickered derisively. "You should have seen her before. She looked like an overgrown chipmunk."

Catherine nodded. Brass could tell she was onto something. "She got braces? With elastics?"

"The whole nine yards," Jill said. "Which didn't exactly help her mood, you know. If anything, they just made her bitchier and more touchy about her looks. And those elastics . . ." Jill rolled her eyes. "They used to get everywhere."

"So I hear," Catherine said dryly.

Brass was curious to hear what the CSI was up to. Clearly, there was some significance to Debra's orthodontic improvements, beyond them being one more reason for Debra to resent Jill's photogenic smile. He looked forward to picking Catherine's brain in private.

But he wasn't done with Jill yet.

"Did Debra know about the gun?" he asked.

"I guess so," Jill said. "She was around for some of that bullshit with Craig." Her face flushed with anger as she put two and two together. "Oh my God, that bitch! She knew I had the gun, but she still set me up for that show!" Her fists clenched at her sides; if Jill had been bitter about the hoax before, she was positively livid now. "I'm going to kill her!"

Brass remembered the way she had lunged at Debra outside the makeup trailer. The redhead's fiery temper clearly lived up to the cliché.

"A word of advice," he counseled her. "That's probably not the kind of thing you want to say in front of a police officer."

Remembering where she was, and who she was talking to, Jill stopped and clapped a hand over her mouth. Her florid complexion subsided as she got her temper under control. "Sorry about that," she said sheepishly. "You know I wasn't serious, right? About killing her?" She tried to dig herself out of trouble. "You've got to understand, I'm just so angry about this whole thing. And the more I think about it, the more pissed off I get. I mean, how could she put me in that position, knowing everything I've been through? Do you think she did it on purpose? Seriously?"

"That remains to be determined," Brass said, declining to fan the flames of Jill's suspicions. Instead he issued her a stern warning. "You probably ought to stay away from Ms. Lusky for the time being. Don't reach out to her, don't talk to her, and don't even think about trying to get even. Let us handle this, okay?"

Jill seemed to get the message. "All right." She glanced at the door, like she was having second thoughts about coming in for this interview. "Are we almost through here? I'm not sure what else I can tell you that you don't already know."

"We're not quite done yet," Brass told her. He moved on to the next topic. "About those threatening calls, have you gotten any more of them since the incident?"

To spare her feelings, he avoided the word *shooting* this time.

"No, actually," she said with a touch of surprise in her voice, as though it hadn't occurred to her before. "In all this awfulness, I hadn't realized . . . there hasn't been a call since that night." Confused, she searched Brass's stony face for answers. "Does that mean something?"

"Maybe," he admitted. The fact that the calls had

ceased after the *Shock Treatment* tragedy suggested a connection between the two events. Perhaps the mystery calls had stopped because they'd served their purpose?

Now that Matt Novak was dead . . .

"Of course, now I'm being pestered night and day by TV reporters and the tabloids," Jill said glumly. "All wanting the inside scoop on what happened that night. Like I really want to talk about that twenty-four hours a day."

The thought crossed Brass's mind briefly that Jill might have conspired to take part in the shooting for the publicity, perhaps as part of a crazed plan to boost her stalled modeling career, but that struck him as a long shot even for Vegas. At least so far, Jill didn't seem to be in any hurry to capitalize on her newfound notoriety. If anything, she sounded like she just wanted the whole scandal to go away.

I've been there, he thought.

"I think we're almost done here," he informed her. He glanced across the desk at Catherine to see if she had any more questions. "Catherine?"

"Just one more thing." A sly smile came over the CSI's face. She turned to face Jill. "What's your Facebook password?"

"'TopModel#1'?" Brass scratched his head. "Seriously, that's her password?"

"Don't complain," Catherine said. "Just be glad that she coughed it up readily enough, and that she hasn't gotten around to unfriending Debra Lusky yet."

Jill had been sent on her way, leaving Catherine and Brass alone in her office. The cop looked over

Catherine's shoulder as she commandeered his seat and laptop to pursue a hunch. Logging in as Jill, she quickly made her way to Debra's Facebook profile–and a gallery of old photos.

"Bingo," Catherine murmured.

Sure enough, a number of old vacation photos depicted Debra wearing a full set of braces. There was even a shot of Debra and Jill together, posing atop the Stratosphere Tower at the north end of the Strip. The metal braces glinted in the bright desert sunlight. Catherine could barely make out the accompanying elastics, but she was sure they were there. A pair of glasses implied that Debra had not yet resorted to contact lenses or laser surgery. Pre-makeover, she definitely came in second to Jill where looks were concerned. Catherine wondered if that had really bothered Debra as much as Jill had maintained. The two women certainly looked like friends in the snapshot.

"Taken during happier times," Brass assumed.

"Apparently," Catherine agreed. "But check out those braces on Debra. Greg and I found the same kind of elastics scattered around Roger Park's luxury trailer-slash-love nest. I'm guessing that Debra and Park have known each other for much longer than they have let on."

"Long enough to conspire to kill Matt Novak?"

"And get back at Jill at the same time," Catherine speculated. "Settling two scores with one unfortunate 'misunderstanding.'"

"Possible," Brass said. "Nasty, but possible."

Was Debra capable of such a heartless stunt? Catherine decided Jill's number-one frenemy deserved a closer look. Noting a link to Debra's personal web page, she clicked over to check it out.

A dark violet background, adorned with black orchids, betrayed a more gothic side to the seemingly innocuous copywriter, as well as more literary ambitions. Catherine skimmed the website, surfing through pages and pages of purple poetry and prose written in flowery cursive type. "Looks like Debra fancies herself an author of sorts . . . of more than advertising copy, that is."

"What?" Brass asked sarcastically. "Hyping new brands of toothpaste doesn't satisfy her creatively?"

"Yeah. Imagine that." Catherine scrolled through Debra's online literary output. "Hmm. She seems to have a distinct taste for the macabre. Get a load of some of these titles. *Ode to a Demon Lover. Graveyard Tryst. Deliver Me to Evil. . . .*"

Brass rolled his eyes. "Slasher movies. *Shock Treatment.* Creepy poetry. Doesn't anybody just watch sports anymore?"

"Debra doesn't look like much of an ESPN fan to me," Catherine said. "But, judging from this, she might be the kind of girl who would be into playing trick-or-treat in bed."

She mentally compared Debra's photos to the unnamed zombie girl in the sex video. A biometric comparison of the *Shock Treatment* footage and the sex tape, conducted by Archie, had confirmed that Jill was not the woman in the zombie mask, but Debra . . . ? *It could be her,* Catherine thought. *Under the mask.*

Brass nodded. "I think we need to have another talk with Ms. Lusky."

"Before or after we show her a movie?"

22

THE DEAD SNAKE wasn't going anywhere.

Fully extended, it occupied a tray on the light table in the layout room. Color photos of the snake, including close-ups of its scarred hide, were mounted on the wall. Its abdomen had been stitched back up following the necropsy. Colored dyes had been employed to trace the depth and contours of the wounds. Leaning over the specimen, Ray gently double-checked the distance between the wounds with a caliper. Magnifying lenses were clipped over his regular reading classes. Concentration showed upon his face. The more he examined the scratches, the less he believed that they had been caused by another snake or a rough set of tongs.

"Spending some quality time with Coral?"

He looked up to see Sara enter the room. Like Ray, she had shown up early this afternoon to get a head start on the next round of their investigation. If they were lucky, maybe they could squeeze in dinner before their next shift officially began. "Coral?"

"Feels odd calling a snake 'Jane Doe,'" she explained. "Coral seemed like a good nickname."

"Except that the necropsy indicated that this snake was a male." Sexing a snake was a tricky business, especially when it was alive, but dissection had cleared up that mystery. A full copy of the necropsy report was spread out on the table next to the specimen. Ray flicked the magnifying lenses up away from his eyes. "Doc Robbins evicted 'Coral' from the morgue. Says he needed the biers for human casualties."

Sara nodded. "So where you keeping her . . . I mean, him?"

"The fridge in the break room," he confessed. "So far, nobody has complained." The snake was still cold to the touch. "Did you know some snake handlers refrigerate live snakes before displaying them? The cold makes them sluggish and easier to handle."

Sara shot Ray a look. "Brian Yun has a fridge in his office."

"Yes," he said. "For his 'private stash' of Snapples. It would have been the perfect place to store Coral until everyone else went home. He could have brought it to work in a cooled thermos bottle or some other container."

Fang Santana had picked Yun's photo out of a line-up, identifying the assistant manager as the individual who had illegally obtained a coral snake from him. Santana was hardly a reliable witness, however, and a good defense attorney could easily make the case that his testimony had been coerced, so Vartann was reluctant to pick Yun up just yet. Questioning Yun now would only alert him that they were onto him. More conclusive proof was required to get a conviction.

"We need to tie this snake directly to Yun," Sara said, thinking aloud. She walked over to the board and examined the photos. X-ray and fluoroscope images looked beneath the snake's scaly hide. "Any progress?"

Ray grinned. "Maybe. The placement of these scratches, as well as their depth, suggest that they may have been made by extendable claws. I'm waiting for confirmation now." He took out his cell phone and dialed the morgue. "Let me check on that."

David Phillips picked up on the second ring. "Hi, Professor," he greeted Ray. "I was just going to call you."

"Did you get those results yet?" Ray asked.

"Yep," David said. "And you were right on target. The tissue samples from the wounds tested positive for *Bartonella*."

That was bad news for Brian Yun. Ray gave Sara an encouraging nod. "Thanks, David. I appreciate you getting right on that."

"No problem, Prof," the assistant coroner replied. "Hope this helps."

"I'll let you know." Ray wrapped up the call, while Sara waited curiously. "That was David," he informed her. "Coral was infected with *Bartonella*."

The name drew a blank with her. She was a scientist, not an M.D. "Which is?"

"The bacteria responsible for cat scratch disease," he explained. "Fairly common in the feline population." Ray had treated more than a few cases of CSD over the years, mostly in small children. "The cats themselves are usually asymptomatic, but can pass the bacteria on via bites or scratches."

Sara glanced at the scarred snake carcass. "Coral was scratched by a cat?"

"From the looks of things, he had a nasty tussle with a feline not long before he ended up in the spa." Ray recalled a framed photo of a scowling Persian cat. "Brian Yun's cat died recently."

He didn't need to spell it out for her. Sara grinned back at him.

"We're going to need a warrant," she said.

23

"To be honest, I'm not sure what I can tell you that you don't already know," Debra Lusky said. "This whole episode has been a nightmare, but I told you before how it happened."

Brass and Catherine faced her across the glass-topped table in the interrogation suite. If Debra really had conspired against Jill Wooten, the intimidating environment might sweat the truth out of her. Or so he hoped.

"Just the same," he said gravely, "we'd like to go over it one more time. Frankly, there are still some details that strike us as a little fishy."

Debra squirmed nervously in her seat. Like Jill, she had dressed conservatively for her visit to the police station. A mustard pantsuit gave her a distinctly professional appearance, quite unlike the naked zombie girl in the video. "Like what?"

"Take the gun for instance," Brass began. "As Jill's former roommate, didn't you know she had a gun?"

"That was over a year ago," Debra protested, "back when she was having all that trouble with Craig. It was ancient history. Besides, how was I supposed to know that she would take a gun to a job interview? Seriously, who does that?"

"Jill, apparently." Brass jotted down Debra's response on a notepad. The session was being taped, of course, but he liked to keep his own records for easy reference. "So why didn't you mention the gun, or Jill's stalker ex-boyfriend, to the crew at *Shock Treatment*?"

"Like I said, that was ages ago. It didn't even occur to me." She sighed ruefully, a contrite expression on her face. "In retrospect, obviously, I should have remembered about the gun. I'm going to regret that till the day I die. But it honestly never crossed my mind. I didn't even realize she still had the gun, let alone that she'd be carrying it around like that."

"Too bad for Matt Novak," Brass said.

"Trust me, I feel terrible about this." She looked anxiously at Brass and Catherine. "Have you spoken to Jill? How is she holding up? I've tried to talk to her, but she's not taking my calls."

"Imagine that," Brass said.

Debra bristled at his tone. "Look, I know I screwed up. There's no need to rub it in. You can't make me feel any worse than I already do." She scooted her chair back. "If you're just going to give me attitude, maybe I'm wasting my time here."

"Let's change the subject then," Catherine said, before Debra could get up and leave. A laptop rested on the tabletop in front of her. She lifted its lid. "There's something we'd like to show you."

Debra eyed the computer apprehensively. "Is this the hidden-camera footage from that night? Because I'm not sure I want to see that again." A shudder worked its way down her all-too-average frame. "Once was enough."

"Nah," Brass assured her. "This is something else. A different kind of candid camera."

Catherine fired up the sex tape and rotated the laptop to face Debra. Brass couldn't see the screen himself, but that didn't matter. The CSIs had already shown him the video before. Right now he was more interested in watching Debra's reaction.

Which was impressive. Her eyes widened in shock. The color drained from her face as her jaw dropped open. Was she just reacting to the explicit nature of the video, he wondered, or to something more?

It was hard to tell. He trusted his gut, but he had also been a cop long enough to know that people could always surprise you. A grieving widower could turn out to be a cold-blooded killer. A slimy creep could prove to be innocent. He was a detective, not a mind reader. He had been fooled before.

Still, in his expert opinion, Debra looked more alarmed than embarrassed by the tape. And was that a flicker of fear in her eyes?

Or guilt?

She watched for less than a minute before looking away. Averting her gaze, she reached out and closed the laptop so she couldn't see the monitor anymore.

"I don't understand," she said, visibly shaken. A tremor rattled her voice. "Why would you show me that?"

Brass raised the screen back into the position. "Do you recognize the man in the video?"

Grimacing, she forced herself to watch some more of the tape. She strained to maintain a neutral expression. Her jaw looked tight enough to grind her teeth to gravel. "Is . . . is that Roger Park? From the TV show?"

"Got it the first time," Catherine said. "How long have you known Mr. Park?"

"I don't really know him at all," Debra insisted. "We met once to plan the wax museum hoax, and then again the night of the shooting, but I don't know anything about his . . . his personal life. Why should I? And what's that got to do with anything?" Her eyes widened again. "Wait a second. You don't think that's Jill in the video, do you?"

"No," Brass said. "Not Jill."

A pointed look got his implication across.

"What? You think that's *me*?" She sputtered in indignation. "You can't be serious!" She leaned forward, trying to convince him. "Look, I applied for the show the same way everyone else does, by volunteering at their website. They got in touch with me, told me they were going to be filming several episodes in Vegas, and we took things from there." She pointed at the erotic antics on the computer screen. "There was certainly nothing like *that* involved!"

Brass wasn't sure he bought her show of offense. Debra's pupils were dilated, a sure sign of dismay. She chewed nervously at her nails. Brass had interviewed a lot of guilty customers in this room. Debra looked like maybe she was on the verge of cracking.

He kept the pressure up. "What about Matt Novak? The man who died? Did you know him before that night?"

"No! Absolutely not."

"Do you know why anyone would want him dead?"

"Of course not. Don't you get it? It was an accident. A stupid, tragic accident."

"Are you sure about that?" he pressed. "Or was the whole thing a set-up to get Novak killed?"

"That's ridiculous," she protested. "Why would I do something like that? I keep telling you, I didn't know that actor . . . and I did *not* have sex with Roger Park."

Catherine weighed in. "Okay, what about you and Jill? We understand that there have been some hard feelings between you two in the past. Maybe enough to want to get her into trouble?"

"Jill is my friend," Debra insisted.

"That's not the way she tells it," Catherine said. "She says you were always jealous of her."

Debra scoffed at the notion. "That was all in her head. Look, I like Jill, but she can be a little . . . volatile sometimes. Paranoid even." Calming down a little, she settled back into her seat to explain her side of the story. "There was this one time, back before she and Craig broke up, when she got up from a nap and found Craig and I watching some old monster movie on TV. It was completely innocent, but she was convinced that we had been making out on the couch, that I was trying to steal her boyfriend or something."

"And were you?" Catherine asked.

"Not at all. But that's Jill for you. She can read

too much into things sometimes. She has a tendency to overreact to the littlest things. Kind of high maintenance, if you know what I mean." Debra looked to Brass for confirmation. "Remember how she came at me the other day, outside WaxWorkZ?"

"And yet," Catherine persisted, "you thought it was a good idea to subject your volatile, high-maintenance friend to a little *Shock Treatment*?"

"Umm." Flummoxed, the prolific writer found herself momentarily at a loss for words, as she struggled to come up with a plausible response. "That's why I thought she would be the perfect victim for the show, that she was sure to have a big reaction for the camera. I figured it would be great television, but it was just for fun. Like I said the other day, I was even hoping that it would help her modeling career. Give her a little extra exposure."

"Uh-huh," Brass said skeptically. "And you weren't trying to get back at her at all?"

"Not really." Debra caught herself gnawing on her nails and yanked her hand away from her mouth. She seemed to be unraveling before their eyes. "And even if I did have a little bit of an ulterior motive, you think I actually wanted her to *kill* someone? I just wanted to scare her, that's all. Maybe teach her a lesson about not jumping to conclusions. But it was just a stupid, practical joke. Why can't you believe that?"

Catherine shrugged. "Help us out then."

"How?"

A portable palm scanner rested on the table. Catherine turned it on. "I need your fingerprints, as well as samples of your voice and DNA."

Debra regarded her warily. "Why do you need all that?"

"Just standard procedure," Catherine lied.

Debra wasn't convinced. She eyed the humming scanner like it was a trap waiting to snare her. "Do I need a lawyer?"

"We haven't charged you with anything," Brass pointed out. "Is there any reason we should?"

"No," Debra said. "That's what I keep telling you."

"Okay." Brass leaned back in his seat, not wanting to scare Debra off. "Then why do you need a lawyer?"

Again, Debra had no ready answer.

Catherine took her silence as consent. She checked to make sure the palm scanner was online. The sleek biometric device could capture Debra's prints without any messy powders or inks. The crime lab had only been using electronic scanners for a few years now, but Catherine already considered them worth every penny she had pried out of the budget for them.

"Just place your right palm here," she instructed.

Debra drew back her hand. "Wait. I need to think about this."

"Nice poems, by the way," Brass said casually.

The unexpected remark threw Debra off-balance, just as he had planned. "My poems?" She blinked in confusion, trying to keep up. Brass guessed that she had not been prepared for the topic of her bizarre literary efforts to come up. No doubt her brain was racing to figure out how much they knew about her various extracurricular passions—and where exactly her attempts at creative writing figured into the investigation. "Which poems?"

"*Graveyard Tryst,*" Catherine supplied. "*Ode to a Demon Lover.*" She placed Debra's right hand on the scanner, palm down. The worried suspect was too distracted to make a fuss. "Hold still, please."

Debra swallowed hard as the device scanned her palm. She looked as though she would have preferred to have been eaten alive by zombies.

"All right. Here they come."

Catherine marveled at the miracles of wireless technology. Nick was miles away, checking Jill's gun box for fingerprints, but she didn't have to wait for him to drive back to the lab to get the results. An electronic chime confirmed that the prints had been beamed to her own computer. An image of a latent print appeared upon the monitor in front of her. She immediately ran them against the prints she had taken from Debra Lusky only hours ago. Labor-saving software zeroed in on corresponding arches, loops, and whorls.

"They're a match," she reported.

"How about that," Brass said, unsurprised. He lounged in a chair in Catherine's office. Several hours had passed since they had interrogated Debra at police headquarters. Moonlight and neon filtered through the window blinds. "Wonder how she's going to explain that?"

The evidence was piling up against Debra, making her look like an accomplice to more than just a harmless TV prank. Catherine made sure to save the results of the fingerprint comparison on to the hard drive. "Want to bet she peeked under Jill's bed recently, to make sure Jill still had the gun? Maybe during a 'friendly' visit to Jill's place?"

Catherine wondered if it was too late to confiscate the bed sheets from Park's trailer. She wouldn't be surprised if Debra's DNA was all over them. She kicked herself for not grabbing the sheets during her earlier search, but, of course, that was before they had stumbled across the X-rated blackmail video. There had been no reason to pry into Park's sex life before.

"Yeah. I'm liking Debra for this," Brass agreed. "But what exactly have we got so far?" He ticked off the clues on his fingers. "Debra's fingerprints on Jill's gun box. Elastics at Park's trailer. Old photos of Debra wearing braces. A masked woman in a sex tape. And a possible motive for Matt Novak's murder." He frowned. "A good lawyer could tear that apart."

"Not exactly an iron-clad case," Catherine admitted. "I ran Debra's voice samples past Archie, and he's pretty sure she didn't make those scary phone calls either."

"Too bad," Brass said. "That would have made things easier."

Catherine mentally ran through their list of suspects. "Maybe Park made the calls. He's the one who cast Novak as the chainsaw maniac, and he's who Novak may have been blackmailing." She sipped coffee from a mug Lindsey had given her two birthdays ago. "The way I see it, getting rid of Novak was the main objective. Making Jill the patsy was probably an afterthought. An extra bonus as far as Debra was concerned."

Brass nodded. "That would explain why Novak was glaring at the hidden camera when he died. He must have realized that Park had set him up to be shot."

"No wonder he tried to give him the finger," Catherine said. She would have felt like doing the same. "Now we just need to prove it."

"What about those elastics?" Brass asked. "Any way to link them directly to Debra?"

Catherine shook her head. "Wendy did her best," she said, referring to the night shift's resident DNA tech, "but she says the DNA on the elastics was too badly degraded. Time and cleaning solutions had done a number on what fragments and base pairs she found, not that there was probably much to begin with. There's no actual DNA in saliva, just trace amounts of epithelials from inside the mouth."

Brass was no scientist, but he understood that you needed a fairly complete sequence of DNA to make a reliable match. "Any idea how much time it would take for the DNA to decay that much?"

"Hard to say," Catherine said. "There are too many unknown variables. Time, heat, moisture, bacteria, chemicals, etcetera. But the degree of degradation suggests that Park and Debra may have known each other for some time, maybe even long before this whole *Shock Treatment* stunt was conceived."

"She wasn't wearing braces the night of the shooting," Brass pointed out. "Wonder when she stopped wearing them?"

"That would help fill out the timeline," Catherine said. "Assuming, of course, that those *were* Debra's elastics we found in Park's trailer—which we don't know for sure." Frustrated by their lack of conclusive proof, she pondered their next move. "You had Debra pretty rattled before. Maybe we should keep the heat on, see if we can get her to flip on Park?"

Brass mulled it over. "You think she's the weak link?"

"Maybe," Catherine said. "I wonder if she fully grasps the legal consequences here. Even if she and Park didn't actually shoot Novak themselves, if it can be proven that they deliberately conspired to get him killed, that's first-degree murder. Perhaps somebody needs to explain that to her?"

"Could work," Brass grunted, warming to the idea. "The fingerprints alone might be enough to make her crack." A ringtone chimed and he fished his cell phone from his pocket. "Excuse me," he said to Catherine as he took the call. "Brass here."

She took advantage of the interruption to sort through the accumulated paperwork on her desk, which seemed to multiply faster than maggots on a corpse, but a sudden edge to Brass's voice caught her attention.

"What?!" he demanded of the person at the other end of the line. His expression darkened and he shot Catherine a glance that made it clear that she needed to hear this. "All right. I'm on my way."

Catherine waited until he hung up. "What is it?"

"Change of plans," he said grimly. "Looks like we won't be grilling Debra Lusky after all."

"How come?"

"She was just found in Sunset Park. Shot in the head."

24

Sunset Park had been closed for hours.

The spacious public grounds usually went lights-out at eleven, but the streetlights around the tennis courts were already back on by the time Catherine and Brass met up with Nick and Greg at the crime scene, which was just a short hike away from the parking lot. Yellow tape cordoned off the vicinity. Uniformed officers stood guard. A frigid wind rustled through the palm trees. A paved footpath traversed browning swaths of lawn. Sunrise was only a few hours away, but the temperature was still too cold for comfort. A winter coat and wool cap helped Catherine hang onto her body warmth.

Unlike Debra Lusky, who was cooling rapidly.

Camera flashes strobed the night as Greg and Nick photographed the scene from multiple angles. David Phillips was already examining the body, which lay prone upon the walkway leading to the tennis courts. Her lifeless face, turned to one side, stared blankly into oblivion. The dead woman had changed clothes since her interrogation several hours ago. A black hoodie, dark pants, and leather boots made it look like she had been considering a new career as a cat burglar. A dropped flashlight had rolled away from her limp fingers. A bullet wound at the back of her skull revealed that she had been shot from behind—a ragged exit wound in her forehead lined up with the smaller injury behind it. Frozen blood glistened in her hair. Debra's newly straightened teeth appeared intact, not that they were going to do her much good anymore. Nobody was going to see her smile at her funeral.

Catherine wondered if Jill Wooten would attend.

"A security guard stumbled onto the body while doing his rounds," Nick explained. He and Greg had beaten Catherine and Brass to the scene by a few minutes. His frosty breath misted before his lips. "Apparently they've been having a problem with teenagers sneaking in after closing lately."

David knelt by the body. "COD appears to be a single GSW to the head. Stippling on the scalp indicates that the weapon was fired at close range, from less than two feet away. She probably never saw it coming."

"Time of death?" Catherine asked.

"Judging from lividity and body temperature, and taking into account that it's way too cold out tonight, I'm saying about three hours ago." He glanced at his wristwatch. "So around one a.m., more or less."

"Well after closing time, in other words." Catherine found the time and location more than a little suspicious. "Which begs the question: What exactly was she doing here at one in the morning?"

"We found her car in the parking lot," Nick informed Catherine. "A green Subaru Forester."

Catherine recalled seeing the Subaru when she arrived, parked alongside the various cop cars and the coroner's wagon. "Any other vehicles that didn't belong there?"

"Nope," Nick said. "No security cameras either."

Damn, Catherine thought. Not that she was too surprised by the lack of cameras; from the looks of things, Debra had wanted to keep things on the down-low. They would have to impound the Subaru, of course, and hope that it contained some clue as to what had brought Debra here sometime after midnight. Chances were, the killer had exited in their own vehicle, or perhaps on foot.

She glanced around for any obvious tracks, but didn't see any. Not for the first time, she regretted that Vegas's arid climate cut down on the number of muddy footprints they found. *Then again,* she reflected, *we don't often have to worry about rain washing away our evidence.*

"You think she was meeting someone?" Brass wondered aloud.

"That's what I figure." Catherine couldn't think of any other reason for Debra to visit the park under the cover of dark. "And secretly."

Brass pulled out his notepad. "Any signs of robbery?"

"Nope," Nick said. "She still had her purse and car keys on her. Ditto for her watch and jewelry."

"No evidence of sexual assault either," David

added, after rolling the body over to conduct a more thorough exam. A trickle of blood streaked her forehead. Cloudy brown eyes gazed sightlessly up at the heavens. Pooled blood had settled on the right side of her face, creating a livid pink eclipse across her features. Her clothing appeared undisturbed.

"So this probably wasn't a random mugging," Nick concluded. "Unless, I suppose, the shooter panicked and fled before looting the body."

Catherine shook her head. "Unlikely. That would be one more freaky 'coincidence' in a case that already has too many of those. No, this has something to do with Matt Novak's death. I'd bet a week's salary on it."

Brass didn't disagree. "So who would want Debra dead?"

"Good question." Catherine considered the possibilities, and an awful scenario popped into her head. "I hate to say it, but do you think maybe Jill did this? She was pretty upset at Debra—with good reason."

"Oh, crap," Brass muttered. She knew he felt sorry for Jill, who had probably been tricked into shooting a stranger. "I hope not."

"Me, too." Catherine couldn't rule out the theory, however. Unfortunately, it wouldn't be the first time an innocent crime victim decided to take the law into their own hands, with tragic consequences. Jill could have just dug herself a very deep hole. "I mean, right in front of us, she *did* threaten to kill Debra. I thought she was just blowing off steam, but . . ."

"Yeah, I know." Brass winced. "We need to find out if Jill has an alibi for tonight."

"Not to mention Roger Park," Catherine said. Jill wasn't the only suspect with a motive for killing Debra. "Maybe he's tying up loose ends?"

She found herself hoping that Park was to blame. If their suppositions were correct, Park was already responsible for one death. She wouldn't mind putting him away for Debra's murder as well.

Her gaze was drawn to the ugly exit wound in Debra's brow. "Any sign of the bullet?"

"Way ahead of you," Greg reported. He moved down the walkway to a swaying palm tree. The beam of his flashlight exposed a gaping wound in the tree trunk, around eye level. Shredded bark circled the impact site. "The security guard spotted the bullet hole after he got the lights back on. We haven't had a chance to extract the slug yet."

"No rush," Catherine said. Great care had to be taken to avoid damaging a bullet when it was being recovered; they wouldn't want to compromise any identifying marks by scratching it themselves. If necessary, they might have to cut out a chunk of the tree trunk to keep the bullet intact until they got it back to the lab. "What about any casings?"

"Haven't even looked yet," Nick admitted. "We've been busy with the body."

"Works for me."

She gave Dave the go-ahead to transport the body to the morgue. While Greg and Nick helped him load Debra onto a gurney, she tried to trace the trajectory of the bullet in her mind. Visualizing Debra standing in front of her on the walkway, Catherine lined up the shot with the tree farther down the path. Her index finger filled in for the gun

as she imagined the killer shooting Debra from behind, the bullet passing through the woman's skull
to strike the unlucky palm tree. Catherine glanced
down at the pavement beneath her feet. *Assuming
no ricochets*, she deduced, *the shooter would have been
standing right about . . . here.*

She started retracing the killer's steps back toward the main parking lot. If the shooter had indeed driven away, that was the way they would
have headed. The beam of her flashlight swept
across the ground before her in slow, deliberate
arcs. The streetlights around the tennis court lit
up much of the surroundings, but nocturnal shadows still cloaked the greenery outside the pathway.
Her eyes and flashlight carefully probed the neatly
trimmed lawn and foliage, which were showing
signs of the winter's rigor. Bare branches and brown
grass reminded her that spring was still months
away. Nick and Greg joined the search, spreading
out from the crime scene in ever-expanding circles.

A row of shrubs ran parallel to the walkway. A
metal waste bin was filled with empty soda cans,
plastic water bottles, soiled diapers, napkins, fast-
food wrappers, and other debris. Catherine made
a mental note to have the trash bagged and processed, just in case the killer had tossed something
incriminating away. It was amazing the things
people would toss in convenient garbage cans and
Dumpsters sometimes. In the past, she had recovered guns, knives, gas cans, and even the occasional
cadaver from the trash. She shuddered to think how
much valuable evidence had been lost to landfills.

And how many missing persons.

A metallic glint caught her attention, only a few feet away from where Debra's body had fallen. She replaced her winter gloves with latex ones, then knelt to investigate. "Eureka," she murmured as she spotted the distinctive gleam of a brass shell casing nestled in the bushes. In her experience, shooters rarely stuck around to clean up after themselves. They were usually in too much of a hurry to get away. "I knew you had to be around here somewhere."

Despite her excitement, she took the time to thoroughly document her find. Snapshots captured the location of the casing, as well as its proximity and orientation to the crime scene. She sketched a map of the park grounds in her notebook, noting the approximate distances involved. As was to be expected, the casing was on the right side of the path, facing toward the distant tree; most firearms ejected their empty cartridges to the right. Not until she was sure she had enough coverage did she gently retrieve the casing and place it in a clear plastic bag. Scooting away from the shrub, she stood up and walked back toward the tennis court.

"That was fast," Greg commented. He broke off his own search to join her. "You got something."

"A brass casing, to go along with the bullet in that tree." She held the transparent bag up to the light. Unfortunately, the explosive heat of the gunshot would have burned away any fingerprints, but hopefully there were still things they could learn from the shell. Ejector marks on the brass indicated that it had been fired by an automatic. "Looks like a 9 millimeter round."

Brass finished conferring with the security guard. His hands were tucked into the pockets of a heavy overcoat to keep warm. "I'm heading out to pick up Jill for questioning," he told Catherine. "You coming?"

"Definitely." She wanted to keep on top of the human element here. Handing the bagged casing over to Greg, she peeled off her latex gloves. "You and Nick finish working the scene here, then meet me back at the lab."

"Will do." Greg took custody of the shell, then looked over at the pavement where Debra's body had been found. A bloody smear was frosting over in the cold. He frowned at this brutal new development. "You really think Jill Wooten shot *another* person?"

"Could be," Catherine said. "For a 'harmless' cable show, *Shock Treatment* is racking up quite a body count."

"I'll say," he agreed. "Who knew reality TV could be so . . . real."

Catherine wondered if he was rethinking his viewing habits.

"Uh-huh," she said. "Not to mention fatal."

This time Jill Wooten got the full interrogation room treatment. They could not afford to go easy on her, not if she had actually killed her ex-roommate.

"Debra is dead?" she asked again, as though she still couldn't believe it. "No kidding?"

"This isn't another hoax," Brass said firmly. "Debra Lusky's body was found in Sunset Park earlier this morning."

"Oh my God." Jill drooped in her seat, the wind

knocked out of her. She wore a red cotton poncho over the T-shirt and sweat pants she'd had on when Brass and Catherine had knocked on her door less than an hour ago. He had been surprised to find her still up, given that it was the wee hours of the morning. She was definitely wide awake now, though. She clutched a steaming cup of coffee as she processed the news of her one-time friend's death. Jill's face was pale, but her eyes were dry. Her voice, when she spoke again, was halting. "I honestly don't know how I feel about that."

Brass found himself in the position of trying to assess her acting skills. Jill certainly appeared stunned by Debra's murder, but he couldn't forget how furious she had been at Debra less than twenty-four hours ago. *At least,* he noted, *she's not pretending to be completely broken up about it.*

Was that a point in her favor?

"I'll bet," Catherine said, sitting in on the interrogation. "You two weren't exactly the best of buds anymore."

"You know we weren't," Jill said. "Still . . . oh my God. I can't believe she's really dead."

"Lot of that going around." Brass took out his pen and notebook. "I have to ask, where were you around midnight tonight?"

Jill tensed up. "Whoa, whoa, whoa . . . you think *I* did this?"

"We're just considering every possibility," he said blandly, avoiding either sympathy or accusations. "You *did* have a motive."

She didn't deny it. "Yeah, I guess so. You got me there. But I didn't do it, I swear."

"So where were you tonight?"

"At midnight?" She didn't need to search her memory. "At home, right where you found me."

"Sleeping?"

"Hah!" She laughed bitterly. "I haven't had a good night's sleep since . . . you know when." Her haggard appearance lent credence to her claim. Dark shadows haunted her eyes, and her hair was a mess. Good bone structure notwithstanding, she wasn't likely to get many modeling jobs these days—unless they were for insomnia cures. "I was watching TV. Just had a movie on in the background. About the only way to avoid stumbling onto a news story about what happened."

Brass could believe it. The media was still having a field day with the *Shock Treatment* shooting. Even people who had never heard of the show before were following the story—and demanding that the authorities get to the bottom of things. Matt Novak had achieved in death the fame and celebrity that had largely eluded him in life, while cheesecake shots of Jill, taken over the course of her modeling career, were all over the tabloids and internet. *Just wait until the news about the sex tape leaks,* Brass thought. *The media will go thermonuclear.*

He prayed he could wrap up the case before then.

"Can anyone confirm your alibi?" he asked.

"Not really," she admitted. "I was home alone all night, hiding from the press."

Too bad the paparazzi weren't keeping watch outside, he thought. *Then we'd have some way to verify that.*

"So when was the last time you saw Debra?"

"That morning at WaxWorkZ." She cracked a

pained, humorless smile. "When you stopped me from kicking her sorry ass. That was the last time I saw her, and the last time I *ever* wanted to see her."

"We spoke with Debra yesterday," Catherine said. "She said she'd been trying to get hold of you."

"*Trying*," Jill stressed. "That doesn't mean I was taking her calls. Or answering her emails."

"Not even tonight?" Catherine showed her a cell phone in a plastic baggie. David Phillips had taken the phone off Debra's body before escorting it to the morgue. "According to her cell phone, she tried calling you several times this evening, only a few hours before her death."

Catherine wasn't bluffing, Brass knew. Judging from the phone records, Debra had started calling Jill almost as soon as she'd left this very interrogation suite. Had they arranged to meet later on, perhaps at Sunset Park after midnight?

"Yeah, sure," Jill said. "But I was screening my calls, especially where she was concerned. There was nothing she had to say that I wanted to hear." Her eyes moistened, and she choked up a little. "To be honest, I feel kind of bad about that now." For the first time, guilt showed upon the hollow angles of her face. "You think I should have given her a chance to apologize . . . ?"

Her voice trailed off as it sunk in that Debra was never going to have another chance to make amends. Brass wondered if Jill would feel better or worse if she knew that her friend had possibly tricked her into killing Matt Novak for her.

"That's not for me to say," he told her. He was a detective, not a priest.

"I don't suppose you own another gun?" Catherine asked. "Maybe a 9 millimeter automatic."

"Not a chance," Jill insisted. "I'm done with guns . . . for good." She leaned across the table. Damp emerald eyes implored Brass and Catherine. "Please, you've got to believe me. I was pissed off at Debra. I still am. No way was I ever going to forgive her for what she put me through. But I didn't want her dead."

"That's not what you said the last time we talked," Catherine reminded her. She took out a handheld digital recorder, which was already keyed up to just the right moment. She hit Play and Jill's angry voice, taped only yesterday, emanated from the recorder:

"Oh, my God, that bitch! She knew I had the gun, but she still set me up for that show! I'm going to kill her!"

Jill blanched at her words. "No, you don't understand! That was just crazy talk. I didn't mean it!"

"I want to believe that," Brass said sincerely. "But we're going to need a bit more proof."

Jill appeared desperate to clear herself. "Like what?"

"Give me your hands." Catherine prepared to test Jill's hands for gunshot residue. "And please roll up your sleeves."

She swabbed Jill's hands and lower arms, concentrating on the palms and the webbing between the thumb and trigger finger. She then inserted the swab into a small plastic cube. A plunger button broke open a glass vial inside the cube, releasing diphenylamine, a chemical reagent that would react to the presence of any particles that might have clung to Jill's skin. A positive result would turn the swab blue.

It did not change color.

"Negative," Catherine announced.

"See," Jill said, vindicated, at least in her own mind. "I told you, I didn't kill Debra."

Brass was relieved by the results of the test, even though he knew that it wasn't conclusive proof that Jill was innocent. At least four hours had passed since the murder, plenty of time for Jill to wash the GSR from her hands. And the instant hands-on test was only the first step in eliminating her as a suspect. Her clothing would also have to undergo chemical and microscopic analysis back at the lab. But at least the GSR test had not caught her red-handed.

There's still a good chance she's not our shooter.

"We'll need a sample of your hair as well," Catherine said. "Plus, whatever clothes you were wearing tonight."

"Geez," Jill complained. "You're going to end up with my entire wardrobe before this mess is over." She shrugged in resignation. "Whatever. You're not going to find anything."

No longer afraid of being arrested, she sank back into her chair. The enormity of Debra's fate seemed to creep up on her again. She sniffled and wiped her eyes. "I don't understand. Why would anyone want to kill her . . . besides me, that is." She looked to Brass for answers. "If it wasn't me, then who?"

He was asking himself the same thing.

"We're working on that."

25

"For me?" Mandy Webster quipped. "You shouldn't have."

"Very funny." Catherine carried the bagged shell casing into the fingerprint lab and placed it down on Mandy's desk. "Think of it as employment security."

Mandy was seated in front of a stack of freshly processed print cards, eyeballing them through a magnifying glass. The younger woman had been the night shift's number-one fingerprint tech for over a decade now. Tortoiseshell glasses, a lab coat, and a no-nonsense haircut gave the appearance of a serious professional scientist, an impression only occasionally belied by her wry sense of humor. Catherine figured if anyone could locate a latent print on the brass casing, it would be Mandy.

"As if I really need to worry about the crime rate dropping around here." Mandy put down the magnifying glass to inspect Catherine's latest offering. "So what do we have here?"

"A shell casing I found near the scene of the homicide in Sunset Park. It may have something to do with the *Shock Treatment* case as well." Closer examination had confirmed that the brass had come from a 9mm automatic, probably a Glock. "As usual, any fingerprints appear to have been vaporized when the bullet was fired."

"Naturally. Organic oils and salts are not going to survive being blasted from a gun. Hence, no latent prints." She gave Catherine a puzzled look. "So why bring this bad boy to me?"

Catherine jogged Mandy's memory. "Weren't you telling me about some new technique you'd read about? One that could conceivably retrieve a fingerprint even after the bullet was fired?"

"Right!" Mandy's eyes lit up behind her glasses. "The British method. I've been wanting to try that."

"Well, here's your chance," Catherine said. "Without a gun, we need to link the bullet to the suspect."

The slug itself had been badly deformed by its collision with the tree trunk, as well as its passage through Debra's skull. Although its weight and composition had verified that it was a standard 9mm Parabellum bullet, any further ballistic evidence was unlikely, even if Catherine had a suspect firearm to try to match it to. Which she didn't.

"This suspect have sweaty hands, by any chance?" Mandy asked. "That will increase our odds of success."

Catherine remembered shaking Roger Park's greasy palm. "I don't think that's going to be a problem."

"Good to hear." Mandy sounded enthused by the task at hand. "I like a challenge, but every little bit helps." She gingerly inspected the casing. "Me, of course, I would have just worn gloves when I loaded the gun."

Catherine arched an eyebrow. "Is that so?"

"Don't give me that look," Mandy said, not at all contrite. "I have to think about something when AFIS is running slow—nobody can work on homicides forty-plus hours a week without developing very definite opinions on the best ways to knock someone off." She peered over the rims of her glasses at Catherine. "Like you've never plotted the perfect murder in your head?"

"Only when Ecklie is on my case," Catherine confessed.

"That often, then," Mandy said. Her point made, she turned her attention back to the casing, shoving her stack of print cards aside. "All right. Let me see what I can do."

"Thanks!" Catherine said. "Do me a favor and don't carry out any of your diabolical plans before you get around to it."

Mandy smirked back at her. "No promises."

Debra Lusky's apartment was located in the basement of a refurbished town house in the University District. The landlady helpfully let Greg and Nick onto the premises once they explained the circumstances. The morning sun had already dispelled last night's frigid cold. Greg wasn't sure he even needed his windbreaker.

"In the park?" the older woman echoed. Helen

Yost was a retired nurse who occupied the floor above Debra's basement digs. The petite, gray-haired senior citizen reminded Greg of his Nana Olaf. "What in heaven's name was she doing there?"

"We're still looking into that," Greg divulged. While Nick made his way downstairs, Greg lingered in the ground-floor foyer to question Mrs. Yost, in hopes that she could provide some insight into Debra's recent activities. "Did she live alone?"

"As far as I know," Yost said. "I don't pry into my tenants' personal lives. Long as they pay the rent, and don't set the place on fire, I don't care what they get up to. No pets, though. I'm allergic."

He mentally filed that factoid away, relieved that he and Nick would not be running into any orphaned four-leggers this morning. A zealous watchdog, or even a freaked-out kitty, could seriously complicate a search of a domicile. He had the scars to prove it.

"Did you see Ms. Lusky yesterday?" he asked. Their timeline had her leaving police headquarters late in the afternoon. Now they needed to fill in the blanks between her interrogation and her death in the park approximately nine hours later. "Maybe in the evening?"

"Afraid not," Yost said. "I turned in early. Slept like the dead." She caught what she was saying and placed a hand to her lips. "Sorry. Bad choice of words."

"Don't worry about it." Greg handed her a card. "If you remember anything, please give us a call."

"All right, young man."

She started to follow him downstairs, but he held up his hand. "We can take it from here, ma'am. Thanks for your cooperation."

Visibly disappointed, she retreated up the steps. He lugged his field kit into the basement apartment, where Nick was already doing a preliminary walk-through. Greg was careful not to disturb anything. Even though the apartment was not a crime scene, it might contain evidence that could point to Debra Lusky's killer—or perhaps her involvement in Matt Novak's death.

Nick looked up as Greg entered. "The old lady tell you anything?"

"Not really." Greg put down his field kit in the entry. "She's not exactly the proverbial nosy land-lady, too bad for us. Apparently, Debra lived alone, though."

"Looks like it," Nick confirmed. "This place is def-initely smaller than the apartment she used to share with Jill Wooten." He opened a closet door. "No men's coats in sight."

Greg looked around. The cluttered basement was pretty basic in its layout: a smallish TV room with an attached kitchenette took up most of the space. Open doors led to a single bedroom, bathroom, and home office. Judging from the lack of housecleaning, Debra had not been expecting company. "I don't suppose you stumbled onto a rubber zombie mask yet?"

"We should be so lucky." Nick grinned at Greg from the bedroom door. "So how was the rest of that video?"

"Don't ask," Greg said. After perusing the sex

tape frame-by-frame, he was glad to be back in the field again. "I'll never be able to watch a zombie movie the same way again, I can tell you that."

Nick had a chuckle at Greg's expense. "I'll take your word for it. You discover anything useful?"

"Just that hidden cameras catch some pretty unflattering angles sometimes." He grimaced at the unappetizing images burned into his brain. "No convenient tattoos, scars, or identifying marks . . . although I did manage to calculate Zombie Girl's height with relation to the bed and headboard. She's shorter than Jill Wooten, but has approximately the same build as Debra Lusky."

"Along with several thousand other women in Vegas alone," Nick observed. "And that's assuming the trailer was here in Nevada when that encounter was filmed, which might not be the case. For all we know, Park hooked up with Zombie Girl at another location in a different city."

"True enough." Greg didn't want to think that he had wasted his time poring over the sex tape, but that was the nature of the job sometimes. You had to go down some blind alleys, and bump into plenty of dead ends, before you found the right path. He glanced around the apartment. "Here's hoping this place is more informative."

"Only one way to find out," Nick said. His gloved hands sliced up the apartment with decisive chopping motions, like a quarterback calling a play. "I'll take the bed and bathroom. You check out the living room and office. First one done gets the kitchen."

"Aye, aye. So what exactly are we looking for?"

Nick disappeared into the bedroom. "Anything that might connect Debra to Roger Park," he called out. "Or explain what she was doing in the park last night."

"Both would be good," Greg said. "Or is that hoping for too much?"

Nick's voice escaped the open doorway. "Probably."

Yeah, Greg thought. *It's never that easy.*

He pulled on his gloves and got to work, starting with the living room, where a dark velvet couch faced a modestly sized entertainment center. Newspapers and magazines were piled haphazardly on a wicker coffee table in front of the couch. Greg noticed that many of the periodicals were folded open to articles on the *Shock Treatment* shooting, almost as though Debra had planned to start a scrapbook.

"Has reality tv gone too far?" asked an editorial in the *Las Vegas Review-Journal*. A bikini-clad Jill Wooten occupied the cover of a supermarket tabloid that billed her as "The Deadly Beauty at the Heart of the TV Chainsaw Massacre." Somebody, Greg noted, had drawn an angry black "X" over Jill's face. A Magic Marker lay on the coffee table next to the newspapers. Debra's fingerprints were probably all over it.

Okay, he thought. *No bad blood there.*

He turned his attention to the couch. A thought occurred to him and he lifted a seat cushion to expose some loose change, a misplaced pencil, the TV remote . . . and a tiny rubber band just like the ones he'd found scattered around Roger Park's trailer.

"Found another elastic," he called to Nick.

"Me, too," Nick shouted back. "Under the dresser."

Granted, they'd already known that Debra used to wear braces, but Greg felt like they were on the right track. In his experience, there was often a tipping point in an investigation when, after the usual false starts and slow progress, things finally started to come together in a big way. Were they reaching that point in this case?

He wanted to think so.

The rest of the living room proved less revelatory. To Greg's disappointment, there was no obvious evidence that Roger Park, or anyone else, had visited lately. Debra obviously hadn't straightened up for a while, but, given all the recent drama in her life, that was to be expected. Several episodes of *Shock Treatment* were recorded on her DVR, but, again, that was hardly a smoking gun. He had actually recorded some of the same episodes himself.

He moved on to the office, which looked like it had once been a smaller guest bedroom. Overstuffed bookshelves sagged under the weight of numerous hardcovers and paperbacks. A rolling office chair was parked in front of a computer desk. Cables connected a newish PC to a laser printer under the desk. A beat-up file cabinet occupied one corner. Post-Its, index cards, and yellow legal pads littered the work area. Paperwork was pinned to a bulletin board. A bronze trophy, in the shape of a crescent moon, occupied a position of honor atop the file cabinet. A shredder was perched atop a plastic waste bucket. All in all, a pretty standard home office.

Eventually, the computer would have to be

packed up and carted off to the lab, so they could conduct a thorough forensic examination of Debra's emails and web searches. Greg began, however, by scanning the titles on her bookshelves. An aspiring author himself, whose magnum opus on the hidden history of Las Vegas was still seeking an enthusiastic publisher, he was always interested in checking out other people's libraries.

You are what you read, he thought. *Or so Amazon tells us.*

His curious gaze glided over the usual reference works you'd expect to find in a writer's office: dictionaries, thesauri, a couple of atlases and almanacs, *Bartlett's Familiar Quotations*, Strunk & White, and so on. His survey paused on what appeared to be an entire shelf devoted to a single author, one "D. L. Dakota." The name didn't ring any bells, but Debra was clearly a fan. She had multiple copies of Dakota's books, which appeared to be paperback romances with a supernatural bent. He pulled out a pristine copy of one novel, *Immortal Passion*, whose spine looked like it had never been cracked. The cover depicted a lithe young woman wearing tight leather pants and a laced corset, silhouetted against a luminous full moon, which was partially obscured by stormy black clouds. Bright red eyes gazed hungrily from the shadowy depths of the cloud. An embossed metallic-gold starburst proudly billed the author as a past winner of the "Moonsong Award for Best Undead Romance."

Wait a second, he thought. Turning away from the shelf, he took a closer look at the trophy on the file cabinet. An inscription on the base read:

BEST UNDEAD ROMANCE
2008
KISSES AND CURSES
D. L. DAKOTA

Greg put two and two together. He glanced back at all the D. L. Dakota paperbacks on display. *That's not a collection,* he realized. *That's a brag shelf.*

"Hey, Nick!" he hollered. "Come check this out."

The other CSI responded quickly. He strolled into the office, holding up a plastic baggie containing yet another elastic. "Look what I found behind the bathroom door."

Greg shrugged, well over the orthodontic evidence already. He sorted through the papers on Debra's desk, uncovering a partial manuscript beneath the general clutter. Red pencil marks indicated that it was a work-in-progress. He hastily perused the title page, then thrust it at Nick. "Get a load of this."

"What've you got?" Nick read the first page aloud. "'Zombie Heat: The Thin Gray Line'."

Greg spelled it out for him. "It's a script for the new TV show. By D. L. Dakota."

Nick gave him a puzzled look. "Who is?"

"Debra Lusky's pen name," Greg explained. "Or so it appears." He showed Nick the bulging brag shelf. "Looks like she wrote paranormal romances under a pseudonym."

"Paranormal romances?" Nick asked, clearly unfamiliar with the genre. Greg couldn't recall ever seeing Nick reading a novel for pleasure. Just nonfiction and history.

"You know," he said. "Boy gets girl. Vampire gets werewolf. Witch gets sexy hot guy."

Nick got the picture. "Zombie gets TV producer?"

"Bingo." Greg handed *Immortal Kisses* to Nick. "Not quite a zombie mask, but definitely working the same graveyard vibe."

Nick nodded, making the same connection. "And the *Zombie Heat* script sure implies another link to Park. Maybe he promised her a TV sale in exchange for her help getting rid of Novak?"

"Could be," Greg said. "Or perhaps she was just trying to capitalize on a certain illicit relationship." He fired up the computer. "Wanna bet we find more of D. L. Dakota's deathless prose on Debra's hard drive?"

"Sounds like a safe bet to me."

While the computer was booting up, Greg took a closer look at the brag shelf. He noticed that the shelf wasn't entirely full; there was an empty gap between *Kisses and Curses* and *Prowling for Love*. He ran a finger over the exposed fiberboard. "No dust. Like there was another book here until just recently."

"Wonder where it went," Nick said. Inspecting the desk, he pulled out a drawer under the keyboard and took out a small pile of correspondence. He sifted through the mail, piece by piece.

Greg tried to make out the return addresses on the envelopes. "Anything from Park?"

"Nope," Nick reported. "Just bills, mostly. Gas, electric, cable . . . hang on." He extracted a single letter from an already opened envelope and unfolded it before his eyes. "Okay, this might be something."

"What is it?"

Nick held up the bill so Greg could see. The letterhead atop the invoice read "24/7 Storage—Safe and Secure."

"Looks like Debra was renting a storage unit." Nick took a second look at the address. "Only a few miles from here."

Greg grinned. They were teetering right on the brink of that tipping point; he could feel it. "I think I know where we're going next."

26

"HELLO, MR. YUN," Ray said. "I hope we're not disturbing you."

Brian Yun lived in a modest stucco house several miles and income brackets away from The Nile. Spanish tile adorned the roof. A fashionably xeriscaped front yard flaunted cacti, agave, and other desert blooms in lieu of a grassy lawn. Only a birdbath required more than Vegas's annual four inches of rain.

"Dr. Langston? Ms. Sidle?" He looked surprised to find them on his doorstep. His casual attire consisted of a polo shirt, slacks, and loafers. A uniformed police officer accompanied the CSIs. Classical music played softly in the background. Yun appeared to have been enjoying a quiet evening at home before they arrived. "What are you doing here?"

Sara presented him with the papers. "We have a warrant to search the premises."

It might not be enough to convict him, but Santana's identification of Yun as the man to whom he had sold the coral snake had been enough to convince Judge Kim to issue a warrant. Especially once they explained what they were after.

"Search?" Yun's eyes grew wide. "I don't understand. What are you looking for?"

"It's all spelled out in the warrant." Sara pushed past him into the foyer. "Now, if you'll just step outside with this officer."

"Wait! Wait!" he protested. He leafed frantically through the documents, before being daunted by all the legalese. His eyes remained bugged out in horror as Ray followed Sara into the house, carrying his field kit. He hurried after them. "Stop! I need to call my lawyer."

"Go ahead," Ray said. "In the meantime, we're going to get started. We may have a long night ahead of us."

He frankly doubted that they would find anything incriminating inside the house itself. Nearly a week had passed since Rita Segura had been bitten; there had been plenty of time to clean house. Prudence dictated that they conduct a full search anyway, after they dug up what they were really looking for. Who knows? Maybe they would get lucky.

"Start with the backyard?" Sara suggested.

Ray nodded. "My thoughts exactly."

"Wait! Where are you going?" Yun looked positively bewildered. Breaking away from the uni, he chased after the CSIs. "What do you want with my backyard?"

"Excuse me, sir," the cop took hold of Yun's arm. Her badge identified her as ORTEGA. Her tone brooked no dissent. "You need to come with me."

"It's all right, officer." Ray wanted to observe Yun's reaction to what they had planned. "You can let him watch."

"Just stay out of the way," Sara warned. "You got that?"

A sliding glass door separated the living room from the fenced-in backyard. Ray glanced around the living room as they passed through it. An even larger portrait of Fala, Yun's late Persian, was displayed upon the mantel of a largely decorative fireplace. He nudged Sara, calling her attention to the photo. With any luck, Yun's sentimental attachment to his cat extended to its burial arrangements.

Ortega kept watch over Yun as the party stepped out into the yard, which was just as tidy as his office back at The Nile. The light from inside illuminated much of the xeriscaped grounds and gardens, surrendering to shadows farther on by the fence. Tasteful terra-cotta statuary stood among the cacti. Patio furniture rested in the shadow of a large red umbrella. Ray swept the area with his flashlight. Sara did the same.

It was a cool night, but Yun was already perspiring. He ran a shaky hand through his thinning hair. "This is crazy," he objected. "Maybe if you just tell me what you're looking for?"

Ray saw no reason to keep it secret. "Your cat Fala's grave. Care to point it out?"

"Over here," Sara said, beating Yun to the punch. "I think I found it."

The beam from her flashlight exposed a small ceramic monument, in the shape of a dozing kitten, nestled in one corner of the yard. A small selection of cat toys, including a green plastic ball and a catnip pillow, lay atop a tiny mound of earth.

Despite their somber mission, Ray was oddly moved by the obvious care and affection shown by the memorial. It was a shame they had to disturb it, but evidence was evidence. Too bad Yun allegedly hadn't shown as much respect for the life of another human being.

"I'll get the shovel," he told Sara.

"Shovel?" Yun gasped as he realized what Ray had in mind. "You can't. That's obscene!" He started to lunge forward. Ortega's hand dropped heavily onto Yun's shoulder, restraining him. Yun could only quiver helplessly, visibly distraught. "I won't allow it!"

"I'm afraid you don't have any choice," Sara stated. "If you look carefully, you'll see that our warrant entitles us to exhume your cat's remains."

"Why are you doing this?" he moaned, his eyes tearing up.

Ray was brutally honest. "We need to know exactly how Fala died."

27

GETTING A WARRANT to search Debra Lusky's storage unit proved easy enough. Now that she was a murder victim as well as a suspect, protecting her privacy took a backseat to finding her killer.

"Here we go," Nick said to Greg as he opened the unit. A pair of industrial-strength bolt cutters took care of the padlock keeping them out. A corrugated steel door rattled up and out of the way, exposing a rectangular vault roughly the size of Nick's laundry room. Cardboard boxes and sealed plastic bins were piled neatly atop each other in order to take full advantage of the available space, alongside a set of dusty exercise equipment, a ten-speed bike, an artificial Christmas tree, and a peeling wooden rocking chair. No dead bodies, though, which put it up on some of the storage units Nick had probed over the years. The air inside the vault, although stale and stuffy, lacked the sour aroma of decomp.

The beams of their flashlights explored the unlit

interior of the unit as they stepped inside. Nick was relieved to see that the vault was only about five by ten. In theory, it wouldn't take too long to search. Even better, the boxes and bins appeared to be clearly labeled.

"A lot more organized than her office," Greg observed. "Sure we got the right unit?"

Nick double-checked the number on the invoice. "This is the place. Guess she just wanted to be able to find all of this stuff again, without having to search through every box."

"Too bad we can't say the same," Greg said. "Unless there's a box conveniently labeled 'Material Evidence'?"

Nick chuckled. "You wish."

In truth, the space was small enough that they didn't really need two CSIs to conduct a thorough search, but it was always better to have a second person to verify any significant discoveries. An investigator operating alone could be too easily accused of planting evidence by an eager-beaver defense attorney. Two CSIs, on the other hand, meant implying a conspiracy, which was a bit harder for juries to swallow.

Nick swept his flashlight beam over the hand-written labels, scanning them along the way:

"High School."

"College."

"Vacation."

"Author Copies."

"Quilts."

"Xmas Ornaments."

"Z.H."

Whoa there, he thought. His beam came to a halt on that last label. "Z.H." he read aloud. "Think that could be short for *Zombie Heat*?"

"More likely than 'Zygotic Helixes,'" replied Greg. He turned his own beam on the container in question, which was a brown cardboard box sealed with masking tape. It rested near the front of the storage space, on top of several flat plastic bins labeled "Tax Receipts/Returns." He walked over and squinted at the carton. "Is it just me, or does this package look newer than some of these other boxes?"

Nick was inclined to agree. The cartons nearer the rear of the unit looked scuffed and battered to various degrees, as though they had been shoved around more than once. There were even traces of dust and cobwebs on the older-looking containers. By contrast, the "Z.H." box appeared freshly packed. "Wonder how long it's been sitting here?"

"Not very long," Greg guessed. "Looks like a recent addition."

Camera flashes lit up the murky vault as they recorded the box's location for posterity, before proceeding to investigate its contents. Greg kept his flashlight on the box while Nick sliced open the masking tape with an Exacto knife. He tugged open the top flaps.

Inside was at least a dozen copies of *Zombie Heat,* "a novelization by Lucia Duske, based on the original screenplay by Roger Park." The lurid cover was basically just the movie poster, shrunk down to size.

Nick eyed the paperbacks dubiously. "There was a book?"

"Adapted from the original movie, apparently." Greg helped himself to the top copy. He peered at the byline. "'Lucia Duske.' Maybe another pseudonym?"

"Probably," Nick said. "But why are these tucked away here, and not on display in her office along with her other books?"

"To hide her prior association with Roger Park, just in case we came knocking on her door?" Greg stepped back toward the sunlight outside, the better to peruse the novelization. "Remember that empty gap on her bookshelf? Maybe she got spooked after Catherine and Brass grilled her and decided to bury the evidence?"

Nick nodded. "Makes sense. Guess she was hoping we'd never make the connection between Debra Lusky and 'Lucia Duske.'"

"And that's not all," Greg said. "Look what I just found pressed between the pages of this copy."

He handed a color photo to Nick, who examined it under the glare of his flashlight. The snapshot showed a smiling Debra, braces and all, posing in front of Grauman's Chinese Theater in Hollywood. A lighted marquee advertised the world premiere of *Zombie Heat*. Debra proudly held up a copy of the novelization for all the world to see.

"Okay, I can see why she'd want to hide this," Nick said. "Even if she couldn't bring herself to destroy it."

"The book is autographed, too," Greg said. "Want to take a wild guess by whom?"

"Roger Park?"

"Give that man a prize."

Greg handed the book over to Nick, who checked out the title page for himself. *Great job!* was scribbled across the page, above Park's flamboyant signature.

Nick grinned. The circumstantial evidence was piling up faster than *Zombie Heat*'s box office returns. He inspected the copyright date, which was over three months ago.

"So much for Debra and Roger not meeting until recently," he concluded. "It's pretty clear they've known each other, and then some, long before they hatched that *Shock Treatment* stunt together."

Greg completed the thought for him. "Which means Debra could have told Park all about Jill's creepy stalker boyfriend . . . and the gun she'd bought to defend herself."

"Giving them a convenient way to dispose of Matt Novak and his blackmail threats," Nick said. The pieces were definitely coming together. "Now all we need to do is find that zombie mask."

Greg stepped back to contemplate the daunting accumulation of junk before them.

"Okay," he said. "Let's get digging."

28

RAY WAS STARTING to feel like a vet. Or perhaps the manager of a pet cemetery.

The cold remains of Fala the cat were laid out on a table in the prep room outside the morgue. Although this was ordinarily David Phillip's domain, he had opted to recuse himself from this particular examination; the helpful assistant coroner was allergic to felines.

Even dead ones.

The arid desert climate, and frigid nights, had helped to preserve the specimen at least to a degree. After a week or so in the ground, Fala bore little resemblance to the fluffy, well-groomed pet in Brian Yun's photo collection. Most of his fur had sloughed off, leaving behind a shriveled, brownish-black carcass. Dry, leathery skin was stretched tightly over the cat's skeleton. Marbled green veins protruded beneath the hide. Ray suspected that the internal organs had already turned to sludge. Determining the cause of death was going to be difficult, but not impossible. Plastic wrap, lovingly taped around the corpse, had largely protected Fala from the elements and insects. Ray smiled grimly behind a surgical mask. Brian Yun might have cause to regret the care with which he had buried his precious Persian.

Nice of him to gift wrap the evidence for us.

Wintergreen oil, rubbed beneath Ray's nostrils, counteracted the foul odor emanating from the carcass. He peeled away the last of the hair around Fala's neck and front legs. According to his research, that was where cats and dogs were most often bitten by agitated snakes. The blackened skin resisted examination, so he deftly removed it to expose the underlying dermis; as was often the case, the inner layer had not decayed as quickly as the outer epidermis. At first, he didn't see anything, but polarized light exposed a faint, horseshoe-shaped discoloration on the cat's withered paw. The shape and size of the bruise reminded him of the bite marks he had measured on Rita Segura. He took multiple snapshots of the mark and collected a sample of the mottled dermis. A microtome could later be used to slice the sample into segments thin enough to be mounted on microscope slides. With luck, histology might find signs of tissue damage caused by the venom.

A mental image of cat versus snake played across his mind. Fala scratching Coral's back with its extended claws, only to squawk in panic as the coral snake's jaws latched onto his paw. Had Brian Yun come running at the sound of the commotion, or had he returned later to find his beloved pet already dead? Had the snake gotten loose somehow, or had the curious cat somehow managed to get his paw into the snake's cage?

Ray suspected the latter.

But the bite marks, if that was what they were, were only the icing on the cake. Most of his hopes lay elsewhere, in Fala's opaque, clouded eyes. He was relieved to see that the frozen eyes were only partially desiccated. It was too late to try to obtain blood or urine from the corpse, but the vitreous humor within the eyes was fairly resistant to putrefaction; it often survived even when the rest of the body was badly decomposed. Using a syringe, he extracted a few cc's of the clear, thick fluid and transferred it to a sterile tube.

Next stop: toxicology.

Fortunately, they already had an exemplar of the poison in question. All the gas chromatograph/mass spectrometer needed to do was match the chemical compounds.

And then, like Poe's fabled black cat, Fala might expose a criminal.

29

"You know what the problem with zombies is?" Catherine asked. "They don't stay buried."

She flung the rubber mask onto the table in front of Roger Park and his lawyer. The producer flinched at the sight of it. The stark decor of the interrogation suite was a far cry from his luxurious trailer, and Park appeared much less at ease in this inhospitable setting. He swallowed hard. "Where did you get that?"

"Debra Lusky's personal storage unit," Brass stated. "Carefully wrapped in tissue paper and tucked away in a box of personal memorabilia." He cracked a wry smile. "Who knew zombies could be so sentimental?"

"Not to mention murderers." Catherine held the mask up so that Park could get a better look at its worm-eaten features, previously seen in close-up on the infamous zombie sex tape. Park had been confronted with the video footage only moments earlier. "Look familiar?"

The attorney, a silver-haired smoothie named Arthur Chou, placed a restraining hand on his client's arm. Chou had a reputation for getting Hollywood celebrities out of trouble; he had once managed to get an A-list date rapist acquitted despite a surfeit of DNA evidence. "Don't answer that."

Brass ignored the lawyer, keeping Park in his sights. "Maybe we should ask your wife if she recognizes the mask . . . or the woman in the video."

"No!" Park blurted. "You can't! She'd ruin me!"

"Quiet," Chou counseled Park again. He dismissed Brass's threat with a wave of a well-manicured hand. "I fail to see the relevance of my client's personal life. I was under the impression this was a murder investigation, not divorce proceedings."

Catherine was unimpressed by the lawyer's haughty attitude. "I think your client just did a pretty good job of demonstrating its relevance. Mr. Park's career would suffer if his wife found out he was cheating on her. That gave him a motive to dispose of Matt Novak—and Debra Lusky."

"We did our homework," Brass elaborated. "Seems Tricia Grantley has a controlling interest in the whole *Zombie Heat* franchise." He gazed knowingly at Park. "She could kill all your big TV plans if she felt like it."

Park blanched at the prospect. Perspiration beaded on his forehead. "Look," he began, over Chou's protests, "I admit I had a thing with Debra. We met at the *Zombie Heat* premiere and, what can I say, we just clicked. There was this amazing chemistry between us. . . ."

"You mean you both liked your sex good and creepy," Catherine translated.

Park glared at her. "That's not a crime."

"So why didn't you mention this to us before?" Brass asked.

"It's just like you said," he answered. "We were trying to keep my wife from finding out, for all sorts of personal and professional reasons." He wiped his sweaty brow with a silk handkerchief. "I had enough catastrophes to deal with after the shooting, and telling you about my affair with Debra was not going to bring Matt back. After all, it didn't have anything to do with Matt's death."

"Even though Novak died with a copy of the video on his person?" Brass was openly skeptical. "Here's what I think happened. Your old drinking buddy somehow got hold of one of your kinky home movies. Maybe he lifted it off your computer. Or maybe you even showed it to him in a careless moment."

Stranger things had happened, Catherine mused, especially where Hollywood types were concerned. According to this movie she'd seen on cable once, Bob Crane, the one-time star of *Hogan's Heroes*, had frequently taped himself having one night stands with groupies, then shared the videos with a long-time crony of his. Come to think of it, that had ended in murder too. . . .

"But then," Brass continued, "Novak decides to blackmail you into making him a star. So you decide to get rid of him in a convenient 'accident.' And, lucky for you, Debra knows just the right person to squeeze the trigger for you. Her old frenemy, Jill Wooten."

"That doesn't make sense," Park protested. "If

I was in cahoots with Debra, why would I kill her, too?" He placed a hand over his heart, feigning grief. "Believe me, what we had was very special."

"Not special enough," Catherine accused him. "Not once she started cracking under the pressure. We interrogated her roughly nine hours before she was murdered, and she was pretty stressed out by the end of the questioning, almost like she was on the verge of coming clean." Catherine could see how it all played out. "I'm thinking she called you in a panic, probably on one of those disposable cell phones you harassed Jill with, and you realized you couldn't depend on her silence anymore."

Brass picked up the narrative. "Of course, there was no time for anything tricky or elaborate this time. So you just arranged to meet her in the park . . . and shot her in the head when her back was turned."

Park started to object, but Chou cut him off. "You two missed your callings, you know that? You should have been screenwriters." He scoffed at their theory. "It's a colorful story, but it's all just supposition. Prove it."

Catherine met his cocky smirk with one of her own. "We're working on it."

"Is that all?" the lawyer demanded. "Are we done here?"

"Just one more thing," she said.

"What's that?"

Catherine took out her cell phone. "I'd like to hear your client say 'nuclear.'"

30

"I DON'T UNDERSTAND what I'm doing here," Brian Yun complained. "I haven't done anything wrong."

An interrogation room at police headquarters was probably the last place the soft-spoken assistant manager was used to spending Sunday night in. He had no police record; this was his first documented brush with the law. He fidgeted nervously in his seat, across the table from Ray and Sara. Vartann had been called away to investigate a drive-by shooting in Pahrump, but Ray figured they finally had enough evidence to pin the snake attack on Yun. A confession would wrap things up nicely.

"Really?" he said skeptically. "Then perhaps you can explain how it is that we found coral snake venom in your cat's remains. Venom identical, by the way, to that produced by the snake that bit Rita Segura."

Gas chromatography and the mass spectrometer had both confirmed that the venom samples were chemically identical. The toxicology reports rested in a folder in front of Ray, along with various photos and statements. Yun looked anxiously at the bulging folder, just like he was supposed to. He had to be wondering what else they knew.

"Guess Fala didn't like having a snake in the house," Sara said. "What happened? Sometime when you weren't looking, the cat got at the snake? Which then retaliated?"

Once again, Ray pictured a moment of hissing, snarling chaos. "A tragic turn of events for Fala. I'm sure you were quite broken up about it, but not enough that you abandoned your plan to sneak the venomous snake into the vivarium at The Nile."

"Why would I do something like that?" Yun argued unconvincingly. He glanced over at the one-way mirror, as though worrying who else might be listening. "There must be some sort of mistake."

"I don't think so," Ray said. He opened the file and slid a photo across the table. The color glossy was an enhanced close-up of the bite marks on Fala's moldering remains. Yun gagged at the photo and looked away. Afraid that he might throw up, Ray reclaimed the picture and tucked it back into the folder. He assumed he had made his point. "Fala was bitten by a snake. A coral snake."

Yun swallowed hard. "Maybe . . . maybe it was a different snake." He groped for an alternative explanation. "She must have been bitten in the yard, when she was playing outside. I didn't realize . . . I thought she had just died of natural causes."

"Unlikely," Ray pronounced. "Coral snakes are not native to Nevada."

Yun's hopes faded. "A rattler?" he suggested feebly.

Ray shook his head. "Completely different kind of venom."

"There's more," Sara added. "We know you bought the snake from Fang Santana. He identified your photo. We can put you in a lineup if necessary, but why drag this out." She ticked off the evidence on her fingers. "We know the snake was in your house. We know who you bought it from. All we need now is the why."

Ray offered Yun a sympathetic ear. "You never wanted to hurt Ms. Segura, did you? That wasn't the plan. You were after your boss. She's the one who was supposed to get bitten, wasn't she?"

"Of course!" Yun threw up his hands in surrender. "She always had her massage every Monday morning, just like clockwork. How was I supposed to know that Rita was going to show up and take her place? I wasn't even there that morning to stop her. I came in late on purpose, so nobody would think I had anything to do with it." Tears streamed down his face. "You have to believe me! I never wanted anybody else to get hurt!"

"But why Madame Alexandra?" Sara asked. "What did she ever do to you?"

Yun looked surprised by the question. "Are you serious? You've met her, haven't you?" Bitterness curdled his face and voice. "She swans around, treating me like a servant, even though The Nile would fall apart without me. I do all the work, and she takes all the credit . . . and all the money. She should've made me her partner years ago, but I'm still just a doormat as far as she's concerned." He snapped his fingers while doing a cruel impression of his imperious boss. "'Oh, Brian! Come here, Brian! Take care of this, won't you, Brian?'"

Obviously, he had been nursing a heavy-duty grudge for some time. "You could have just quit," Sara observed.

"And let her reap the rewards of my creativity?" he scoffed. "The success of the serpentine massages was the last straw. I told you before, that was all *my* idea. But did I even get a bonus or a cut of the profits? Of course not! Instead she acted like the whole notion sprang from her own deep spiritual wisdom, spouting off about the sublime healing properties of snakes." He laughed harshly. "*I* pulled all that bullshit off the internet for her!"

Sara still didn't get it. "So you decided to kill her?"

"No!" Yun exclaimed. "I just wanted to scare her, maybe make her sick for a while. I looked it up: coral snake venom usually takes hours to take effect. I figured she'd make it to the emergency room in time . . . but not before she got a taste of her own medicine."

"I see." Ray wasn't sure if he believed that Yun expected Madame Alexandra to survive, but it didn't really matter. Yun had shown a reckless disregard for human life; it would be up to the district attorney's office if they wanted to press for attempted murder. "Well, you lucked out in one respect," he informed Yun. "I just heard from the hospital. Rita Segura has finally regained consciousness and is breathing on her own again. She's going to need plenty of observation and follow-up, but she's expected to make a full recovery in time."

"Good thing," Sara told Yun. "Otherwise, you might have been looking at a lethal injection of a different sort."

31

"So how does this work again?"

Nick watched with interest as Mandy Webster set up her experiment. She placed the shell casing at the end of a short wooden wand. The rest of her apparatus was set up in a cardboard box lined with aluminum foil. A metal contact plate was wired to a 2,500-volt battery. Nearby a metal scoop, with a wooden handle, rested atop a tray of fine black powder.

"It's pretty ingenious," Mandy enthused. "Ordinary fingerprinting techniques require some sort of sweaty residue to be left on the metal, but this British inventor, Dr. John Bond, has developed a technique that can sometimes retrieve prints even after they've been wiped or burned away. It's based on the idea that the salt in the original fingerprints actually corrodes the metal underneath. That corrosion remains even after the sweaty prints are gone."

"And the sweatier the hands, the deeper the corrosion?" Nick remembered reading something about the process in a forensic journal.

"Yep," Mandy said. "Good thing most people tend to get a little nervous when they're planning to murder someone."

She flicked a switch and placed the casing against the electrical terminal. The wooden wand kept her from being shocked herself, although she was also wearing rubber gloves just to be safe. "The corroded areas are too small to be seen by the naked eye, as in microns," she continued, "but they pick up less of an electrical charge than the clean brass."

She scooped up a small quantity of the black powder and sprinkled it over the casing, rolling the 9mm cylinder across the electrode as she did so to make sure all its surfaces were exposed to the powder. "These are actually tiny ceramic beads, about a half a millimeter in diameter, coated with a very fine conducting powder. In theory, they should cling to the microscopic corrosion pattern left behind by the fingerprint."

Nick was impressed by how relatively low-tech the apparatus was, as opposed to some of the expensive DNA scanners that busted the crime lab's budget. "You built this set-up yourself?"

"You bet," Mandy said proudly. "Not really that hard. The original inventor constructed his prototype out of cardboard, masking tape, and popsicle sticks."

"Ecklie's going to love that," Nick observed. The stingy undersheriff was forever complaining about the cost of keeping the lab's hardware up-to-date.

Mandy flicked off the current and held the cartridge up for inspection. Sure enough, inky black whorls and ridges stood out against the brass exterior of the casing. The uncorroded metal, which had held a stronger charge, gleamed by comparison.

Mandy subjected the prints to her expert eye. "Probably a forefinger or thumb. From when the shooter loaded the gun." She passed it over to Nick, so he could admire her results. "Now we just need to heat the casing to bake the powder in place and compare it against our exemplars."

Nick couldn't wait to compare the fingerprint to Roger Park's. The smarmy TV producer was possibly responsible for at least two deaths. It would be great to pin him to at least one of them.

"Thanks, Mandy. You may have just cracked this case."

"Don't thank me," she said. "Thank our friends in Scotland Yard."

"Right." Nick looked forward to reporting their success to Catherine and Greg. "What was the name of that inventor again?"

Mandy took off her glasses and affected her best Sean Connery impression.

"Bond. John Bond."

32

TUMBLEWEEDS ROLLED DOWN the dusty streets of the abandoned ghost town. Moonlight shone down on ramshackle brick buildings that had been slowly falling apart for over a century. Cacti sprouted in the middle of the street. Desert weeds poked through gaps in dilapidated plank porches and sidewalks. Sagging roofs tempted gravity. Rusty chains were draped over askew hitching rails. A derelict dance hall leaned precariously to one side. Wooden shutters banged in the wind. A noose dangled from a hangman's tree.

An airborne figure came hurling through the swinging doors of an old saloon. He flew over the rotted timber porch to crash down hard on the baked dirt street, the impact of his landing raising a cloud of ochre dust. Torn modern clothing, better suited to a twenty-first century gangbanger than an old-time gunslinger, clashed with the decrepit western decor. A bloody stump protruded from a shredded sleeve, where the man's left arm appeared to have been torn from its socket. Pain and fear contorted his sweaty face, which was now caked with grime. Blood spurted from his ghastly wound. He whimpered pathetically.

A second figure stomped out of the saloon after his victim. The tattered remains of a blue LAPD uniform clung to his tall, bony frame. Merciless crimson orbs glared at the wretched gangster sprawled in the street. A skeletal hand clutched a severed arm like a police baton.

"No! Keep back!"

The panicked man reached beneath his scuffed leather jacket with his remaining hand and drew out a Beretta semiautomatic. The sharp report of the pistol sounded as he opened fire on the fearsome apparition stalking him. Bullet holes erupted across the creature's moldering blue shirt, but no blood spewed from the wounds, only puffs of grave dust. A dry, sepulchral voice escaped a withered larynx.

"Benny Salucci," Officer Zombie addressed the fugitive. "You have the right to remain silent . . . forever."

The gangster screamed in mortal terror.

"Cut!" Roger Park barked. "Great work, guys!"

A full film crew was in place to shoot the scene, which was being shot on location in one of the many abandoned frontier mining towns within a day's drive of Las Vegas. Mounted spotlights simulated moonlight. A wind machine churned up the atmosphere. Production trailers were parked discreetly out of view of the cameras. Tumbleweed wranglers scrambled to get the prop weeds back in place for the next take. No longer lurching like a dead man, Officer Zombie helped his "victim" get up off the ground.

"You okay, Duane?" Park asked the stuntman.

The dust-covered "gangster" gave him a thumbs-up with the hand that wasn't hidden beneath the torn jacket. His terror-stricken expression gave way to a cocky grin. "No problem, chief."

"Cool," Park said. "I think we need to do one more take, though." He got up from a folding director's chair. "This time I really want you to dial it up to eleven. I want to see sheer dread on your face and maybe even a trace of remorse. Salucci is guilty as hell and his sins have finally caught up with him."

"I couldn't have put it better myself," Catherine said, intruding on the conference. "Maybe you can give him some pointers on what it feels like."

"What the hell?" Park spun around to see Catherine and Brass striding toward him, with Nick and Greg lagging right behind them. His eyes bulged from their sockets. Angry veins stood out on his neck. "This is a closed set!"

Brass held up a polished copper star. "Tell it to the badge."

"This is harassment," Park objected, while the rest of the film crew milled about awkwardly, uncertain what to do. Park pulled out an expensive-looking smartphone. "I'm calling my lawyer."

"Tell him to meet you at the station." Brass kicked a stray tumbleweed out of the way. "Roger Park, you're under arrest for the murder of Debra Lusky . . . and possibly Matt Novak."

The fingerprint on the shell casing had proved a perfect match for Park's right thumb. Catherine wasn't sure they'd ever be able to prove beyond a shadow of a doubt that the corrupt producer had conspired to get Novak killed; just pronouncing *nuclear* correctly wasn't enough to make a conclusive voice analysis. But that was for the D.A. to decide. What with the blackmail tape, the evidence linking him to Debra, and his print on the bullet that had killed her, however, Catherine was pretty sure they had him on at least one count of first-degree murder.

I can live with that, she thought.

She stepped forward to confiscate the stuntman's gun. They'd have to bring in all the firearms being used by the production. If they were lucky, maybe ballistics could match one of them to the weapon that had killed Debra. Not that they really needed it. She smirked at the noose dangling from a nearby tree branch. As far as she was concerned, they already had more than enough to hang Roger Park.

Figuratively speaking, that is. Nevada had switched to lethal injection years ago.

"This is insanity," Park babbled. "I didn't do anything." Panicked eyes darted back and forth, looking in vain for a way out. The cast and crew backed away from their agitated boss, not wanting to get involved. Catherine spotted Bill Hamilton in the crowd, decked out as a dead rodeo clown. The zombie peeled off his latex mask. He didn't look a thing like Matt Novak.

She glanced around the set. A rubber arm, smeared with blatantly phony blood, lay forgotten in the dust. She shook her head.

Two people died . . . for this?

"Don't even think about running," Brass warned Park. He stepped around to cuff the producer's hands behind his back. "There's nothing but desert for miles around anyway."

Sweat streamed down Park's face. He looked just as terrified as the unsuspecting victims on his other TV show. Catherine couldn't resist delivering the *coup de grace*.

"Surprise," she told him. "You got *Shock Treatment*."

ACKNOWLEDGMENTS

I want to thank my editor, Ed Schlesinger, and the good folks at CBS for giving me a second chance to test the wits of the ace investigators at the Las Vegas crime lab; I tried hard to come up with cases worthy of the original TV show, which I look forward to watching every week. I particularly enjoyed the opportunity to write Ray Langston and Sara Sidle for the first time.

Researching a CSI novel is always an education. This time around, I can thank the friendly doctors and staff at the Applebrook Veterinary Clinic in Oxford, Pennsylvania, for answering my questions about cat scratches, and the Hand & Stone Massage and Spacial Spa in nearby Kennett Square for letting me tour their premises. I promise I didn't see any dangerous reptiles on the loose at either location.

As always, I can't forget my agents, Russ Galen and Ann Behar, for handling the contractual details. And my girlfriend, Karen, for all her support and patience, even when I kept talking her ears off about voiceprints, coral snakes, elastic braces, and interrogations.

Finally, our four-legged family—Alex, Churchill, Henry, Sophie, and Lyla—did their best to distract me, but somehow I managed to get the book done anyway.

ABOUT THE AUTHOR

GREG COX's previous CSI novel, *Headhunter*, received a Scribe Award from the International Association of Media Tie-In Writers. He is also the *New York Times* bestselling author of numerous novels, including the official movie novelizations of *Daredevil*, *Ghost Rider*, *Death Defying Acts*, and all three *Underworld* movies. In addition, he has written books and short stories based on such popular series as *Alias*, *Batman*, *Buffy the Vampire Slayer*, *Countdown*, *Fantastic Four*, *Farscape*, *Final Crisis*, *52*, *The 4400*, *The Green Hornet*, *Infinite Crisis*, *Iron Man*, *The Phantom*, *Roswell*, *Spider-Man*, *Star Trek*, *Terminator Salvation*, *Xena: Warrior Princess*, *X-Men*, and *Zorro*.

He lives in Oxford, Pennsylvania.

His official website is: www.gregcox-author.com.

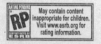